Ocean's Embrace

Maritimo Island Book 1

Lisa Stanbridge

Crystal Brook Publishing

OCEAN'S EMBRACE

ISBN: 978-0-6456673-7-0

Abandoned Hearts

Navigate to the link below to read more about her books.

https://lisastanbridge.wixsite.com/lisastanbridgeauthor/books

For you, my wonderful reader.
Thank you for picking up this book.

Chapter 1

T enika glanced out the window as the plane descended through the clouds. Through a gap she could see aqua blue ocean, sand bars visible beneath the water, and strips of exposed land covered in tropical foliage. The Pacific was certainly a marvel.

With her nose pressed against the glass, she peered out over the wing down at the sparkling ocean, a beat of excitement thrumming through her. She hoped, after an unsuccessful trip to Fiji in search of her birth parents, this would be more successful. Then again, it *was* a holiday...with a school reunion thrown in.

When clouds obscured her view again, she looked away. Her stomach roiled as nausea washed over her. She could do this. Time to put her past to rest. Soon, the future would be hers. She *wanted* this. To finally stop feeling so...so...*disconnected* from life.

With no family, and only a few friends, she had little to show for her twenty-seven years on earth.

Behind her, three jovial Scotsmen talked loudly and laughed about their latest adventures. Intrigued, Tenika removed her earbuds. Their thick Scottish accents filled the small cabin, and a little shiver ran along her spine. There was something sexy about a Scottish accent. She only caught snippets of conversation as they reminisced about some adventure they'd been on.

"Dougie, you were navigatin' like a blind bat while Angus held on for dear life!" one said in his strong Scottish burr.

The three men burst into laughter, and Tenika peered over her right shoulder.

It was a small, six-seater seaplane with three seats on each side and only four passengers occupying them. Two behind her, who she couldn't see, and one on her right who'd been talking. She caught his gaze, his eyes sparkling. Sun shone in through the window, catching on his ginger hair. Short at the temples, longer and styled but loosely curled on top, it looked soft enough to run her fingers through. Emerald-green eyes beneath rounded eyebrows on a masculine face with an angular jaw smattered with a three or four-day stubble made her heart skip. What was it about stubble that was so sexy? He winked at her and grinned, displaying faint laughter lines around his eyes.

Cheeks burning, Tenika smiled and turned away.

She'd known Scottish men were good-looking but, he was...*woah*.

The seaplane dipped and shuddered as it descended further. A glance out the window showed they were beneath the cloud, the ocean seemed only metres away. Tenika gripped the armrest, a mixture of excitement and anticipation pulsing through her. A medium-sized island came into view. White sands, fishing boats, and piers dotted the coastline. On the south-east side of the island stood a large mountain covered in trees and other tropical foliage. She caught glimpses of water from a pond on top and a waterfall cascading down from it.

Several buildings built up the rest of the island, but she couldn't see what they were from this distance, along with patches of rainforests and other agriculture areas for growing crops. A large white structure on the northern side stood out. It could only be the resort.

As the descent continued, she lost the aerial view and finally, the plane touched down on the sparkling waters of Maritimo Island. Fiji had been stunning, but this, its neighbouring island was next level. She would never have thought to visit—didn't even know it existed—until she'd received the reunion invite. The little research she conducted told her the island was growing in popularity and becoming a tourist hotspot only the best of the best visited.

Yep, that explained her schoolmates. Rich. Only ever wanted the best.

She gritted her teeth as memories resurfaced. They were not her *mates*. They were her enemies.

Her breathing turned uneven. She glanced out the window again, drawing in a breath through her nose and out through her mouth, and let the memories pass. As excited as she was about the holiday, she *really* didn't want to go to the reunion. Her best friend Brenda talked her into it, convinced her it'd be worth it. That she'd get 'closure.'

Tenika wasn't convinced, but she couldn't back out now.

She'd almost said no, but the tropical paradise location, and the fact it was one of Fiji's many islands, sold it to her. Desperate to find out more about her own Fijian heritage, she couldn't pass it up. Worst-case scenario, she didn't have to turn up on the day.

This thought calmed her and regulated her breathing.

The plane taxied towards a floating pier, about eighty metres long, with a floating dock on the end in a T-shape, about twenty metres across. She could already see Brenda standing on the pier, waiting to meet her.

This was a unique situation. The mega rich organisers, the ex-school peers she despised, footed most of the costs. The attending alumni would pay for their own all-inclusive package, but at a discounted rate.

She sighed. The reunion was a week away, then she had a week afterwards to continue her holiday. That meant she had a week to relax and prepare herself for what awaited her. She was a grown woman, and she wasn't afraid of those people anymore.

Aren't you?

She hushed her inner thoughts as the plane stopped beside the dock. When the seatbelt sign flicked off a few minutes later, she unclicked hers and stood. The three Scotsmen continued to laugh and talk as they stood. As she removed her two bags of overhead luggage, she cast a casual glance down the aisle of the small plane.

The three red-headed Scotsmen were tall, well built, broad, and *smoking* hot. And...*were they brothers*? The one who'd been sitting on her right turned and caught her gaze. He grinned at her again and her face grew hot. They *had* to be brothers. They looked too alike. The other two glanced over, smiled politely, and nodded in greeting. Actually, they looked *so* similar, almost like they were...twins? She returned the nod, caught the first one's eye once more, and he had the nerve to wink...*again*!

She blushed and giggled as she turned around. She walked on trembling legs towards the exit, sensing his gaze boring into her back.

With the help of the friendly crew, Tenika stepped out onto the dock. She placed a backpack strap on one shoulder and the duffel bag strap on her other. She liked to pack light when she travelled. She could wash her clothes and buy anything she needed. Spotting Brenda a few feet away on the pier jumping up and down waving, Tenika grinned and rushed towards her.

When she drew closer, she dropped her bags on the pier as they lunged at each other in a long hug. They hadn't seen each since Tenika left for Fiji two weeks ago.

"This place is *amazing*!" Tenika exclaimed when they pulled apart. She inched to the edge of the pier that had no barrier, and glanced out over the ocean, the afternoon sun glistening on the water. The warm breeze tousled her tight, black curls.

"Wait until you see the resort," Brenda said. "And everyone is so…" She trailed off, her gaze catching on something behind Tenika.

Tenika spun around, watching the three Scotsmen making their way down the pier towards them, laughing and bantering.

"Holy smokes," Brenda said, her voice breathy.

"Uh huh," Tenika said. "One of them winked at me. Twice!"

Brenda gasped, but before she could speak, the man who winked at Tenika pushed one man a little too hard. He stumbled, tripped over her dropped luggage, and collided with Tenika.

Still standing too close to the pier's edge, she gasped when the impact sent her toppling back towards the water. With nothing to hold on to, she shrieked, "Brenda!" and held out her hand.

It all happened in slow motion. Brenda's light brown eyes widened as she reached out. Their fingers brushed, but they couldn't clasp. The man who'd collided into her reached out for her too, his fingers closing around hers briefly, but there was no grip. Then time sped up and she fell, landing in the water with a *splash*.

The floating pier meant it was a short fall and warm water smothered her. Salt stung her eyes, but despite being fully clothed, it was wonderfully warm. How could she be annoyed when it seemed like she was being embraced by the ocean? Coming up for air, she found Brenda doubled over in laughter and three Scotsmen looking down at her wearing contrite smiles.

"That's one way to make an entrance," Brenda said between giggles, doubling over again.

Tenika treaded water as she stared at the three men. "What the hell?" She laughed, wiping water off her face and pushing her hair back.

"Sorry, lassie," the one who'd winked at her said, his eyes sparkling. "But in our defence, I'm pretty sure that's not our luggage."

She bit her lip, then giggled. "Oh yeah. Sorry."

He held out his hand. "Let me help."

She reached out to him, but before her wet hand could grip his, he lost his balance and toppled forward. His eyes went comically large as he fell in with a gasp and a *splash*. The other two laughed loudly and high-fived each other.

He came up for air and shook his head, water spraying everywhere.

"It's lovely, isn't it?" Tenika quipped.

He chuckled, then they considered how to get out of the water. It was no easy feat. Their clothes were waterlogged, and there were no stairs, but with the help of Brenda and the other two men, they soon were back on the pier, dripping wet and laughing.

He held out his hand. "I think this calls for a proper introduction. I'm Hamish."

Tenika grinned and took it, an electrical current surging through to her core as their gazes clashed. Held. "I'm Tenika." Her voice broke.

She delicately cleared her throat as they stood, hands slowly shaking, staring into each other's eyes. For a few long seconds, neither of them let go as the warm tropical breeze whipped around them.

A not-so-subtle *ahem* from beside Tenika sent her crashing back to earth. Blinking a few times, she reluctantly removed her hand from his and drew in a calming breath.

"Uh, this is my friend, Brenda."

"Brenda, hello," Hamish said. "These two loons are my brothers, Angus and Douglas."

"Well, hello," Brenda growled, yes *growled*, and looked at all three, nearly drooling.

"Nice to meet you all," Tenika and Brenda said, shaking their hands.

Tenika noticed Brenda and Douglas locked in a stare-off, holding onto each other's hands a little too long. Brenda's cheeks were tinged pink. Well, well, well.

"Oh, my boys!"

Brenda whipped her hand away and spun around, her face turning beet red. Tenika bit back a smile as she turned to see a middle-aged Polynesian woman bustling down the pier towards them, an enormous smile on her round face. She had short, curly black hair peppered with grey and wore a wraparound skirt, or lavalava, which had bright, tropical flowers printed on it, and a matching blouse.

Tenika's heart lurched. Wait. Was that—?

"Look at you all grown up!" the woman rushed forward, only having eyes for the three men as they smothered her in a group hug.

Tenika stood frozen for a moment, trying to see the woman, but it was impossible.

"Nika," Brenda said, "you ready?"

Tenika glanced at her friend, then back at the woman. "Uh, yeah, let's go." She shook her head, concluding she must've been imagining things, then grabbed her luggage and followed Brenda down the pier. Her shoes squelched and her clothes dripped seawater. Despite the warmth of the sun, the humidity was thick. It would take a while to dry, so she wanted to change into fresh clothes.

December was probably the worst time of year to visit, but it was a ten-year school reunion and the organisers insisted it had to be the same date as the high school formal.

"Do you know where to go?" Tenika asked.

"Of course I do," Brenda said. "I have a golf cart to take us back to the resort."

"A golf cart?"

Brenda grinned, her frizzy, light brown hair catching on the breeze. "It's easier to get around for those of us who can't or are too lazy to walk. You can borrow them from the resort any time."

Tenika chuckled. That was so Brenda. She hated exercise, whereas Tenika lived and breathed it. She couldn't wait to start her morning jogs again.

"What the hell just happened back there?" Brenda asked once in the cart and heading back to the resort.

Tenika looked at her blankly.

"The fall-in-the-water trick," Brenda said with a flourish of her hand.

"Oh," Tenika giggled, squeezing water out of her hair, "I have no idea. One second I'm on the pier, the next I'm in the water."

Brenda shook her head and laughed. "You crazy woman." She grinned and turned her attention back to the path. "Take everything in. We'll catch up later, but for now, just enjoy this stunning island. I'll take you on the scenic route back to the resort."

Tenika did so with wide eyes. Apart from the golf carts, there was no other transport on the island she could see. The carts used the same concrete paths as the visitors, with lanes for both. There were paths all over that led to various points on the island. Lush, tropical foliage presented a stunning view with coconut palms, ferns, shrubs with various colours of hibiscus flowers, and other plants Tenika didn't recognise. There were even benches and picnic settings dotted around overlooking the ocean.

As they navigated towards the centre of the island, local islanders waved and greeted them in their native tongue. They passed the village where people lived, markets, and a small shopping precinct. It had everything. Like a small rainforest town.

Brenda turned down a palm-tree-lined driveway, and Tenika gasped when the resort came into view at the end. Even from here she saw the large, white-washed structure with terracotta roof tiles, elegant archways, and ornate balconies. She'd never seen so much green grass as she did on the lead up to the resort, along with even more tropical foliage. Golf carts came from the resort with staff waving and grinning.

"Everyone's so friendly," Tenika said.

"They're beautiful people, and they'll treat you like royalty."

Tenika swallowed, then asked, "Is anyone else here? You know...for the reunion?"

"No, not yet. I did some digging, and it looks like no one else arrives until Thursday, so you can relax."

That gave her five days to prepare. She didn't know about relaxing, but she'd try.

"Thanks, Brenda. I appreciate you helping me out."

Friends since primary school, Brenda knew all about Tenika's sordid past.

"What's the plan for our trip?" Tenika asked, her tone upbeat.

Brenda waggled her eyebrows. "I've got *so* much planned, but if one of those Scottish Gods is single, I may just leave you to fend for yourself. Sorry, Nika."

They burst into laughter because that's what Brenda would do. Always looking for 'the one' and failing. This might finally be her time to shine.

"Seriously though," Brenda said, "tonight we'll check out the restaurant at the resort for dinner. I didn't get to visit last night, too zonked after travelling, but I hear it's great. Did you know the main produce here is fish?"

"It makes sense. I saw all the fishing boats and piers as we were landing."

"They grow sugarcane too, and some other crops, but fish is their primary source of income."

Tenika closed her eyes and drew in a deep breath, inhaling the earthy aroma of the tropical foliage and the ocean's salty tang.

"I think I'm going to love it here," she said. "Maybe it's in my blood." Tenika glanced down at her brown-skinned arms.

"Well, you are an island girl."

Born in Australia to Fijian parents but given up for adoption, she was thankful to have grown up with a loving adoptive family. She'd never truly known who she was, though, and something was missing.

Maybe she'd find it here.

Chapter 2

♥

"Look at you three," the friendly woman exclaimed, stepping away and wiping her eyes.

This must be Litia, Ma's longtime friend. Hamish remembered meeting her a few times when she visited Scotland, but he was just a wee lad and only had vague memories.

Hamish wiped his brow where a sheen of sweat had already formed. It wasn't too hot, but the humidity was heavy and stifling.

"Litia?" Douglas asked.

"Yes, yes, you remembered!" Fresh tears filled her eyes. "Oh, forgive me. I've been so emotional lately. Ever since your ma..."

Tears trickled down her cheeks, and she turned away to compose herself. Sadness descended on them all. Hamish glanced over at his two brothers, knowing their thoughts without having to ask.

They all missed Ma.

Litia turned back around. Tears stained her cheeks, but she fixed a bright smile on her face. "I'm so sorry. You boys don't need the constant reminder of her passing. Follow me. Taito is waiting for us."

She bustled off down the pier with Douglas striding alongside her, chatting away in his normal ease. Of the three, he handled his emotions a lot better. Or maybe he hid them? Hamish never knew.

Before walking off, Hamish turned to Angus. Unshed tears shimmered in Angus' eyes and his jaw twitched from clenching it. "Hey." Hamish rested a hand on his shoulder. "It's alright to be upset. I miss Ma as well."

Angus nodded, his bottom lip quivering, but he pulled his shoulders back and nodded, jutting his chin out. "Come on," he said. "Let's get settled, then we can see what this place is all about."

They walked to the end of the pier where Douglas and Litia waited for them in front of three golf carts.

Hamish glanced to his right where another cart disappeared around a bend with the two women he met earlier. Tenika and Brenda. A smile tugged at his lips as the image of the pretty, dark-haired woman flashed up in his mind.

A large, beaming Polynesian man came forward and held out his hand, interrupting his thoughts.

"You're Hamish and Angus, right? I'm Taito, Litia's husband. I'm so pleased to meet you. After everything I've heard, it's like I already know you."

Angus shook his hand and Hamish followed. He had a strong, friendly shake.

"Good to meet you, too," Hamish and Angus said.

"Let's take you three to your bungalow," Taito said. "And for the record, these carts are available for use any time."

Hamish joined Litia in her cart while Douglas went with Taito, and Angus went with a porter who didn't speak English. Hamish chuckled to himself. Typical Angus, go with the one who required the least effort.

"I'm sorry for making it so awkward back there," Litia said as she followed the other two carts.

"You didnae," Hamish said. "We know you and Ma were close."

She sighed this time. "Very. She was my best friend. Did she tell you how we met?"

"Just that she was holidayin' here before we were born and you became instant friends."

After a long pause, she added, "I know she asked you boys to come here and follow her journey. She sent me a letter too."

Hamish wasn't surprised. He'd sent a lot of letters for Ma before she died. He saw a handful go to Maritimo Island but thought nothing of it until after her passing and he'd read the letter and itinerary she left him and his brothers.

"Do you know what it's all about?" Hamish asked.

Apart from Ma saying she'd been on a life-changing journey and wanted them to experience it too, he knew nothing else.

Litia glanced at him with a secretive smile. "I do, yes, but I've been sworn to secrecy. Your ma had her reasons for doing this, and you will learn about everything while you're here. Just enjoy your trip. Trust me, you won't regret it."

"I understand."

But did he?

He respected Ma's wishes, but did he understand her request? No, not really. Maybe he was just impatient. It was a bad time to travel. He and his brothers had big plans to get off the ground once they returned to Scotland. This holiday was their last hurdle before it came to fruition.

Litia turned down a path leading into the centre of the island. She waved at the other locals with a cheery, "*Bula!*" then to Hamish, she said, "You three will be staying in a self-contained bungalow. It's part of the resort, but it's away from the main building. It's the same place your ma stayed at during her visit. You're welcome to pop over to the main building any time, but the guest areas inside are for those attending a private function."

Hamish nodded. Were the women he met here for that function?

On the drive to the resort, he and Litia continued to chat generalities. The more they spoke, the more he remembered. He recalled warming to her easily the last time he saw her. So much like Ma—happy, kind, easy to talk to, exuberant—it's why they were such close friends.

The three golf carts stopped on the path with palms on their right, the resort and a pool visible through them, and the beach on their left. A long jetty extended out into the sparkling turquoise water in an L-shape with bungalows coming off it. Built from wood panelling with a thatched roof, each one had its own deck at the back, with rail stairs leading into the water.

"Here we are," Litia said, getting out of the cart.

Hamish jumped out, grabbed his luggage, and followed Litia, Taito, and his brothers across the sand to the jetty.

"Home sweet home!" Taito announced when they stopped at a bungalow in a deeper part of the water. "You'll each have your own space to sleep, and all essentials have been supplied. If you need anything, just pop over to the front desk inside the resort." He pointed to the resort through the trees. "Or you can use the phone."

"We'll let you get settled," Litia said. "Do you have your itinerary?"

Hamish patted his backpack pocket. "Right here. We start tomorrow, right?"

Litia nodded.

Someone called Taito's name and he waved. "I must go," he said. "See you around boys." With a grin, he disappeared.

"Would you like breakfast at the restaurant or room service?" Litia asked.

"Room service!" Angus and Douglas said.

"I think that answers it," Hamish said.

"The menu is inside," Litia said. "Just call through your order the night before." She turned to walk away, but then came back and gave all of them a hug. "It's so good to see you again."

She clasped her hands in front of her, sighed, then bustled off.

Hamish looked at his brothers and they all shrugged. Angus went inside first, then Douglas and Hamish followed. They walked into an open plan area that included a kitchen, dining area, and lounge. The bungalow had varnished floorboards and modern wooden furniture throughout, and island decorations in browns, whites, blues and greens. Double doors opened out onto the deck with a table and chair setting overlooking the ocean.

While his brothers unpacked, Hamish investigated the bungalow. Taito was right, they had their own sleeping spaces, but everything was open plan with only walls and fancy screens for privacy. Only one bed had nearly full privacy, and a screen separated the other two. It had everything they'd need, but it was cramped. It wouldn't take long until they drove one another crazy. Hamish was thankful they had a packed itinerary.

Before Ma's death, all three had their own lives in Scotland. It had been many years since they had to live together. Angus lived with his long-term girlfriend, Skye, and Douglas lived in an apartment in Edinburgh. Hamish had done the same at one point but when Ma got sick, he moved back into the family home to care for her.

When they returned home after this holiday, they would start on bringing their long-awaited plans to life—opening a whisky distillery. This would mean they'd spend a lot more time together.

While his brothers chatted and bantered, Hamish stepped out onto the balcony to take in the stunning view. Aqua blue ocean. Clear blue sky with only a few fluffy, white clouds, but the heat and humidity would destroy him.

He sat on a wooden chair in the shade overlooking the ocean. Strangely, even though he'd never been here before, he sensed Ma's presence. She only passed away a few months ago, but she'd said this trip was urgent. Adamant they must follow it step by step and visit on the exact dates. Hamish had no clue why.

He wondered if there was something in the Maritimo Island air, because even though he longed to go back to Scotland, he couldn't deny the pleasure of taking a break. It was hard work being a carer, and watching his beloved ma deteriorate day by day. His brothers would never understand the pressure and emotional stress it caused. He loved Ma more than life, and her death devastated him, yet there was a sense of relief knowing she was no longer suffering.

In her final days, she wasn't the same robust woman—pale and sunken cheeks, only skin and bone. Her long, beautiful red hair had fallen out during treatment, and it had started growing back in patches of grey.

A shell. The only way to describe her.

The pain of grief spiked in his chest, and he rubbed at it absentmindedly. Oh, how he missed her. So, while Hamish didn't understand what this trip meant, he'd do it in memory of her. At the end, they would scatter her ashes over the Pacific Ocean as she'd requested.

It grew quiet, and Hamish assumed his brothers were resting or had gone for a walk. He stood and went back inside, finding the only unoccupied bed, and unpacked his things in the closet provided. When he spotted the itinerary, he scanned over it for the umpteenth time, then put it aside.

There was a knock at the door. He went to answer it and noticed an envelope being pushed underneath. He picked it up, then opened the door, spotting a resort employee walking away. They turned back, waved, then ran off. On the front of the envelope was Ma's familiar handwriting.

Hamish's heart rate spiked as he went looking for his brothers, finding them laid out on the double beds separated by a screen. He appreciated they'd given him the one with the most privacy. They had earbuds in their ears and scrolled on their phones.

Hamish tapped on the wall, both looking at him, and held up the envelope. "This just came. It's from Ma."

They removed their earbuds as Hamish sat on a long ottoman at the end of a bed. He read the letter aloud.

To my sons,

Hamish's voice broke, and the words blurred through his tears.

"Get on with it," Douglas said impatiently.

Clearing his throat, Hamish continued.

I cannot tell you how proud I am of you three. You are the light of my life and I only have one regret. That you never knew your father…

He trailed off on the last word and looked up at his brothers with wide eyes. Ma was never one for secrets except when it came to their biological father, whom she never talked about. They learned from a young age to never ask about him because it always upset her.

"Well, this is unexpected," Angus said, shuffling to sit on the edge of his bed.

Hamish continued reading.

Talking about him was difficult for me. I still remember the times when you were boys and you'd ask why you didn't have a daddy like your friends. I couldn't answer, so I told you I didn't want to talk about it.

It was wrong of me, and I'm sorry I let you down. You should not have grown up without a father, but it was not that simple. It is painful to talk about, but you deserve the truth. That's why I wanted you to follow this journey as I didn't go alone. Your father, Duncan McNeill, was with me.

In fact, it was our honeymoon.

Hamish looked up to gauge his brother's reaction. Douglas appeared unimpressed, but Angus was wide eyed in anticipation.

"Keep goin'," Angus said eagerly.

Right now, all you must know is that he was a wonderful man, but you will learn this yourself along the way. Please follow our footsteps on this life-changing journey, and it will answer all your questions.

My friend Litia, who you will have met already, owns the resort with her husband Taito and they are more than willing to help with this request.

I love you all so much.

Ma

Hamish put the letter aside, his stomach all jumbled. He was thirty years old and had adapted to not having a father, but a part of him always noticed the void in his life.

Douglas muttered something under his breath, then stormed out of the bungalow. Hamish glanced at Angus, who shrugged. Ma only ever said not to talk to her about their father to her, but they never talked about him with each other either. It had become an unspoken rule, almost like Ma would know if they dared to breathe a word.

Now they'd been sent on an unexpected journey and they were going to learn about him, whether they liked it or not.

Chapter 3

♥

"Wake up, wake up!"

Tenika sat up with a gasp. "Wha—?"

As she came to and found Brenda bouncing on the bed, she groaned and flopped back, resting her arm across her eyes.

"Who are you, and what did you do with Brenda? She's never this chirpy in the morning."

Brenda stopped bouncing. "That's before we met three *extremely* hot Scotsmen yesterday."

"Good point." Tenika sat up again, running her hands down her face.

Brenda sat on the bed with her legs crossed. "I woke up with this overwhelming desire to get fit. What's the likelihood we can exercise *all day* and I'll have abs of steel?" Brenda pinched the tiniest bit of flab around her belly, only there because of how she sat, otherwise she was flat as a board.

Tenika snorted a laugh and pushed the covers back. "Oh stop. You look great. I am *not* exercising all day, thank you very much. I had hoped to sleep in and start jogging tomorrow."

"Nope, not gonna happen. If I can't get abs of steel, I've got to at least look like I'm trying to make it happen."

Tenika scoffed as she stood. "Fine, let me go to the loo and get changed." She turned to the window and opened the blinds with a gasp. "Oh my God, Brenda, it's not even daylight yet! What time is it?"

"It's like five a.m. or something." She bounded off the bed and pulled her hair up into a ponytail using a tie from around her wrist. "Think of it this way. We'll get to see the sun rise."

Tenika muttered as she grabbed her exercise clothes and made her way to the bathroom. She loved jogging, but she'd usually get up a little later or do it after work.

When she left for Fiji, she quit her casual waitressing job at a Melbourne restaurant. She'd planned to kick-start her life when she returned, sick of flitting from job to job and never finding her feet. She'd been a Sous Chef (badly), a kitchen hand, a bartender, and an actual Chef once in an emergency. That also went badly.

She was sick of the same old jobs and wanted something she loved, or at least enjoyed. Tourism would be right up her alley since she loved travelling. Working at a resort like this would be perfect. For now, she had a little money saved, but it wouldn't last forever.

Five minutes later, she was ready. After stretching, she and Brenda started their jog. For a little while, all she heard was their even pants as they jogged on the hard ground, and the waves in the distance lapping at the shore. Brenda had earbuds in, but Tenika enjoyed listening to nature, so different to the usual traffic sounds.

The morning air was cool without being too cold. They soon emerged through some palm trees onto soft sand with the ocean only a few metres away. The sky began to lighten, the stars fading with it.

"Let's try and jog around the island," Brenda called.

Tenika nodded. They moved to wetter and firmer sand. She had no idea how big the island was, but she was up for the challenge.

Sand kicked up behind them as they jogged side by side. Tenika came alive when she exercised, even when sweat dripped down her face, back and chest. She noticed the distance by the ache in her calves as they rounded a bend and the sky became brighter. When they were about halfway, Tenika stopped for breath.

"Wait, wait," she called out. "I...need...to...breathe."

Bending over, she placed her hands on her knees as she breathed deeply and slowly. When she'd pulled herself together, she stood up straight and looked at her friend who jogged on the spot.

"I'll ask again, what have you done with Brenda?"

Brenda laughed and removed her earbuds. "I can't believe how much energy I have! It must be the island."

"Or three hot Scotsmen," Tenika muttered the same time Brenda said it aloud and they laughed.

Tenika looked at the sky and gasped. The rising sun cast a warm and magical orangey-yellow glow over the coastline, the ocean losing its darkness.

"You mentioned something about a sunrise," Tenika said, sitting on the sand and patting the spot next to her.

Brenda plopped down next to her. "You twisted my arm."

"Like it took a lot of effort." She breathed in the fresh, salty air and watched a boat on the horizon. A fishing boat?

Pastel hues of orange, pink, and blue painted the sky as the sun rose above the horizon.

"It's like paradise on earth," Brenda whispered.

Tenika nodded. "Thank you. This was so worth the early wake up."

"You're welcome. We can do this every morning if you like."

Tenika tore her eyes away for a second to give her friend a death glare. "Not *every* morning. I'd like to sleep in sometimes. Besides, we could watch some sunsets too."

"I'll agree to that. I want to sleep in too. Shall we play it by ear then?"

Tenika nodded and turned back to the horizon. "We're on holiday, no schedule and no phones, remember?"

She didn't realise how much her phone ruled her life until now. She was getting antsy not checking her messages or emails and it hadn't even been a day. This cleanse was exactly what she needed.

"Well, no schedule apart from the reunion," Brenda said but then groaned when she noticed Tenika tense. "Sorry, Nika."

"No, it's fine." She breathed out. "You should be able to talk about it. I'm happy to be here, but I can't relax knowing we've got a week to stress about it."

"Well, technically it's only six days now."

She turned back to the sunrise as a seagull squawked and flew overhead. "Splitting hairs, are we?"

Brenda got to her feet. "You know what I mean. Look, I get it. Trying to have fun while dreading something isn't easy, but do you really want to spend the next few days stressing about it?"

"Of course not, and I'll try not to." Tenika stood as well.

It helped knowing she could always back out of attending at the last minute. She'd paid her share. Not turning up wouldn't change anything. She kept this to herself though. If Brenda found out, she'd only rant about closure again. Tenika had heard it a dozen times before.

"Let's make our way back to the resort. I'm starving," Tenika added. "We can jog around the island another day when I'm not so hungry."

Brenda's face flooded with relief. "Oh, thank God. Can we walk. Please? My motivation has taken a dive into the ocean and my legs are killing me. Remind me not to overdo it next time. I'm so unfit."

Tenika chuckled and started walking. She took in the area which apart from palm trees lining the shore, a pier and some boats docked, there wasn't much else. Through the palms she saw some fields with crops growing and some buildings. Even this early, there were islanders getting to work.

"Let's keep following the coast for now," Tenika said.

As they chatted, warmth from the morning sun washed over her. Two figures rounded the bend, appearing from a gap in the trees and jogged on the sand towards them.

"Oh look!" Tenika pointed. "There's an entrance there."

Brenda gasped. "No way! It's the Hot Scots, well, two of them at least."

"Mornin' lassies," they greeted as they approached.

"Morning," Tenika and Brenda replied, turning to watch them jog past.

The men turned, jogging backwards, and grinned. One of them—Tenika thought it was Hamish—winked at her. Correction, it was *definitely* Hamish. Her knees turned to jelly and her cheeks grew warm. Even metres apart their chemistry was off the charts, crackling between them.

"You got a wink?" Brenda stage-whispered.

"That's Hamish," Tenika said, his name rolling off her tongue so naturally.

"How can you be sure? They look the same."

"He looks different enough, plus he's the same one who winked at me yesterday. Now, come on." Tenika looped her arm through Brenda's. "What's the word for when you're more than starving?"

"Dying."

After a full breakfast of bacon, eggs, toast, and local fruit, Brenda and Tenika made their way back to their room.

"Why did we bother jogging if we were going to eat all that crap?" Brenda asked.

"Because now we won't feel so guilty about it."

"True. Well then, I call dibs on a lazy day. We've done the fresh air, exercise, and food. From now on it's movies and room service."

"Hell yes. But if we're doing that, I'm changing back into my pyjamas."

They both showered and changed then Tenika put the 'do not disturb' sign on their door.

"I can't remember the last time we did this," Brenda said when they settled back on the sofa.

"High school, probably." Tenika grabbed the remote and switched on the TV, flicking through the channels.

"Shame we don't have any snacks—" Brenda gasped. "Mini bar!" Then she jumped to her feet.

For the rest of the day, they ate everything in the minibar, ordered lunch a few hours later, and watched romcoms. At the end of another movie, silence filled the room and Tenika got up to stretch. She was relaxed and ready to talk.

In Fiji she'd dealt with everything alone. Brenda made herself available, always ready to be a listening ear, but Tenika hadn't been ready to face the truth. Until now.

"They're dead, Brenda," Tenika said, her back to her friend.

Silence.

"Your parents?" Brenda finally asked. "But...but your birth certificate listed them."

Tenika ran her finger along the spine of some books on the bookshelf. She'd have to find something to read. Her poor eyes needed a break from the TV. Choosing an Agatha Christie book, she turned back to Brenda.

"That's just a historical record, Brenda." Tenika held the book against her middle. "It's not updated if they die. It only holds their details at the time of my birth."

Tears stung her eyes, her bottom lip trembling. She bit down on it. She'd cried after learning the truth, but the pain was too intense. She dealt with it by burying it, locking it away in a secret compartment in her heart.

"Oh Nika." Brenda jumped up and came over, wrapping her arm around Tenika's waist and resting her head on her shoulder.

"After all the research I did, the careful planning, it all came to nothing."

"How did you find out?" Brenda led her back to the sofa.

They both sat and Tenika placed the book on the coffee table in front of her. "I visited the house where my mother used to live, only to get a slammed door in my face."

The pain in her chest returned and she rubbed it. She shouldn't have got her hopes up, but she'd concocted a story in her mind that involved them welcoming her into their lives with open arms. Stupidly, she'd convinced herself it was true and hadn't been prepared for the actual truth.

In her mind, she'd imagined them being Fijian refugees who'd come to Australia. Gave birth to her but because of living in poverty, couldn't raise a child, so they gave her up. The fact they hadn't specified no contact gave her some hope.

Ironically, she hadn't been far off from the truth. That's what hurt the most.

"You tried again?" Brenda asked.

Tenika stood again and paced the floor. "Stupidly, yes. I gave it a few days, then tried again. That only resulted in another slammed door." She rubbed her nose at the memory, still feeling the whoosh of the door.

"After a few more attempts, she finally spoke to me and told me the truth. Turned out she was my aunt, my mother's sister. She had the gall to blame *me* for their deaths." Tenika shuddered, the words still echoing in her mind.

"*What?*"

Tenika shook her head. "Sorry, I'm getting ahead of myself." She released a slow breath. Once composed, she continued, "Apparently my mother was from a traditional and very religious household where she felt suffocated. When she was eighteen, she moved to Australia with her boyfriend, my father, for a better life."

She stopped in front of the open balcony doors, glancing out at the tropical gardens with the ocean sparkling in the distance.

Calmness washed over her, giving her the strength to continue. "I don't know the details about their life in Australia because they had no contact with their families for a while. My family in Fiji didn't even learn about me until after my birth. My mother made contact when I was two months old, around two years later. She asked for financial help because they weren't eligible to receive government benefits because of their residency status."

She drew in a deep breath.

"That aside, my parents weren't married and had me out of wedlock, which didn't go down well as you'd imagine. The family only agreed to help if they returned to Fiji, but they had to..." Her throat clogged and she swallowed roughly. A stray tear slipped out of the corner of her eye, and she wiped it away. "...they had to give me up for adoption."

She turned around and shrugged. "When they arrived in Fiji, they were in a bad accident on the way home and died instantly. The rest is history."

"And that's your fault, how?" Brenda frowned and folded her arms.

"It's my fault because they were only struggling financially after having me."

She didn't want to believe it, but her aunt was so forceful about it and spoke with such disgust, Tenika couldn't help but take the blame. If she hadn't been born, her parents might still be alive.

There were so many questions she'd never get answered. Like, why did they give her up so easily? Why didn't they return to Fiji with her anyway and screw the judgemental families?

But if they did, you'd be dead too.

She shuddered and shook her head. Somehow, she had to accept she wouldn't get anymore answers. This was it.

"What a load of bull crap," Brenda blurted. "If anything, it's your family's fault because they insisted they give you up. What did your father's family have to say about it?"

Tenika shrugged. "My aunt didn't know anything about them." She rubbed her forehead. She stumbled back over to the sofa and collapsed onto it with a heavy sigh. "Honestly, I really don't care right now. All I know is I don't need people like her in my life and she made it clear she wanted nothing to do with me. At least I know, right?"

When she smiled, it felt forced. Another tear escaped. She swiped it away, emotion bubbling away deep down. She wasn't ready for the compartment to open again. Wasn't sure she could handle that pain, so she drew in a long breath and squashed it back down.

Brenda shuffled closer and looped her arm through Tenika's. "They're so not worth it, Nika. You've got your own family now."

"I know that, and my adoptive parents are great, but—"

"You wanted a *real* biological family."

Tenika nodded. "I want what you have with your family." She winced. "Please don't tell Mum I said that."

"Of course I won't. Look, I get it, but you've found the missing pieces. Now it's time to put it to rest. With that *and* the reunion, you'll have so much closure. Think about what you could do with your life once this is over."

Tenika pulled her shoulders back. "I know. This is my path to self-discovery."

"And I'm happy to come along for the ride." Brenda checked the time. "It's nearly dinner time. Why don't we check out the tidal restaurant? If we're lucky, we might encounter the Hot Scots."

Tenika laughed and shook her head. "Is that likely?"

"Uh, duh, of course it is. This place isn't exactly a bustling city. I don't know why those sexy men are here, but I'm determined to find out."

Tenika's stomach fluttered. "Well then, I guess some fresh air will do us some good. We *have* been cooped up all day."

Brenda grinned, her eyes twinkling. "Exactly."

Chapter 4

♥

Arriving back at the bungalow, Hamish leant over and caught his breath. Douglas wiped his brow and placed his hands on his hips, breathing deeply. When they recovered, they stretched their calves and thighs. He jogged occasionally in Edinburgh but preferred to go to the gym. He'd forgotten how refreshing jogging was.

Even more so when he got to see Tenika again.

Something stirred inside his chest as he envisioned her dark chocolate eyes and that stunning smile that lit her up like an aura. Her brown skin glowed in the early sunrise. When their eyes met and they passed each other, Hamish was certain she experienced the same connection he had.

Hell, they'd only just met but there was certainly something there.

Although he suspected Douglas had his eyes on Brenda after their meeting yesterday.

"So," Douglas said when they stopped stretching and faced each other, "what's with you and that woman? I forget her name, not Brenda."

Sometimes the fact his brother could read his mind was both terrifying and annoying.

Hamish laughed. "That says a lot about you if you remember Brenda's name. Shouldn't I be askin' you that question?"

Douglas shrugged nonchalantly. "I asked you first."

"Tenika is her name. I barely know her, but we had a spark."

"Ooh a spark?" Douglas mocked in a high voice.

Hamish punched his arm. "What would you call it then?"

"Sexual tension. That's what I experienced when I met Brenda." He raked his fingers through his hair. "A holiday fling sounds good right about now."

"Yeah right," Hamish said. "You're as likely to have a fling as I am."

As in, never.

Ma raised her three sons to treat women right and respect them. That's why Angus was the only one in a stable relationship while Hamish and Douglas were long-term singles.

Douglas smiled weakly, uncertainty passing across his features, then walked inside. He never talked about it, but Hamish knew he wanted what Angus had with Skye. They both did, but finding 'the one' was no easy feat. If a fling happened between Douglas and Brenda, it would be her idea not his. He'd be more likely to wear his heart on his sleeve and beg her to return to Scotland if they hit it off.

Hamish followed Douglas inside, finding Angus at the table reading a book while he ate breakfast. Spread out on the table was the food they had ordered last night. They sat and dug in. Even after eating, Angus continued reading while Hamish and Douglas talked. It was nice to have this time with his brothers. It had been too long since the three of them had gone away together.

It was mid-morning when they considered getting ready for their first itinerary item.

"Hey, what's this?" Angus asked as he tidied up the table. He held up an envelope that had been mostly obscured by the tray.

He opened it and Hamish and Douglas crowded around him to read it.

My dear boys,

I hope you're settled into the bungalow at Maritimo Island. I'm certain Litia would have made you feel welcome. Do you remember her?

Today is the first day of your journey. Or should I say the journey your father and I took 31 years ago? The beautiful bungalow you're staying in became our home for a week.

First thing today you will go on a hike—

"Oh, hell no," Angus cried.

Douglas slapped his shoulder. "Quit it and let us read."

—to the peak of the mountain. Trust me, it'll be worth it and you will love it. Even you, Angus.

Hamish chuckled and ruffled Angus' hair.

"Stop it," he said, swatting Hamish's hand away.

Last I heard the hiking guide is the same one your father and I had. His name is Scott, and he's a lovely Australian man who ended up on the island around the time we were visiting when he married one of the local girls.

After lunch, you'll enjoy a picnic of local delicacies, then the afternoon is yours to do whatever you please. Tonight, you'll have dinner at a tidal restaurant and watch the sun set. I hope the food is as delicious as it was all those years ago.

Enjoy your day, my boys.

Love, Ma

They stopped reading the same moment a knock sounded at the door and they looked at each other with wide eyes.

"That was spooky," Angus whispered. "It's not...Ma...is it?" Then he sang the opening bars to *The Twilight Zone* tune.

Everyone laughed and Hamish opened the door, finding a tall and slim middle-aged gentleman standing on the porch. He wore shorts, hiking boots, a beige button-up shirt, a wide-brimmed hat, and a backpack on his back.

"Hello, I'm your hiking guide, Scott. I hope you're ready for a long hike."

"Not on this planet," Angus called from the background.

"Bring it on," Douglas said.

"We'll be ready in five minutes," Hamish said. "We lost track of time, so we need to change."

Scott grinned and tipped his hat as he stepped back. "I'm happy to wait."

Hamish shut the door, and they rushed to get ready, Angus dragging his feet. Yet despite his reluctance, five minutes later they were following Scott who was a fast walker. Douglas and Hamish kept up, but Angus struggled, panting and muttering fifteen minutes into the hike.

The trail led them deeper into the island through dense tropical foliage, the air filled with birdsong and the tropical fragrance of exotic flowers mingled with the earthiness of the vegetation, moisture, and soil. It grew steeper as they hiked, glimpses of the azure ocean peeking through the emerald canopy.

The air grew crisper and less dense the higher they got. After just over an hour of hiking, they reached the top and were greeted with a breathtaking view of the Pacific Ocean and the small islands dotted around. Even Angus stopped grumbling.

"This is the peak of Maritimo Island," Scott said. "The only place that gives a 360-degree view of the entire area."

While Douglas and Angus wandered around, Hamish stood on the spot, slowly spinning to take it all in. His shirt dripped with sweat, but the cool breeze took the edge off the heat. It was a different world out here. Not just the view, but life in general. Relaxed. Slower paced. *Hotter*. But strangely invigorating.

"It's quite a view, isn't it?" Scott asked, coming up to him.

Not only could Hamish see the ocean and other little isles dotted around, but he had a great view of the island itself—the resort, village where the islanders lived, and community areas.

Hamish nodded. "Sure is. You come out here often?"

Scott stood with his legs apart and hands on his hips. "Most days, unless the weather's bad. I moved here from Australia the same time your parents visited."

Hamish nodded, remembering what Ma had written in her letter.

"They were the first couple I brought up here," Scott added wistfully. "They were both much loved around here. Isla, your ma, she was very quiet, but Duncan brought her out of her shell. It also helped that Isla and Litia became instant friends. After—" He stopped, cleared his throat, "—They kept in contact often after she returned home and Litia always kept us updated with news and photos."

Hamish turned to face him, brow furrowed. What was he going to say?

"What was he like, our father?" Hamish asked.

"A real larrikin," Scott said, his Australian accent strong on that last word.

"A what?"

Scott removed his hat, wiped his brow on the back of his hand, then put it back on again. "A larrikin. Someone who's a joker, easy-going. Everyone liked him. He was very extroverted and loved to have fun. He was a great guy."

Sounds like Douglas takes after our father.

"Right," Hamish said, "but then why—"

Scott held up his hands. "I'm sorry. It's not my story to tell, mate. Isla wanted you to find out this way. Now, I'll show you to the picnic area." He put two fingers in his mouth and whistled to get Angus and Douglas' attention. "Come on boys, let's go!"

Scott led them to a clearing a short distance away for the picnic with a stunning ocean view and a picnic table and chair setting. He removed his backpack and made quick work of lining the table with a checked tablecloth laid out and containers of food in the middle.

"This is your picnic lunch," Scott explained. "The same lunch your parents shared all those years ago."

"Has nothin' changed here?" Angus asked.

Scott shrugged and removed his hat to scratch his head. A wistful expression clouded his features. "Maritimo Island is its own world. It has fast internet and modern amenities, but it doesn't move the same way the rest of the world does. Life here is an escape from reality. So, no, not much has changed. We have maintained everything to retain its natural feeling." He placed his hat back on. "Enjoy your lunch. When you're done, just bring the items back down and leave them with the reception staff. You can follow this path." He pointed to a path leading into the foliage.

Scott disappeared with a wave, and the brothers sat down to eat.

"I'm starved!" Angus said, rubbing his hands.

"We had a huge breakfast a few hours ago," Hamish said.

"I walked it off."

The brothers dug in. Hamish wasn't hungry to begin with but once he saw the local delicacies, he couldn't stop himself. Lemongrass chicken skewers, spring rolls, cassava chips, and a tropical fruit salad for dessert. For a drink, they had sparkling passionfruit mineral water.

The brothers spent the next hour talking, laughing, and reminiscing about their childhoods. They didn't talk about Ma's final days. Instead, their memories were fond ones of what she used to be like.

"Ma would've definitely loved this," Angus said wistfully. "A part of her is still here, dinnae you think?"

Hamish nodded but Douglas just stared into space, his eyes glassy.

A little while later, they made their way back down the mountain to their bungalow, dropping the picnic supplies off on the way. Even Angus didn't complain this time, probably because the walk down was much easier than the walk up.

Angus spent his afternoon reading a book while Hamish and Douglas played poker. When dinner time rolled around, they visited the tidal restaurant where the sun inched closer to the horizon. It wasn't far from the pier and dock where the seaplane landed and looked to be a restaurant they set up and packed away as they needed it.

The wooden dining settings had a small candle in the middle of each table. Dotted around the tables were solar lights for when it got dark. A long floral rug lined the sand, which led to a podium with a sign asking guests to remove their shoes and wait to be seated. While they waited, Hamish stared out over the ocean as the sun sunk lower in the sky.

Douglas elbowed him in the ribs and Hamish glowered at him. "What was that for?"

"Look who's here." He lifted his chin toward the restaurant.

Hamish followed Douglas' gaze, and his breath caught when he saw Tenika sitting at a table with Brenda. She laughed at something her friend said. Her long, black, ringlet hair hung past her shoulders, and she wore a knee-length white dress. She. Was. Stunning.

"Cannae deny your woman is a bit of alright," Douglas said.

Hamish shook his head. "She's not *my* woman."

Douglas grinned mischievously. "I beg to differ. You haven't seen your face." The hostess arrived and Douglas asked, "Any chance we can sit with those two lovely ladies?" He pointed to them.

The hostess nodded, instructed them to leave their shoes on the sand, and led the way over to them.

Chapter 5

"Don't look," Brenda whispered, "but the Hot Scots are heading our way."

Tenika looked.

"I said *don't* look!" Brenda hissed.

Tenika turned back with a chuckle. Seconds, later the men stood in their line of vision.

"Evenin'," one said.

By the way he ogled Brenda, it had to be Douglas. Tenika remembered the quieter one was Angus.

"Evening," Tenika and Brenda said.

"I hope we're not interruptin'," Angus said.

"Not at all," Tenika said. "Please join us."

Brenda sat straighter in her chair and mouthed a 'thank you'.

The men dragged another table and some chairs across. Hamish sat next to Tenika, and Douglas next to Brenda, leaving Angus at the end. He picked up his phone and started typing a message.

"Dinnae mind him," Douglas said, sending daggers to his brother. "He can be a bit anti-social."

Angus' cheeks turned red, and he put his phone face down on the table. "Sorry."

"It's okay." Tenika said. "No offence taken. Keep going."

Angus smiled in thanks and when his brothers didn't argue, he picked up his phone again. She understood him. He was introverted and not as confident around new people as his brothers. She used to be like that once upon a time. Still was sometimes depending on the situation.

Her stomach somersaulted when she glanced across at Hamish, cheeks burning when he gave her that devastating grin and wink. Her breath hitched and she looked away. It took all her willpower not to fan herself.

"Alright, I have to ask," Brenda spoke up. "Are you two twins? You look so similar."

Thankful for the diversion, Tenika looked up to see Brenda pointing between Douglas and Angus.

The three brothers glanced at each other and nodded once.

"We're triplets," they said in unison.

Tenika and Brenda gasped.

"No way!" Brenda exclaimed. "But Hamish, you look very different."

"We're fraternal," Angus explained. "But me and Dougie look alike."

"But in personalities we're so different," Douglas said.

"Who's the oldest?" Tenika asked.

"I am." Hamish grinned. "*And* I was born on a different day."

"At 11:59 p.m.," Angus and Douglas said.

"He never lets us live it down," Angus said with a roll of his eyes.

"Let me guess..." Brenda looked between Angus and Douglas. "I bet you're the youngest." She pointed at Angus.

His eyes widened. "How'd you know?"

"Lucky guess. The quieter ones usually are. Always in the shadow of the older siblings."

"You're not the youngest in your family then?" Douglas quipped.

Brenda laughed. "I'm an only child. I guess that's the same."

"Angus is forty-five minutes younger than Hamish," Douglas explained, "and fifteen minutes younger than me."

Food orders were placed, and while they waited, they enjoyed drinks and easy chatter. It ended up being Tenika and Hamish talking and getting to know each other, Brenda and Douglas doing the same, and Angus on his own. He never once seemed to care, and happily joined in when the conversation warranted it.

"Where are you and Brenda from?" Hamish asked during a lull in conversation.

"Melbourne, Australia."

"Hey, we landed there before we flew to Fiji. Got a chance to have a wee look around the city for a bit. Seems nice."

For some reason, this made her heart swell with pride. "It's a great city. So, where in Scotland are you from?"

"Edinburgh."

"I've heard Scotland is a beautiful place. I'd love to visit one day."

"I might be a wee bit biased, but it really is stunnin'. You're not much of a traveller?"

"Not really, but I want to travel more. I love it, but never had much of an opportunity. I was in Fiji recently, and now I'm here. The first time I've ever been overseas."

He sat up straight. "What were you doin' in Fiji?"

Crap. The last thing she wanted was to bore him with her family woes. Thinking quickly, she said, "Researching family heritage."

"You're from Fiji?"

"Born in Australia, but my parents are Fijian." *Were*. She gritted her teeth but kept it to herself.

"Did you find out much?"

"Um, a few things." Shuffling in her seat, she moved to a safer topic. "What brings you to Maritimo Island of all places? It's very specific when coming from the other side of the world."

He looked at her curiously, his eyes full of questions. She held her breath, anticipating them while hoping he didn't ask.

"Aye, it is, but we're on a journey," he finally said, and Tenika breathed a sigh of relief.

The table grew quiet. Tenika glanced around, noticing Angus and Douglas had been listening in. The three brothers looked at each other, as though speaking telepathically, and nodded.

"Our ma passed away a few months back," Hamish explained, a sadness to his tone. "She visited here over thirty years ago, before we were born. Litia was Ma's best pal. When Ma passed away, she had one wish for me and my brothers to follow her journey and learn more about our birth father, who we dinnae ken."

Tenika stared at him, wide-eyed, then at Brenda who looked just as awestruck. Maybe she didn't have to be worried about revealing too much about her parents after all. Then she recalled the name he used...Litia. Why did it sound so familiar?

She dismissed it for now and focused on the conversation. "I'm sorry about your mother." Tenika looked at the three brothers. "The journey sounds exciting though."

"Far too much exercise," Angus spoke up, wrinkling his nose. "We had to hike *all* the way to the peak of Maritimo Island."

"You what?" Tenika asked. "There's a hike?"

"Oh no, not you too," Angus said, and everyone laughed.

Tenika made a mental note to find out how to get there.

As if reading her mind, Hamish leant in and whispered. "I'd be happy to show you the way if you're interested. We had a guide, but I remember where to go."

"I'd love that."

Brenda sighed and went all dreamy-eyed as she rested her elbow on the table and placed her chin on the palm of her hand. "I could listen to you guys speak *all* night. That accent is pure heaven."

"Amen to that," Tenika said.

The brothers looked at them, then each other and laughed.

Their food arrived and all casual conversation ceased as they focused on eating. Entree consisted of coconut prawns followed by a main of grilled mahi-mahi with breadfruit chips, and a pineapple and coconut sorbet for dessert.

"Oh, my goodness." Tenika leant back in her chair. "I haven't eaten that much in *forever*."

"Liar," Brenda said with a snicker. "I think you ate more than that today alone."

Tenika shrugged good-naturedly. "What can I say? I'm on holiday."

Hamish eyed her appreciatively. "I like a lassie who enjoys her scran."

They shared a smile, and her heart did a little flip. The alcohol had loosened her up to the point of being confident and happily flirting. *And* he was returning it. There was something magical about this place. She never wanted to leave.

"I'll go for a long jog in the morning so I can do it again tomorrow." She grinned and Hamish laughed.

Angus stood and announced, "It's been grand, but I'm callin' it a night so I can call Skye."

"His girlfriend," Douglas explained.

Once he left, Brenda said, "You all seem close."

"We have our moments," Douglas said. "But I suppose they're not so bad. Now, Brenda, how about a wee walk along the beach?"

His hooded gaze held Brenda's and Tenika silently cheered for her friend. Brenda looked back once and Tenika nodded, their silent agreement that she understood.

Occasionally they'd go clubbing in Melbourne and they always agreed to check in on each other before doing anything that meant being apart for a few hours or overnight.

Alone with Hamish, Tenika gazed out over the ocean. The sun had set, the horizon a mixture of dull oranges, reds, yellows, and blues. Their feet were in the water as the tide came in. They'd left their shoes further up the beach when they arrived. She loved the concept of a tidal restaurant. They cooked the food under a marquee on outdoor barbecues and firepits. Everything, including the dining tables and chairs, and solar lights, were assembled and disassembled each night if the weather and tide were good.

"How about you, Tenika?" Hamish asked, his voice low. "Would you fancy a wee walk as well?"

Butterflies swooped in her stomach. She gazed into his eyes, the solar light next to their table making them shine brightly. He stood and held out his hand. How could she say no?

She took his hand, and he helped her to her feet. Zaps of electricity shot down her arm and spread throughout her body, leaving her breathless. They picked up their shoes but his warm hand never let hers go as he led her down the beach in the opposite direction to Brenda and Douglas.

The balmy breeze caressed her skin. The sky grew darker, the remains of the sunset nearly gone, with stars littered across the velvety blackness like floating diamonds.

"It's so beautiful out here," she said.

"The nights are great," Hamish agreed. "The days not so much."

She looked at him, her brow furrowed in question.

He rubbed the back of his neck. "The humidity is not fun. It's a bonny place and all but we're lookin' forward to goin' home."

"Oh."

She added a chuckle, but deep down it created a chasm between them. It reminded her they had limited time together. It was a holiday and they had lives away from Maritimo Island. Whatever happened here couldn't be long term.

Brenda had flings sometimes, but Tenika didn't. She preferred her men to commit *and* live in the same country.

They stopped at the edge of the water as it lapped at the shore and wrapped around their ankles. The warm breeze whipped through her curls and kissed her skin.

"How about a swim?" Hamish asked, his voice soft. Husky.

Tenika spun around to stare at him, her eyes wide. "Um...what?"

He inclined his head to the water. "It looks invitin', doesn't it?"

She swallowed, her heart racing, head fuzzy. She remembered it beckoned to her earlier, but...*night* swimming? There wasn't much light apart from the quarter moon and stars, and a few twinkling lamps visible through the palms, but not enough to reach them.

"Yes, but I-I don't have my swimmers," she explained lamely.

Hamish grinned and dropped his sandals onto the sand. "Come on, that's no excuse."

Before she could argue, he ripped off his shirt revealing a lightly defined six-pack and a chest of light, red hair that trailed down below his shorts. *Eyes off, woman.* Her mouth turned dry and she froze, speechless. She broke out of her trance, shrieking when Hamish waded into the water and turned back to splash her.

"Come on," Hamish called. "It's bonny and warm."

Live a little.

She *did* have a sensible bra and undies on under her dress, nothing too skimpy, and *not* white, so it could pass as a bikini. Hamish grinned mischievously and splashed her again.

"Hey!" She jumped back.

"Are you chicken?" he asked.

She puffed her chest out and put her hands on her hips. "No one calls me chicken."

"Well then, what are you waitin' for?"

Fine. Two can play this game. After placing her sandals on the sand, she ripped her dress off and stood staring at the water for a moment. Why was she so nervous? It was just a swim.

Yeah, a swim with a hot Scotsman.

Hamish glanced back at her, his appreciative gaze raking over her. Her whole body came alive as though engulfed in flames, yet goosebumps broke out on her skin. Now she *had* to swim to hide the effect he had on her. She stepped into the water and he came forward, taking her hand as they waded in further until they were chest deep. She dove under the depths, enjoying the same watery embrace she experienced yesterday. She was home. At one with the ocean, and Maritimo Island.

"This is amazing," she exclaimed when she came up for air.

"Told you." Hamish came up to her. "So, Tenika, what brings you here? I hear there's an event happenin', is that it?"

"Unfortunately, yes." When he looked at her in question, she elaborated. "It's a school reunion and I don't have a very good history with my peers. This is the last thing I want to do, but I think I need to. For closure if nothing else."

"Closure for what?" His eyes were full of interest, concern, and confusion. He took her hand under the water.

Her breath hitched. She couldn't move away. Didn't want to. She barely knew this Scottish stranger, but there was a magnetic pull to him.

"I-I'd rather not say," she whispered, edging closer to him with the aid of the gentle movement of the water. His face only centimetres away.

He pulled back a little, his brow furrowed. The cool air sizzled with chemistry. Questions burned in his gaze but he didn't pry. The desire to spill everything was strong, but if she didn't want to scare him off, she had to keep it quiet. For now, at least. Who knew what the next few days would bring.

His gaze hadn't moved from her face, as though memorising every detail. She swallowed hard, struggling to breathe. There must've been something in the air because she suddenly wanted to kiss this man. To see what he tasted like. How he kissed.

Was a fling really so bad?

She stepped closer the same moment he did and gasped when their skin connected. The balmy breeze caressed them as the water moved lazily around them. They linked their fingers together, lips mere inches apart, and she gave in to the magic of the island. His warm breath brushed her lips before he claimed them. So soft and warm and beautiful. He tasted of salt and pineapple.

A little whimper sounded from the back of her throat. Hamish let go of her hands and pulled her flush against his chest. His hard, muscled chest.

Oh. My. God.

But as the world faded away, her heart pounded in her ears. The taunts from her high school bullies crowded her mind. It might've been ten years ago, but it was still clear as day.

"You're fat."

"You're ugly."

"You're useless."

"You're worthless."

She pulled back with a gasp, heart racing. She and Hamish stared at each other, her mouth opening and closing.

"I-I'm sorry," she stammered. "I'm so sorry."

Then she turned and waded back to the shore as fast as she could, cursing the slow movement through the water.

"Tenika, wait," Hamish called, close behind her.

She shook her head and did her best to pick up her pace. Once in shallower water, she took larger strides. On the sand, she grabbed her things and ran.

Chapter 6

♥

"**W**akey, wakey, rise and shine!"

Tenika grumbled and grabbed the spare pillow, holding it over her head.

"Go away, Brenda."

"Today we're going snorkelling."

"You can go. I'm staying in bed." Tenika put the pillow back.

Brenda ripped the covers off and Tenika groaned.

"You're on holiday, come *on*! There's a place called Coral Cove and apparently the snorkelling is *amazing*. Come on, it'll be fun."

A vivid memory of Hamish's soft lips on hers flashed in her mind, and Tenika's cheeks burned.

"Will the brothers be there?" she asked.

As much as she wanted to see Hamish again, she didn't think she was ready. At the memory of her runaway act last night, guilt settled like a lead weight in her gut. What *had* she been thinking? Kissing a man after only knowing him for less than a day? It was so out of character!

Is that really such a bad thing?

"They've got plans, apparently." She leant against the wall and folded her arms, eyeing Tenika curiously. "What's got into you? I thought you'd want to see Hamish."

Tenika sat up and positioned herself on the edge of the bed. "Alright, I guess snorkelling sounds good. But I might—"

She stood but Brenda moved to stop in front of her. "Tenika Ballentine, I demand you talk to me."

"Ugh." Tenika sat back on the bed and covered her face with her hands, quickly mumbling, "Hamish and I went swimming last night, and he kissed me, and I ran away."

"What? I didn't catch a word of that."

Tenika lowered her hands and repeated it slower.

Brenda gasped. "Oh my god, you've been holding out on me. I thought it would be Douglas who wouldn't be able to keep his hands to himself, not his older-brother-by-fifteen-minutes. Seems Douglas is more of a gentleman than Hamish is." She waggled her eyebrows.

Tenika threw a pillow at her friend. "Hamish is the perfect gentleman, thank you very much. It's just...there's something about this island. Something *magical*."

Brenda turned serious and nodded. "You like it here, don't you?"

"It's like I've come home. It must be in my blood."

"It is, silly. You might've been born in Australia, but you're an island girl through and through." She shrugged and inspected her nails as she casually said, "Maybe you should move here."

"Don't even say it! This place is tiny. There's no way I could find somewhere to live comfortably. The wages probably pay pittance too."

Brenda shrugged. "You don't know if you don't find out. You haven't officially met Litia yet, have you? You should speak to her. I think you'd love her."

That name again. Why was it so familiar? She shook it from her mind and focused on Brenda's words. Move here? To Maritimo Island? Was it even possible? It wasn't the right time to think about it. Right now, she had to focus on getting through the reunion then re-evaluate her life.

Then there was Hamish.

But the seed had been planted and it would continue to live in the back of her mind.

Tenika groaned. "Alright, fine, snorkelling sounds fun."

Brenda ducked into the bathroom, leaving Tenika to find her clothes.

"And as for running away, I know exactly why you did it," Brenda called out.

"Oh, do you just?" Clothes in hand, Tenika stood outside the bathroom door.

"Yep. You're worried about the distance, and you're worried about how he really sees you because you're still scarred from school."

Tenika didn't respond straight away but started bouncing from foot to foot. "Stop knowing me," she finally muttered. "And will you please hurry? I'm busting."

The door opened a moment later. Brenda had pulled her frizzy hair into a bun and had changed into in a knee-length pale yellow dress with swimmers underneath, and sandals.

"Tell me I'm wrong," she said, hands on hips.

"I'm not saying you are. It's all moot anyway. You already planted the 'move here' seed in my brain so there's no way it'll work."

"*He* might move here too."

Tenika pushed past her friend and shut the door. "Nope, it won't happen. He made it clear last night he hates the weather and is desperate to get home."

She sat on the toilet and sighed in relief.

"Hmm," came Brenda's reply through the door, "and Douglas told me last night that he and his brothers have a plan to set up a distillery in Scotland when they get home."

"See?" Tenika flushed. "It won't work. For either of us."

She'd showered the previous night, so she washed her hands, then tidied up her hair and changed. When she exited the bathroom, Brenda was sitting on the end of her bed.

"Good thing *I'm* only after a fling," Brenda said breezily.

"You say that, but if Douglas is anything like Hamish..." She let it hang in the air.

"You're a cow," Brenda said behind her.

"**A**lright, I take it back," Tenika said as they returned their rented snorkelling gear. "I'm glad I came."

Brenda grinned. "I knew you would be. I suppose it helped that the Hot Scots had their own thing to do."

Brenda looked glum but Tenika was relieved.

They'd run into them when they arrived at Coral Cove as they headed off on a planned deep-sea diving adventure. Even though Hamish had smiled at her in greeting, implying no hard feelings, Tenika still wore the guilt. She owed him an explanation.

With the snorkelling things put away, they laid their towels out on the sand and lathered sunscreen over their skin. Time moved so much slower on the island. *Bliss.*

"What did you and Douglas get up to last night?" Tenika asked, rolling onto her side and resting her head on the palm of her hand.

"No kissing, if that's what you mean." Brenda threw her a wink.

"Does that mean I had the better night?"

"Sounds like it. We walked for ages, just talking and flirting. It was…nice." She frowned, confusion marring her pretty features. "I don't remember the last time I had a 'nice' time with a guy."

In her periphery, Tenika spotted a dive boat coming into dock. She sat up when she spotted the brothers under the cover, returning from their adventure. When they disembarked and strode down the floating pier to the sand, Angus was the only one fully clothed in shorts and a top. Apparently, he didn't like *any* exercise, including diving. Hamish and Douglas had pale skin, but still appeared all glistening and beautiful in only their swimming bottoms.

"Well, hello," Brenda growled for Tenika's ears only as she sat up, placing her sunglasses on top of her head.

When they came over to them, Hamish invited them along to the next itinerary item—a visit to the waterfall. It was in the same vicinity as the hike, but only halfway to the top.

On the way there, Brenda and Douglas followed the guide with Hamish and Tenika in the middle and Angus lagging.

When they arrived, a waterfall cascaded from the highest cliff and showered into the stunning emerald-green pond. Surrounded by lush tropical foliage, rock faces with moss, and creeping vines, Tenika couldn't remember ever seeing anything so beautiful.

"Let's go swimming," Brenda announced.

Everyone agreed, even Angus. After dressing down to their swimmers, they slipped into the chilly water. At its deepest, the pond came to their chests. Together they talked, laughed, and joked around, splashing each other, and having fun. When Angus had enough and went to dry off, Brenda and Douglas went for a walk, which left Tenika and Hamish alone.

They'd been getting along fine, no awkwardness, but now it was only the two of them and no one to eavesdrop, Tenika grew nervous.

They swam towards the tumbling water but Tenika stopped before they got too close so they could still hear each other speak. "Hamish, I'm sorry I ran off last night," Tenika said, keeping her gaze averted. "I barely know you and I freaked out, I guess."

She let those words hang between them as she considered what else to say. She'd stopped herself from revealing too much about her school years the previous night, but as the reunion grew closer, it wouldn't be a secret for long.

Something deep down told her he'd find out, if not from her, from someone else. She'd rather it came from her...just not today.

She glanced up at him. His beautiful eyes, a similar colour to the pond, were intense as he held her gaze, smiling in understanding. Hamish didn't appear to hold grudges and for that she was thankful.

"You dinnae have to explain anythin' to me, Tenika. I'm sorry if I made you uncomfortable."

She shook her head. "No, it wasn't that. I wanted to kiss you." Her cheeks grew so hot, she half expected the water on them to sizzle. "I'm not used to men being interested in me...genuinely."

He frowned, a crease forming between his eyes. "Why not?"

So much to say but no idea where to start. "Maybe I'll tell you one day."

He reached out to stroke her cheek. "Okay." He gestured to the waterfall. "Let's check out what's behind it."

The pond grew shallower as they approached the tumbling water, droplets forming on her face from the spray. When they went under the rushing water, Tenika couldn't hear anything at first, then they entered a cave. They stood on smooth rocks looking into it with stalactites hanging from the ceiling, and the walls dripping with moisture and covered in moss. A small river continued to flow between sharper rocks and pebbles. With their bare feet, they couldn't proceed much further.

"This is amazing," she yelled over the water tumbling down behind them.

Grinning, she turned to Hamish whose gaze had turned intense again as he stared at her, pupils dilated. "You're too irresistible, Tenika. All I want to do is kiss you and never stop."

She barely heard him but she didn't need to. His gaze said it all. She wasn't sure what came over her, but she grabbed his face, his stubble rough under her hands, and pressed her lips against his. He kissed her back, water dripping down their faces, the rushing waterfall drowning out any noise. His lips were warm, the water cool. The perfect combination.

She was the first to pull away and he rested his forehead against hers, huffing out a short laugh. "I'm not takin' the blame for that one."

She laughed too and put some distance between them. Her heart raced, and her insides were all jumbled as anxiety gripped her. Grabbing his hand, she led him out of the cave and back into the pond.

When they were far enough away to hear better, she turned to him and ran her hands down her face. "I don't know what any of this means, Hamish. I barely know you, yet I like you a lot, but we're from two different worlds."

His bright eyes shone from the light streaming through the foliage. "What if our worlds were meant to collide? Let's just enjoy these few days together and see what happens? No strings, no pressure, just some fun and get to know each other. If anythin' eventuates, we'll figure it out."

She breathed in sharply but nodded. "I'd like that."

"How about joinin' me for dinner tonight followed by a bonfire? I hear there'll be dancin' and everythin'."

"That sounds great, I'll be there."

"Bring Brenda along if you want, though I'm sure Dougie will ask her."

"Thanks, I'll let her know."

Needing some time to think, she said, "If you don't mind, I'm going to head back to my room for a while. I have a lot to think about."

Hamish nodded. "Aye, of course, but I will definitely see you tonight?"

"Yes, I'll be there."

Tenika had a skip in her step, even though anxiety knotted her stomach. Perhaps some time apart before dinner would help ease it. She wasn't used to this relationship stuff. But was it a relationship?

No strings, no pressure, just some fun, were Hamish's words. It sounded suspiciously like a fling, but he also hadn't shied away from the possibility of more. For once in her life, she would stop being so afraid. The time had come to dive in headfirst. Let her hair down and have some fun.

Following the sand to the dock and pier, she stopped when she heard a buzzing sound. She looked up, spotting the seaplane coming in to land on the water. Her heart skipped and bile rose in her throat. No way! Were the other alumni arriving already? What happened to them arriving later in the week?

Anxiety spiked as she remained rooted to the spot, watching the plane dock and three passengers disembark. From this distance she couldn't see them clearly, but one definitely had blonde hair. Something inside her clicked.

Her fear ramped up to one hundred and she ran.

Chapter 7

♥

Back in her room, Tenika paced the floor as her heart raced and tears trickled down her cheeks. She wasn't even sure who the arrivals were, but the memories came back with such force. Still so much terror buried.

She wiped away her tears, only to make way for more.

How was she supposed to deal with this? Why had she even agreed to do this in the first place? Bloody Brenda talking her into it, spouting crap about closure. Tenika would never be able to seek closure. Too much damage had been done.

You don't have to go, remember? You have full control.

She hiccupped and this thought helped her to stem the relentless tears. Finally, she stopped crying and sat on the sofa.

The door opened and closed then Brenda waltzed in. "Hellooo!" she cried, spinning on the spot. "Where'd you disappear to?"

Tenika didn't respond.

"Nika?"

The sofa dipped and Brenda said, "Nika, what's wrong? Are you okay?" A pause, then, "It's not Hamish is it? He didn't..." She gulped. "He didn't *force himself* on you, did he? Because if he did—"

This got Tenika's attention and panic spiked in her chest. She couldn't let that thought ever take hold. Blinking, she shook her head and forced herself back to the present.

"No, nothing like that." Her voice was hoarse from crying but that didn't stop more hot tears from dripping down her cheeks.

Brenda's shoulders slackened, her pale face gaining some colour. "Good, because I'm growing rather fond of those men."

Tenika managed a weak smile, but it fell again. "Me too, but I'm not good enough for any of them, let alone Hamish."

Brenda's eyes widened. "What the hell has brought this on? You're plenty good enough, girl." She stared at her hard, calculating, then realisation dawned on her face. "Oh, of course, I saw the seaplane."

Tenika scrubbed her hands down her face. "Some people disembarked, but I couldn't see them, just that one was blonde. I thought it might've been one of the twins, and I freaked. You said no one was supposed to be arriving yet."

She didn't mean to sound so accusatory. Images of the three people who bullied her in school entered her mind and she shivered. Davina and Belinda were twin sisters and Zachary was Davina's boyfriend at the time. Evil. All three of them.

Brenda shrugged. "I only went by the last update I saw on social media. If anyone changed their minds, they didn't post it."

"I bet they did it on purpose. That would be bloody typical."

"Hey, now you're being paranoid. It's been ten years, Nika. They're probably *nothing* like they used to be?"

"You really think so?"

Brenda slipped her arm around Tenika's shoulders. "Okay, fine, I have no idea. I've only seen posts from Davina who organised everything, and she seems a bit more level-headed. I don't know about the other two though. They kept very silent."

Tenika breathed a little easier as her anxiety eased.

"You can't let this ruin your holiday, Nika. We're here for two weeks, remember? There's less than a week until the reunion, then we have time to forget all about it."

Tenika nodded and flopped back on the sofa.

"So, tonight we're going to join the boys for dinner over a bonfire. There'll be dancing apparently. It's going to be epic." Brenda checked the time on her watch. "Douglas said to be there by six and it's now five-thirty."

Tenika shook her head and sent her friend an apologetic smile. "I'm sorry, Brenda, I don't think I can face it. What if one of them *did* arrive, and they're there?" She gulped, fear traipsing along her skin, making goosebumps rise.

Brenda sighed and shrugged. "I want to say it's unlikely, but obviously I don't know. What about Hamish?"

Tenika winced. Looked like she'd have to break a promise. She'd also have to bite the bullet and tell him about her past. It was a risk because what if it scared him off? But one she needed to take. If she wanted any chance at finding out what they could have, she had to be honest. Warts and all.

"I'll explain everything to him tomorrow." She gave Brenda a pleading look. "Will you send him my apologies? I don't expect you to tell him anything." When Brenda sighed in frustration and hesitated, Tenika begged. "*Please?*"

Brenda threw her head back and sighed. "*Fine*, but you owe me one. And you can't keep letting the past rule your life. You're here for closure, to get over it once and for all. You can't hide every time you see them. It's time to prove you're better than them."

"I won't hide anymore, I promise. I'll be okay by tomorrow."

Brenda looked at her through narrowed eyes. "Okay, but I'm holding you to it. Unless you're spewing your guts up due to some island sickness, you are *not* getting out of anymore holiday fun."

Tenika laughed this time. It felt good. She meant what she told Brenda. She *would* be okay. She just needed some time to come to terms with it.

"Deal."

Brenda pulled the tie out of her hair and winced. "Holy crap, my hair feels so gross. I'm going to shower, then I'll get ready. Are you sure you'll be okay?"

"I'll be fine. Go, have fun, and tell Hamish I'll see him tomorrow. Tonight I need to do the introvert thing by ordering room service and watching romcoms."

Brenda hesitated. "Tempting."

"Go! You've got the other Hot Scot to woo, remember? He trumps room service and romcoms, surely?"

Brenda pretended to think, then grinned and ran to the bathroom. "You're right!"

Hamish and his brothers returned to the bungalow two hours before they were due to return to the beach for the bonfire and dinner.

"Look, another letter," Angus announced.

Hamish approached him standing at the small table in the living area. Angus picked up an envelope like the one they received yesterday morning.

Douglas sidled up beside Hamish. "Open it."

Angus ripped it open and pulled out a piece of paper, reading aloud.

My dear boys,

I hope you're loving Maritimo Island as much as I did all those years ago. This day thirty-one years ago was a day I'll never forget. The day I learnt I was pregnant.

Of course, I had no idea then that I carried three wee babies. I'd been feeling fine, no symptoms of pregnancy, but I only took a test because my period was late.

Anyway, it was a shock. I told Duncan about it and he didn't react well. We had a future planned, but we'd never discussed having children. Little did I know he didn't want them, so the news didn't go down well.

Hamish glanced at his two brothers who looked as shocked as he felt. Angus started reading again.

We still followed our itinerary for the day, but our hearts weren't in it. Duncan's reaction shocked me, and I was questioning our relationship. How did we forget to discuss something so important?

We barely spoke, but I was okay with that. We'd only argue if we did, so it was good to have some time apart to let the news sink in. When we returned to the bungalow later, our next itinerary item was dinner and a bonfire on the beach with entertainment. I was so looking forward to it, but Duncan didn't want to go. He said he'd stay in but for me to go if I wanted.

So I did. I met Taito, and he was such a lovely man. Well, he was barely a man back then. I had only recently turned twenty-one and he was a year younger than me. That's not relevant. What is relevant is that we clicked. He made me laugh, and he had a way to tell the best stories while keeping everyone engaged.

Angus stopped reading again. "Dinnae tell me Ma—" He shook his head. "No, I cannae imagine that."

"She totally slept with him," Douglas said. "Why else would she mention him?"

"Dinnae make assumptions, Dougie," Hamish chided. "We dinnae ken, and it's not fair on Ma to think she cheated on Da."

Douglas muttered something about knowing he was right, and Angus continued.

It's not what you think, boys, get your heads out of the gutter. He only had eyes for Litia, and as you already know, they're married.

"See?" Hamish interrupted.

Douglas flipped him the middle finger.

I was still upset after the way Duncan reacted and Taito provided entertainment and a listening ear, which I needed. I told him I was pregnant, about Dunca's reaction, and Taito listened. He was so much wiser than his twenty years. The island life aged men differently.

That night he became my friend. He was logical and calm, like a man should be. If I'd gone to Litia first, it would've got too emotional, and I would've made a stupid mistake. But Taito told me to give Duncan time.

After that, I let it go and had so much fun at the bonfire. When I returned to the bungalow later, Duncan was asleep, but I was ready to tackle what our lives had to offer. That's what Taito did. He gave me strength to work through this.

So, my boys, enjoy tonight and I hope you enjoy Taito's stories.
I love you all, forever and always.
Ma

"I still think she slept with him," Douglas said when Angus put the letter away.

"Stop it." Hamish punched Douglas' arm. "It's not fair on Ma. You dinnae ken what happened. That's what this holiday is about, remember? Learnin' about our father."

"He's soundin' like an arse so far," Douglas said.

"In *one* letter," Angus argued. "Ma has only hyped him up before now. If they hadn't talked about havin' kids, it would've been a surprise to him. Didnae Taito basically tell Ma the same thing?" He held up the envelope.

Douglas' eyes grew wide in surprise. Angus rarely spoke up, but Hamish was proud. He agreed with him, even if Douglas didn't.

Douglas grunted and shrugged but left it alone.

"Well, let's check out this bonfire then," Angus said. "Sounds right up my alley." He checked the time on his phone. "We have just over an hour until we need to be there. I might check if Skye's awake and we can leave a bit before six."

"I'm goin' for a swim," Douglas muttered.

As they went their own ways, Hamish flopped down on the sofa with a sigh and a smile on his face. He couldn't even think about Ma's letter and what its contents meant. He was too preoccupied with thoughts of Tenika.

Chapter 8

♥

The sun inched closer to the horizon as Hamish and his brothers emerged from the trees onto the sand where the large bonfire crackled away. Large logs spaced around the fire acted as seats. Taito threw more wood into the flames, sparks flying and fire licking the air.

Hamish hadn't spoken to him much, but he looked at him as though for the first time. Through his mother's eyes. He was a large Polynesian man with a friendly face and tattoos on his arms and legs. When he'd finished building the bonfire, he turned and spotted them.

"Ah!" He held up a large hand in a wave and grinned broadly. "The McNeill triplets, good to see you again." He came forward and shook their hands, reciting their names as he did so. "Hamish, the one who looks the most different. Douglas, the outgoing one. Angus, who has a soft, younger face."

"Yeah, a baby face," Douglas quipped, and Hamish snickered.

Angus glowered at them, but humour sparkled in his eyes.

"You know it's true," Hamish said with a grin. "We've been tellin' you that for years."

Angus sighed and shrugged, holding his hands palms up. "I dinnae hear Skye complainin'."

Hamish and Douglas laughed, slapping him on the back.

Taito watched on with wide eyes. "Very good." He clapped his hands together and pointed to the two spits on the right. A man stood over a large one basting the pig while a woman stood next to the smaller one basting three rods of chicken wings.

"Dinner is still being prepared. We have some new guests joining us tonight, and some of the local islanders will come by too. We'll huddle around the fire, tell some stories, and put on a dance for you."

Angus strode over to a log and plopped himself down in front of the fire. Douglas joined him and Hamish hung around to talk to Taito.

"I hear you knew our ma," Hamish said.

He didn't share Douglas' beliefs that their ma had an affair, but he believed they'd become good friends.

Taito looked up in surprise, then laughed. "You ain't backwards in coming forwards, are you?"

"I dinnae want to assume anythin'. We're receivin' letters each day that she's pre-written. Today's letter said you were a good friend to her durin' a tough time with our da."

His smile tightened as an emotion Hamish couldn't make out passed across his face.

"Your mother was a wonderful woman, Hamish. She was a good friend, and as much as I'd love to tell you everythin', I have been instructed not to."

Hamish swore under his breath. "I really dinnae understand the secrecy. Why didnae she tell us before she passed?"

Taito slapped his arm good-naturedly. "I can't answer that, Hamish. I'm sorry. Just know this is what she wanted and we're respecting her wishes."

This silenced Hamish and he nodded.

When Brenda turned up a few moments later, Hamish's spirits lifted. Tenika must be close! Brenda approached, her face taut.

"Tenika sends her apologies," Brenda blurted without a greeting. "She can't make it and will explain everything tomorrow." He went to speak, but she held up a hand. "Dinnae ask me anything. I can't answer it. That's all I can tell you."

He sighed and shrugged. "Okay, thanks for lettin' me know."

Brenda skipped off to sit on a log. The moment Douglas spotted her, he left Angus to join her.

Disappointed Tenika wasn't coming, he joined Angus. He'd been so looking forward to seeing her, but he'd be patient. She'd warned him she had things going on. He just didn't understand what had changed in a few hours.

As the evening progressed, Hamish relaxed as he reflected on their journey. Ma's secrets. Would she really hide something that could change what he knew about his family? What if it destroyed everything they'd built?

But what if it didn't?

Ma loved her sons, and he couldn't believe she'd do anything to hurt them on purpose. One thing was certain though, this journey awakened an emptiness inside him. The kind he used to experience as a wee lad when he'd wished he had a father. How he'd been teased at school when his voice changed. When he had his first crush on that girl in fifth grade. His first heartbreak in high school.

Ma did her best, but she didn't offer the male perspective he'd needed sometimes.

And now he'd met someone special. A wonderful woman named Tenika, who he'd only known for such a short time, yet she'd woven herself around his heart and filled up every crevice of his mind. He'd never grown attracted to someone so fast. She must be special.

Then why wasn't she here? How did he ask her what was going on without frightening her off? This was where he wished he had a male figure he could talk to.

On the other side of the bonfire, Hamish spotted Brenda and Douglas sitting next to each other, their arms pressed together. He said something and she threw her head back in laughter. Hamish smiled, a little bit of envy clawing away at his insides. He wanted to be carefree like that.

Beside him, Angus pocketed his phone. "Where's your woman?"

"She's *not* my woman." He bumped Angus' shoulder. "Apparently, she couldn't make it. How's Skye?"

Angus grinned, his smile almost reaching his ears. "She's great." He kicked off his sandals and wriggled his toes in the sand. "I'm thinkin' of proposin' when I get home."

Hamish gawped at his brother, a wide smile crossing his face. "Angus, man, that's amazin'." He pulled him in for a side hug.

"Cheers." He took his phone out of his pocket, which was lit up and ringing. "This is her now. I'll be back. Save me this spot, will you?" He slid his feet back into his sandals and walked off.

Hamish shuffled to sit in the middle of the log.

The bonfire crackled and popped, growing when Taito added another log. A rich, savoury aroma of roasting meat caught on the breeze, making Hamish's stomach growl. As he took in the area, he noticed some local islanders had arrived, holding drinks and hovering around the fire. To the right, he spotted three people who looked like tourists. Reunion attendees perhaps?

One, a blonde woman, glanced around and spotted Brenda the same time Brenda spotted her. Even on the other side of the fire, Hamish saw Brenda's shoulders tense. Douglas said something and she shook her head. She sat upright as the blonde approached and stopped in front of Brenda, her arms folded around herself.

The words spoken appeared heated, but mainly from Brenda. The girl couldn't make eye contact and when she stopped talking, she held out a hand. Intrigued, Hamish glanced at Brenda, whose eyes were wide. She appeared reluctant at first, but then took the girl's hand and they shook.

The blonde walked off with a bright smile and a skip in her step.

Brenda appeared confused and shook her head when Douglas asked her something. What was going on?

At that point, Taito stood and clapped his hands to get everyone's attention. "Good evening, everyone!" There was a chorus of greetings then Taito added, "Food will be ready to enjoy soon, but until then, I'd like to share a story with you. Some call it folklore. We call it a guardian."

Drums sounded from behind trees, and a shiver ran down Hamish's spine. As they continued beating, some local dancers in Polynesian tribal garb came out dancing in time to the drumbeats.

"The story is about the Maritimo Mermaid, a mythical creature which resides in the azure waters."

Whispers rippled through the small crowd of about a dozen people. Hamish saw firsthand what his mother saw in this man. A storyteller, someone charismatic.

"The Maritimo Mermaid protects our precious islanders and the sea. Once upon a time, this island faced great calamity from a category five cyclone. Never had it experienced such a terrible storm. Cyclones were common, but not devastating."

The drums beat a rhythmic tune that had Hamish tapping his toes. Angus returned and Hamish shuffled over so his brother could sit. They sat in companionable silence, watching the dancers and the flames flickering over their faces as Taito continued his story.

"The cyclone threatened to destroy everything. No one would have survived. The emergency services were too far away to help in time. We were all alone. But then—"

A loud clap of thunder overhead made a few people shriek.

Taito grinned at the sky and held up his arms as though praising it. "—The Maritimo Mermaid emerged from the depths of the water, her luminous scales shimmering in the moonlight flitting in and out of the stormy clouds. She had an ethereal beauty about her. Her long, flowing hair made of seaweed, eyes that held wisdom of the ocean. She sang a song that soothed the turbulent seas and calmed the storm, saving the island and its residents."

Another rumble of thunder caused goosebumps to rise on Hamish's skin and some small drops of rain landed on his arms and face. No one moved though. It had been a humid day, and the rain was a welcomed relief.

Everyone applauded and Taito grinned as he bowed. The dancers left, but the drums continued a new beat that set the tone for dinner.

"Thank you, thank you," Taito said. "Now, help yourself to the food and enjoy!"

"Yes!" Angus jumped to his feet and dashed to the spread behind them.

Hamish chuckled and joined his brother. The drops of rain come faster now, but still no one was deterred. The wind was cooler and bore a mix of briny salt and fresh rain. While Hamish waited in line for food, he glanced up at the dark sky. The clouds moved quickly, stars peeking in and out.

After piling up his plate with delicious spit roasted meat, salads, and plenty of island fruit, he sat back down with Angus. The wind tousled the flames and the rain fell steadily, but not enough to put out the fire.

As the evening continued and Taito told more stories, Hamish concluded life on the island wasn't so bad. He missed home, but life here ran at a different pace. Besides, he was quite besotted with a particular woman.

Tomorrow. Tomorrow, he would encourage her to talk. If he was on a journey to learn about his biological father, why not make it a journey of love too?

Chapter 9

♥

"Come on, Nika." Brenda pulled at the covers. "You told me last night you'd make an effort today."

Tenika groaned. "I was younger and full of hope then."

Brenda tugged on Tenika's arm to get her into a sitting position.

"Okay, okay, I'm getting up." Tenika sat up and Brenda let her go. She grabbed her clothes and made her way to the bathroom.

Once changed, she came out and asked, "Did you get your kiss from Douglas?"

Brenda got to her feet. "Sadly, no, but we had a great night." A smile lit up her face. "He comes across all loud and macho, but he's actually quite sensitive. All the brothers are."

Tenika hesitated. "What did Hamish say? Was he angry?"

"Honestly, I don't think he's capable of being angry. He seemed fine, disappointed though. Are you ready?"

Tenika nodded. Outside, they began their pre-jog stretches. It was cooler this morning and the ground was wet. She didn't realise it had rained overnight.

"I promise I'll talk to him today and apologise," Tenika said.

"You'll tell him about the reunion and—"

"Yes, I'll tell him everything."

Brenda stopped stretching, standing with hands on her hips. "Good. By the way, Douglas asked if we wanted to join them today. Kayaking this morning, lunch, and a boat tour to spot dolphins and sea turtles, then dinner at the resort. If the weather is good, then possible stargazing too."

"That sounds amazing. Count me in."

They set off at a walk, and Tenika said, "Hey, if we're stargazing tonight, maybe it'll be the night for some kissing." She made kissing sounds.

Brenda's cheeks turned red. "Oh stop it, you." But as she was about to put in her earbuds, she grinned. "That *was* the plan though."

When they stepped out onto the sand, they broke into a jog. Brenda put her earbuds in, and Tenika enjoyed the natural sounds. Birds chirping. Waves lapping the shore. The gentle breeze rustling the palm fronds. Occasional voices floating on the breeze from the fishing boats coming back to land. When they reached the eastern side with the sun rising above the horizon, they spotted Douglas and Hamish approaching.

They waved as they passed but no one stopped. Tenika looked back the same time Hamish did. She smiled and waved, then turned back, but as she did, she tripped over her feet, yelping as she landed face first on the sand. Brenda burst out laughing and Tenika heard feet stop beside her.

"Are you alright?" came Hamish's voice, helping her to her feet.

She spat out some sand, gritty on her tongue. "I'm fine." She brushed herself down, shooting daggers at Brenda and Douglas, who were both laughing at her expense. "Just my pride is hurt."

Hamish chuckled lightly. "I'm sure we can fix that."

"Why is it I always seem to make a fool of myself around you?" Tenika placed her hands on her hips.

"What did I do?"

"You distracted me and made me trip." She grinned at him.

"I did not! You looked back and tripped over your own feet. I saw the whole thing."

That makes it even more mortifying. "Damn it." She chuckled. "I can't blame you for anything, can I?"

"No, definitely not."

She glanced over at Brenda and Douglas who were now talking and flirting.

"They've hit it off," Tenika said.

Hamish appeared nonplussed. "They have. I haven't seen Dougie taken with anyone for a long time."

"Me either, for Brenda."

"Did she tell you our plans for today?"

"Yes, I'm looking forward to it."

Hamish smiled. "Good. I'd hoped we could...talk."

She swallowed and nodded. Her behaviour last night, while justified, still wasn't fair on him. She should've at least found him and told him she wouldn't be there. Surely she could let him in a little. She had no reason to distrust him.

"I'll see you soon then. Dougie, you ready?"

Douglas looked over then leant in to say something to Brenda, who smiled coyly and nodded.

The boys disappeared and Brenda and Tenika jogged back to their room, neither of them speaking. Brenda in a love-struck haze, Tenika contemplating possibilities she never thought possible.

Within a couple of hours, they'd showered, changed, had breakfast, and made their way to the northern side of the island. When they rounded a bend, they saw some kayaks laid out on the sand. Tenika stopped, her heart leaping into her throat.

"What is it?" Brenda asked, stopping beside her. When Tenika didn't answer, Brenda followed her gaze. "Oh."

A few feet away stood one of her three nemeses—Davina Parish. So it *was* her yesterday? Where were the other two? They wouldn't be far behind, and this did nothing for Tenika's anxiety.

Dressed in appropriate gear for kayaking, Davina was clearly joining the morning adventures. Tenika's stomach rolled, threatening to bring up her breakfast. If she hadn't promised Hamish she'd be here, she'd be running for her life.

On cue, Hamish appeared with his brothers, stopping near Davina. He spotted Tenika and grinned, lifting his hand in a wave. Frozen to the spot, she could only stare, her heart racing.

You're stronger now. This isn't high school.

She shook the fear and anxiety away and pulled her shoulders back. With a jut of her chin, she managed a smile and wave at Hamish.

"Oh my God! Tenika! Hi!" came Davina's overly cheery voice.

Tenika whipped her head around, her breath catching. Davina waved and grinned at her like they were old friends. Was she delusional?

Her racing heart made her head spin, so she turned away and focused on breathing. If she'd learnt anything from school, ignoring the bullies was the best approach. Davina might be friendly now, but Tenika didn't trust her *at* all.

She wouldn't hide anymore, but she refused to interact. It was the only way she could grow stronger emotionally.

Everyone huddled on the sand as the instructor gave them a rundown on how to row. Davina stood on one side of the group and Tenika purposely stood on the other side.

"You okay?" Brenda whispered.

Tenika nodded but stared ahead, listening to the instructor. After a brief lesson, he informed everyone it was time to leave. Tenika glanced around once more, surprised to still see no sign of Belinda or Zachary. She didn't know what to think.

Don't think. Enjoy your day.

Everyone carried their kayaks to the water and climbed in. As Tenika set a rowing rhythm, an uncomfortable sensation settled in the pit of her stomach. Only one bully was there. What did it all mean? Maybe it was too early to tell. For all she knew, they were arriving later.

So much for no thinking.

Tenika heard a shriek, and she stopped rowing. Glancing back, she spotted Brenda rowing around in circles.

"Nika, help!" Brenda cried, laughing.

Relieved for the distraction, Tenika chuckled and rowed back to her friend. Douglas arrived at the same time. He flanked her right while Tenika flanked her left and they stopped her spinning. It took a few attempts for Brenda to get the rhythm right, but eventually, she did and set off in a straight line with Tenika next to her.

Davina watched from a few feet away, a small smile on her lips. She lifted her hand in a wave and this time Tenika returned it. She wasn't even sure why.

"Come on," Brenda called over her shoulder, speeding ahead.

Douglas caught up and he rowed alongside Brenda, Angus not far behind. Davina followed but stayed separate from the group. It was an unusual sight because Davina always demanded attention in school. Yet here she tried not to interfere with a group she wasn't part of. *Had* she changed somehow?

Lost in her thoughts, Tenika's anxiety subsided as she rowed at a slower pace behind them, following the shoreline of the island. Apart from the splashing water from her oars, they rowed in silence. Below the boat, the water was so clear she could see the sand, shells and rocks on the ocean floor.

Soon it changed and coral gardens appeared. A kaleidoscope of colours and coral formations, a diverse range of fish and marine life. Looking back at Maritimo Island, they passed an area of wild rainforest and a stunning aquamarine lagoon visible through the trees. She hadn't been around that part of the island yet.

In the distance, voices and laughter caught on the breeze as the group rounded a bend. They were about halfway now and she wasn't far behind. The sound of splashing made her heart leap. She glanced back and sighed in relief when she spotted Hamish following her. So caught up in her own thoughts, she thought he'd overtaken her.

"Why are you following me and not saying anything?" Tenika called out, slowing down so he could catch up. "It's a bit stalkerish, isn't it?"

"Stalkerish?" He joined her and raised an eyebrow. "Quite the contrary. I was lookin' out for you, but I dinnae ken if you wanted to talk, so I kept my distance."

Her heart warmed at the kind gesture, but she grimaced. "Look, I'm sorry about last night. I suppose you can tell I don't trust people easily."

Hamish nodded. "I think I'm startin' to understand. I saw someone talkin' to Brenda last night, and it seemed like there might be some bad blood there."

What happened? Brenda didn't say anything, but now Tenika needed to know.

"I will tell you, it's just not easy to open up. I'm sorry."

"Come stargazin' with me tonight," Hamish blurted.

Tenika whipped her head around to look at him. "Uh—"

"Just the two of us, away from people of the past. If you're up for talkin', you can. If you're not, I'd love your company either way. But just so you know, I dinnae scare easily."

Her breath caught and their gazes locked.

"I'd like that," she said, and she meant it.

Chapter 10

♥

Hamish was glad to be talking to Tenika again, *and* he'd learnt something.

She hadn't had an easy life.

He'd seen the way she'd frozen when the same woman he saw last night called out to her. There was a history, and not a pleasant one.

Apart from a few spoken words between them, the last hour of their row was in comfortable silence. Once they returned to the island and put their kayaks away, they had a light lunch on the sand. Tenika was much more relaxed, and the four of them chatted like they'd known each other forever.

While the secrecy on this journey bothered him, he was enjoying it overall. He especially enjoyed each moment with Tenika, and he willed the time to continue moving slowly, not wanting this to end too quickly.

Half an hour after eating, they boarded a medium-sized silver and dark blue motorboat moored at a nearby dock with hollow metal pontoons attached to the bottom of the flat deck, and a dark blue canopy. On board were upholstered beige seats that looked like it allowed up to around twelve people.

Tenika and Brenda sat on one bench on one side of the boat, chatting quietly while they cruised to their destination. Hamish desperately wanted to talk to Tenika, but it would have to wait until later. It wasn't the right time or place.

He sat on another bench with his brothers opposite the girls, only chatting when something caught their interest. They all seemed content to drink everything in. They hadn't received a letter from Ma yet, but he expected it would arrive soon.

The blue water became darker the further they cruised away from Maritimo Island. They passed a few small, uninhabited islands. Most were sandbars, as their skipper Krishneel announced, that disappeared under water each time the tide came in. Some larger ones had rock faces and greenery, while others had nothing but a few palms.

"Dolphins spotted!" Krishneel announced after about half an hour of cruising. He slowed the boat and anchored it.

The girls were the first to jump to their feet and turn around to peer into the water. Their excited gasps had Hamish joining them, his brothers only seconds behind.

"Are we allowed to swim with them?" Brenda asked, glancing back at Krishneel.

The middle-aged Fijian skipper, smaller and shorter than Taito but about the same age, nodded. "Yes, but please don't initiate touch. They will do so if they are interested. We come out here often so they are familiar with people, but we must respect their home. The sea turtles can be a bit hit and miss. If you see them, please do not touch."

Brenda nodded and grinned at Tenika, her face displaying a silent message only Tenika understood because seconds later they stripped down to their swimmers. Hamish tried not to stare at Tenika, but how could he not? Her bright tropical floral bikini showed off her beautiful curves and her brown skin glistened as she reapplied sunscreen.

He drew in a shaky breath and looked away, willing his heart to stop racing. His whole body was on fire, and not from this blasted humidity either. His fingers itched, wanting her in his arms again. Her lips on his.

He was in *big* trouble.

"When you are ready," Krishneel said, interrupting Hamish's thoughts, "you can enter the water through this gate." He pointed to a gate at the front of the boat. "Sit on the edge and slide in slowly so you don't scare the dolphins away."

Brenda was the first to do so, with goggles and snorkel on top of her head. She seamlessly did as Krishneel instructed. Tenika followed.

Hamish and Douglas stripped down to their board shorts. Angus did too, much to Hamish's surprise. He hadn't been interested in their diving expedition yesterday, but maybe dolphins interested him more.

When Hamish had lathered sunscreen on his unfortunate Scottish-pale skin, he slipped into the water. Douglas, then Angus entered after him. Tenika and Brenda were only a few feet away, treading water with a couple of playful dolphins frolicking around them, swimming, jumping, and showing off.

They spread out and let the dolphins swim around them, bumping their legs and wrapping around their waists. One dolphin in particular would swim around Hamish, then swim over to Tenika and repeat this process as though inviting them to join. Surely, he must be going mad. But it didn't let up. Then again, who was he to argue? He needed no invitation to join Tenika and the opportunity to hold her again.

He swam over, the dolphin still weaving between them. When he was close enough, he reached out for Tenika's hand. Startled, she jerked her head around in surprise but then broke out into a brilliant smile, as bright as the afternoon sun, when she noticed him.

He didn't give her a chance to speak. Mesmerised by her, the dolphin now swimming around them, he let the gentle embrace of the ocean push them closer until their bodies touched. As they trod water, their legs brushing, he wrapped an arm around her. He didn't care about the onlookers. Let them watch.

Brenda's excited laughter pierced the air followed by that of his two brothers, but everything became a haze as Hamish lost himself in Tenika's chocolate eyes. He inched closer, flicking his eyes to her lips, needing...*wanting* to kiss her.

The look she returned, one of not just interest, but complete attraction, tested his strength. He'd promised himself he wouldn't kiss her again until he was certain she wanted it. Was now the right time? Reluctantly, he let her go, not missing the disappointment in her eyes before she averted her gaze. He started to swim back when something heavy and rubbery bumped his back, nudging him closer to her again.

"What the—?"

"Why you little—" Tenika said as she too was pushed closer to him.

The same boisterous dolphin popped out of the water and chattered at them before disappearing again. Tenika's laugher pealed around them, and Hamish couldn't breathe for a moment.

"It was the dolphin?" Hamish asked.

She nodded, still laughing as the dolphin swum around and around, not letting them separate but pushing them even closer together. Their legs brushed and he gathered her into his arms, the desire to kiss her returning with force.

"Maybe we should give it a show?" he murmured.

Promises be damned. If a bloody dolphin could see it, why the hell was Hamish shying away? Tenika turned serious, her lips slightly parted as she caught Hamish's gaze, an array of emotions in her eyes. Fear was prominent but he could see she was warring with something.

The dolphin swam a little closer again, bumping them then came up and sprayed water over them.

"Oh my god!" Tenika shrieked, laughing.

That beautiful melodic laughter did Hamish in. He pulled her flush against him, her skin soft against his, lips only inches apart, their legs brushing. The dolphin kept swimming around, popping up occasionally and chattering as though encouraging them.

"I dinnae think we have much choice," Hamish said, his gaze searching Tenika's.

She swallowed and laughed softly, but the fear in her eyes was gone.

"You're giving in to a dolphin?" she quipped with a quirk of her lips.

He shrugged one shoulder. "It's makin' it clear what it wants. How can I argue with a dolphin? It seems to know what *I* want."

"Just you?" she asked, looking at his lips before raking her gaze up to meet his.

"Is this what you want?"

She opened her mouth. Stopped. Then cleared her throat and nodded. "I'm scared."

His heart shattered into a million pieces as he cursed whoever hurt her. He gently brushed his lips against hers in a fairy kiss and she shuddered in his arms.

"Dinnae be scared," he whispered. "I'm not goin' to hurt you."

She met his gaze then gave a single nod. Permission. Nothing held him back. He tightened his hold around her, both treading water, and pressed his lips against her warm, soft ones, the taste of salt and sunshine his undoing.

The world disappeared as the ocean's embrace drew them together along with a happy, frolicky dolphin. This was no fairy kiss. It was heated. Passionate. Full of promise. And he knew that while they were in this magical place, they didn't need to worry about real life.

It was time to take a leap of faith and see where this relationship would go. Everything else could be worked out later. Right?

The dolphin swam between their legs, pushing them apart, and popped up, spinning on the spot and chattering.

"Really?" Hamish said, reaching out to run his hand gently along its smooth but rubbery skin. "Now you're jealous?"

The dolphin chattered again, and Tenika laughed. Hamish would do anything to hear it every day. So carefree and full of life. He caught her gaze, relieved to see she didn't seem afraid or unsure. If anything, she glowed.

Krishneel popped his head over the boat and called out to them, "It's time to return to the island."

Hamish and Tenika both gave the dolphin one last rub then swam back to the boat, the dolphin showing off one last time before swimming off to join its pod. Not a sea turtle in sight. At least, Hamish didn't see one. He had been too interested in kissing Tenika.

Back on the boat, Tenika and Brenda sat on the same bench they arrived on, their heads together as they talked. Hamish sat with his brothers, noticing Douglas held an envelope. *The* letter. Krishneel must've had it.

"Your turn to read it," Hamish said, sitting down as Krishneel turned the boat around.

Douglas nodded and opened it.

My dear boys,

You would have been kayaking this morning and now you're on your way back from swimming with the dolphins and sea turtles. I hope you loved it as much as I did.

It's probably unlikely, but there was one dolphin who was particularly friendly. Duncan and I were still not entirely on speaking terms, but we went swimming together and the dolphin was in a very playful mood and kept trying to nudge us together. Eventually we were forced together, and we talked things out.

Today was the day we got on the same page. He apologised for his behaviour and admitted he'd been scared but he was ready to step up and be the best father he could.

I can't imagine that dolphin still being around, but if it is, be prepared for an adventure. We dubbed it Daisy though we had no clue what gender it was.

Douglas stopped reading and looked pointedly at Hamish, smirking.

Hamish shrugged and held his arms out wide. "I've got nothin' to hide." Then looking up at the sky, he said, "Yes, Ma, that dolphin has a lot to answer for."

His brothers chuckled. The girls looked over once, smiled, then went back to talking. Duncan continued reading.

Your evening will be an easy one. Enjoy dinner at the resort restaurant, then find somewhere to stargaze. If you can get up to the peak of the island, it's worth it. You'll get the best view of the stars there. If not, anywhere on the beach is just as beautiful. And if you can, take someone special with you. It's even more magical with the person you love.

Today was a fabulous day because your father and I promised we'd raise this baby together and be a happy family. Everything was good, and tonight was special because we bonded on a whole new level. But I won't go into details.

"Ma!" the three said at once and burst out laughing.

All I can say is there's something magical about Maritimo Island and it's a place where anything is possible. If you're struggling with a life decision, or not sure what you want to do next, let Maritimo Island work its magic on you. Soon enough you'll figure it out.

With love, Ma

Douglas put the letter away and the three brothers sat in silence, contemplating their mother's words. The only thing going around Hamish's mind was: if she and her father were in such a good place, what in the world could have gone wrong?

Chapter 11

♥

"Nika, oh my god," Brenda whispered as the boat took them back to Maritimo Island. "That was *hot*."

Tenika's cheeks flamed, but her stomach swirled with fluttering butterflies. "It's the dolphin's fault."

Brenda giggled and nudged Tenika's shoulder. "Sure, whatever you say. You two have been on *fire* since you met. You don't need a dolphin to encourage you."

Tenika groaned and buried her face in her hands. "I'm not equipped to deal with this. We're on holiday, I'm not the type to have a fling, what's going to happen after—"

"Stop it, Nika," Brenda warned. "You're too practical for your own good. You over think *everything*. For once, just embrace the moment. Maybe he can keep your mind off the reunion."

Tenika sighed and rubbed her forehead. "Maybe." She rested her head back and closed her eyes against the sun trying to break through the clouds.

She sat upright again, too unsettled to relax and glanced across to where the brothers sat. Hamish and Douglas chatted, and Angus joined Krishneel at the front.

Remembering what Hamish said earlier, Tenika asked, "Brenda? Hamish said someone approached you last night. You didn't tell me."

Brenda shuffled around to face Tenika, eyeing her critically. "I wasn't sure if you were ready to talk about it."

"I want to, especially after seeing Davina today. She seems...different somehow. Nicer perhaps? And what's with the absence of Belinda and Zachary?"

Brenda shrugged. "I have no idea. I do believe Davina has changed, though. I told you that she seemed more level-headed in her posts. Then last night, well, she came up to me at the bonfire and apologised."

Tenika's eyes widened.

"We shook hands and that's all."

"Huh." This was a big deal. While Brenda didn't cop it as badly as Tenika, she still suffered her fair share of teasing and name calling. She deserved the apology as much as Tenika did.

"She asked after you," Brenda said slowly. "I said she'd have to find you herself but that it was unlikely you'd want to talk to her. She understood."

"Thanks, Brenda."

They sat in silence as Krishneel took them back to the island. Tenika once again rested her head back on the bench, her mind full of thoughts from the past. The butterflies turned into knots of anxiety, making her nauseous as the boat rocked.

So far she had found no closure, but maybe she was being too hasty. Or maybe Brenda was wrong and this whole expedition was a waste of time.

How can it be a waste of time when you met Hamish?

His handsome, smiling face popped into her head and reduced her anxiety a little. She breathed out and let the newly made memories overtake the ones of the past.

Half an hour later they docked, and everyone disembarked. Hamish waited for her at the bottom of the pier. Brenda nudged her arm with a snicker before running ahead to meet up with Douglas. Tenika had relaxed, and the rocking of the boat, along with thoughts of Hamish, had put her in a better mood. She must've been grinning like a fool when she approached him.

He casually took her hand, sending sparks shooting up her arm and turning her legs weak. It was so easy with him. Everything was so natural. So nice. So *real*. They wandered slowly along the sand towards the centre of the island. The clouds continued to gather across the sky, the heat increasing and decreasing each time the sun reappeared and disappeared.

They reached the resort entrance and stopped, turning to each other.

"Shall we meet here at seven?" Hamish asked. "For dinner?"

Tenika nodded, losing herself in his emerald eyes. "And stargazing afterwards?"

Those beautiful irises twinkled as he nodded and smiled, his eyes creasing at the corners. He looked up at the sky then back at her. "As long as the weather holds out."

Tenika's whole body warmed as he leant in and left a lingering kiss on her lips. They grinned at each other as he pulled away. With a wink, he strode off and Tenika released a shaky breath, holding her fingers against her lips.

She floated back to her room.

After a delicious buffet dinner with a selection of local delicacies and fish, Tenika followed Hamish out of the restaurant for an evening of stargazing. Thankfully it was just the two of them tonight. She loved Brenda like a sister, and really liked Hamish's brothers, but they'd spent a lot of time together and she wanted some time alone with Hamish.

She looked up at the sky, not convinced they'd get a great stargazing session in. The breeze picked up, as though a storm was brewing. Clouds sped across the sky, the stars and quarter moon popping in and out of view, but never lasting long.

When they reached the beach, the bonfire was burning again and a few local islanders stood around chatting. As they passed it, Davina came into view on the other side, sitting on a log beside the fire by herself.

Tenika tensed and Hamish, who held her hand, must've noticed. He looked at her with a furrowed brow. "You alright?"

Tenika nodded and squeezed his hand but looked away when Davina glanced across at them. Tenika sped up, tugging on Hamish's arm, eager to find a spot away from the fire, away from Davina, and somewhere darker for a better view of the sky. Her breaths came out in short bursts.

They followed the coast to the eastern side where it was darker and settled on the sand a few feet away from the water lapping the shore. The waves were bigger than normal as the wind picked up and the storm rolled in.

They laid on the sand staring up at the sky, Hamish's hand still holding hers. Tenika considered what to say. She appreciated he didn't push, but she needed to do this. This was a good learning experience for her. A chance to trust a man again, a chance to open her heart.

Brenda was right. She needed to have fun and enjoy the moment, stop overthinking it.

"I was bullied in school," Tenika said softly, her voice carrying on the breeze. "I was adopted as a baby, and I had a different skin colour. It made me a target because I wasn't like everyone else. Anyone who was different, or friends with anyone who was different, became automatic targets."

Hamish said nothing but he squeezed her hand, telling her that he was listening.

"That woman by the fire is Davina. She was one of them." She swallowed a lump that formed in her throat. "There were three of them in school. One was her twin sister, and the other was her high school boyfriend. They're not here, which is...strange, but all three of them were my worst enemies."

She stopped for a breath and continued looking up at the night sky. The stars scattered across it like a blanket of diamonds. The bright moon shone down on them. Until the clouds closed in on the final clear patch.

Silent too long, Hamish asked, "What did they do?"

Tenika's laugh was bitter, humourless. "What *didn't* they do?" She closed her eyes, flashes of memories crossing her vision. Over the years she'd blocked them but occasionally they popped up in dreams...nightmares. Tonight, they were real. Taunting.

Tears pricked her eyes, and she blinked them away.

"If you dinnae want to—"

"It's okay." She shook her head and released a slow breath. "Brenda and I were in school together. She was bullied too but not as badly. She knows everything by default, but you're the first person I've ever opened up to."

Tenika heard him moving next to her and turned to see him leaning on his arm, his head resting on his palm. His serious eyes were on her.

"I appreciate that," he said. "If it's too difficult, I understand."

She copied his position and faced him, wanting to see his expression. She wasn't sure why, maybe to witness his reaction? Perhaps to see if he genuinely believed her?

"No, it's okay." She paused. "At first it was typical school yard bullying. Pushing, kicking, stealing and throwing food, pulling hair, you know, the 'normal' stuff."

Hamish's eyes grew wide. "That's *normal*?"

"Well, 'normal' in the sense of that's what's usually associated with bullying. It's tame considering how bad it got. We lived in a small town. The teachers didn't know how to handle bullies and the victims weren't allowed to fight back. If they did, *they* got suspended or expelled, never the bullies."

When emotion rose in her chest, she stopped and took some deep breaths. "That's not the point here though," she said. "I'm just setting the scene, so you understand why it got so bad. Why nothing was ever done."

He nodded but his jaw twitched.

"Over time it got so much worse. Pushing me down the stairs, forcing my head into a toilet bowl and flushing, locking me in a hot shed in the peak of summer." Her skin crawled as memories consumed her.

So many times, she was so afraid she'd die. Drown by the flushing if they didn't lift her head in time. Break her neck when falling down the stairs. Overheat or dehydrate from being in the shed too long. But she never did because Brenda always saved her. Her ever-loyal best friend. If Tenika ever went missing, Brenda knew to come looking.

Until the day she couldn't.

"One time," she continued, "it was late spring and unseasonably hot. They found a shed on a farm, a long way from town. It belonged to the parents of one of our classmates, Travis. We were teenagers then, senior year in fact. Zachary had his provisional licence so he could drive without supervision. After recess one day they kidnapped me, took me out there, and tied me up, leaving me there to..." she shrugged as goosebumps rose on her skin, "...die, I guess." At Hamish's wide eyes, she smiled weakly. "I wish I could say I was joking, but I'm not. Brenda couldn't save me this time because she didn't know where they'd taken me."

Tears seeped out of the corners of her eyes and she sat up, wiping them away. Hamish sat up too, sitting opposite her with his legs crossed. He took her hand and gave it a squeeze, running his thumb over her knuckles. She squeezed back in an unspoken thank you.

"What happened? Who found you?" he asked.

"Travis, actually."

She still remembered Travis' shocked expression at seeing her in his shed. It was late afternoon by the time he found her when he came out to do his chores. At least eight hours had passed, and she had become severely dehydrated. On the verge of passing out, she remembered her heart rate slowing. That was the closest to death she'd ever been.

"Poor Travis couldn't figure out why I was there or how I got in there. We hadn't shared any classes together that day, so we hadn't crossed paths, and I was too sick to explain." She swiped away more tears. "He got help and I was rushed to hospital. When I came to the next day, everything came out."

She sighed and looked out over the ocean. The wind blew her hair across her face and the waves crashed against the shore, the spray of saltwater kissing her skin. It was overcast now. Lightning flashed on the horizon.

"He saved my life," she continued. "We're still friends to this day. We live too far away to see each other often but we text or FaceTime often. It was then things started to change. I only had a few weeks left of school, but he basically became my bodyguard for the rest of the year." Her cheeks flushed when she admitted, "He was my first kiss, too."

Hamish chuckled, and she breathed a sigh of relief. Some men didn't like hearing about exes, even if they were high school ones who no longer meant anything. Although that wasn't entirely true with Travis. She'd always have a place in her heart for him because he did so much for her. They didn't love each other like that though, so nothing ever eventuated but she cared for him. Loved him like a brother.

"Obviously it didnae work out?" Hamish asked, his eyes searching hers.

"I think it was the highly emotional situation that drew us together. I viewed him as my saviour and he viewed me as his damsel in distress. He's married now with a baby on the way and we're like brother and sister."

She smiled wistfully, wondering when the baby was due. She should message him after the holiday. Would he come to the reunion?

"Those *people*, if you can call them that, the bullies I mean, still tried to hurt me even with Travis looking out for me. But it reverted to the 'tamer' bullying, and let me tell you, that was better than what I previously endured. Of course they got the last hurrah. They were all on the newspaper team and during the last week of school, they wrote an article that defamed me and accused me of cheating on Travis. It went around the whole school."

She gritted her teeth. Even though Travis didn't believe the article, the attack on their relationship made it fizzle out. Travis took her to the school formal, but after that, they parted as friends. Tenika held no resentment towards him. He was still her hero.

"After we graduated," she continued, "I left them for dust. I want to say I forgot them and moved on with life, and in a way I did, but the memories never disappeared. Seeing them, well, Davina, again..."

She shook her head, unable to put it into words.

"It must be difficult," Hamish said. "Did you ever report them?"

Tenika's spine stiffened as shook her head. "I was scared," she admitted in a whisper. "All I wanted was a normal school life and if I reported them, it would've made everything so much worse."

Hamish nodded in understanding but didn't push it, much to her relief. "Why did you come to the reunion?" he asked instead.

"Closure." She shrugged. "It was Brenda's idea, and I reluctantly went along. I feel stuck, like I've lost control of my life. Perhaps going through with this reunion will fix something in me. In just over a week, I need to return to Melbourne and figure out what I'm doing with my life. I don't want to keep jumping between different hospitality jobs."

It started to rain lightly, and she held her arms out, the water dripping onto her skin.

"Maybe this will be my new home," she said, a sense of freedom washing over her. Confessing her past to Hamish was therapeutic. "For the first time in my life, I belong. I've never known much about my heritage, and I still don't, but being here is so natural. Like it's in my blood."

She shivered as a gust of wind whipped around her, as though agreeing with her.

She looked back at Hamish to gauge his reaction. He had a soft smile on his lips but what she didn't expect was the sadness in his eyes.

Chapter 12

❤

Maybe this is meant to be my home.

Hamish's skin prickled as the words washed over him. An overwhelming sadness weighed heavily on his shoulders.

This trip was supposed to be a simple journey to learn about his father. Meeting Tenika changed everything. Still so new, still so much to learn, but he liked her. A lot. Was this a pointless path they were on?

If she viewed this island as her home, and he had plans back in Scotland, what future did it hold for them? His heart hurt just thinking about it. He'd rather not think at all and enjoy what time they *could* have. Cross that bridge when they came to it, in about six days' time.

"Are you okay?" Tenika asked.

He shook himself out of his reverie and stared into her beautiful brown eyes that resembled pools of chocolate. Those eyes could lift any flagging spirit and his smile came easily, melting away his sadness. He reached out to touch her soft skin, damp from the rain.

"Of course I am." He leant in to kiss her softly, her full, soft lips melding perfectly with his own. "I'm sorry for all you've suffered," he murmured, resting his forehead on hers. "You can trust me. If anyone ever hurts you, or Brenda for that matter, they've got me and my brothers to answer to."

Tenika laughed, warming him from the inside out.

"Thank you." She stood and held out her hand. "We should head back before the storm turns bad."

He glanced out over the ocean where lightning flashed and forked on the horizon followed by a long rumble of thunder. He took her hand, and she pulled him up. They walked hand in hand back to the resort.

"So, now that you know my sordid past, do you have one?" she asked, glancing up at him.

"Nothin' compared to yours. Ma gave us a great life, but our high school years were tryin'. We went to a large school but bein' triplets came with its challenges." He smiled ruefully. "Polar opposite to you, we were popular by no choice of our own. Girls wanted to be our girlfriends, boys wanted to be our pals, all in the name of popularity."

Tenika smiled softly. "I bet you three broke a few hearts."

He winced, remembering a few occasions he'd had to let girls down only to upset them.

"Never intentionally. You know how cruel some teenagers can be. Rumours and lies spread, makin' girls believe they had a chance with us, and we had to let them down gently.

"That's horrible." Tenika's face was a mask of sorrow.

"Ma always instilled in us the importance of respect and not leadin' someone on if we weren't interested. We really tried our best to live by that. Of course, we weren't perfect and sometimes we got caught up in the moment. It was flatterin' to get so much attention."

Tenika shrugged one shoulder. "I don't know anyone who'd be able to completely resist that sort of attention. I think it's commendable you even tried to do the right thing. But it's ridiculous, isn't it?

Honesty should be a good quality, but if you want to fit in at school you've got to lie and be who you're *not*."

"Exactly. My brothers and I were relieved when we graduated. We attended different universities too. It was a great opportunity to find our independence."

"You live different lives then?"

"Yes of course. We'd drive each other mad if we were in each other's space every day."

Tenika hummed in response. "It makes sense. I just never thought about what life must be like as a twin or triplet or whatever. I guess I wondered if you always lived together until you found that special someone." She laughed softly. "Sounds pretty stupid, huh?"

He shook his head. "Not at all. My brothers and I are close, but we're different people and live different lives. Angus, as you've probably noticed, is much quieter. He's a temp and moves between office jobs. He has a long-term girlfriend he's plannin' to propose to. Dougie flits between pub jobs and is more outgoin' and unsettled. People think he's a serial dater, but he's only had a couple of serious girlfriends. He's picky about who he dates and hasn't found a job he can settle into yet. And me—"

"Ooh wait, let me guess," Tenika interrupted. "You're a jack of all trades—"

He raised his eyebrows. "Good guess."

Like his brothers, he'd never settled into a career since the distillery *was* their goal.

She grinned. "I'd also say you're not as quiet as Angus but less outgoing than Douglas. You're more..." She tapped her chin in thought.

"The voice of reason?" He offered. "That's usually what I'm told."

"Yeah, but I was going to say you're a combination of your brothers. You have your quiet, level-headed side, but you're confident too." She paused and looked at him, her eyes dark and smouldering. "I like you, Hamish. I like you most out of your brothers."

He laughed loudly and stopped, pulling her into his arms. "I would hope so. If you were tryin' to date all of us because you couldn't choose, I'd have somethin' to say."

She stepped back, grinning. "No way! I like that you're a mix. I sometimes find Douglas overwhelming. The larger-than-life personality tires me out. It's why I need to have a break from Brenda sometimes too. But the quieter type in Angus would drive me crazy."

Hamish chuckled and he took her hand when they started walking again. "Tell me about your family."

For the rest of the walk, they talked about their families. Or lack thereof when it came to Tenika's. His heart went out to her. He was glad she had a loving adoptive family, but sad she would never know her biological ones. He told her of his own beloved Ma and the stress of caring for her in her final days. It was a relief to get it off his chest.

When they reached the resort, they stopped. The rain fell faster now, dripping down their faces. Neither of them cared.

"I love my Ma and I miss her, but I'm happy she's no longer sufferin'. Now, perhaps my brothers and I can finally implement the goal we've had for years."

She raised an inquisitive eyebrow. "What's that?"

He swallowed. Dare he tell her? Because this was where the great divide between them would widen. But he didn't want secrets. This relationship, or whatever it was, needed to be open and honest.

"We want to open our own whisky distillery," he said in a rush. "It's been a dream of ours since high school. We've been makin' whisky on the side for years, tryin' to perfect it, and we're close. We just need a proper setup to get it off the ground. Ma left us some money in her inheritance, and we agreed to put our portions towards our project."

"Wow!" she looked impressed but then he saw the moment realisation dawned on her, the shine leaving her eyes. "Ooohh." She released her hand from his and stepped back.

"Tenika." He reached for her, but she stepped further back. "Tenika, please, this doesn't have to change anythin'."

"Doesn't it? What are we doing then, Hamish? What's this?" She gestured between them. "I can't imagine you ever wanting to live here. I've got island blood, and this island is beginning to feel like my lifeline. My home. If I end up living here, there won't be an *us*."

He winced. "We won't know if we dinnae find out."

She stopped. Opened her mouth, then closed it again. For a nanosecond something flashed in her eyes. Like she was seriously reconsidering.

Then a shutter came down and she straightened her spine.

"We don't need to find out, Hamish." She took another step back. "It's already obvious and it's not fair on either of us to risk finding out when it's only going to lead to heartbreak."

"But what if—"

She held up a hand. "Don't Hamish, please. Let's leave it here before we get in too deep. Let's save the heartbreak, okay?"

Before he could say anymore, she turned and disappeared into the resort the same moment the heavens opened, and rain came down in a gush. Lightning flashed and thunder roared overhead. Hamish took a shortcut through the resort, past the pool area, and ran back to the bungalow, cursing the turn of their conversation.

What he'd wanted to say was, "What if I grew to love it here too?"

Of course, he couldn't know that. Yes, he and his brothers had a dream, and being in Scotland would make it easier to get it off the ground but what if they could work something out? Hamish was quickly learning that he'd do anything for Tenika, including moving to a secluded location. But how could he say that when they were still getting to know each other?

He reached the bungalow and ducked inside, his clothes and hair dripping. It was quiet, apart from the gentle snoring from his sleeping brothers. A glance at his watch told him it was nearing midnight, so he pushed his worries aside and decided to sleep on it.

Ma used to say sleep could fix anything. It was time to put her theory to the test.

The next morning loud banging on the wall woke Hamish from a deep sleep. He groaned and pulled the covers up over his head. He'd tossed and turned all night, barely able to sleep as he recalled how he and Tenika had parted.

More loud banging made him jump, and he cursed. "What is it?"

"Get up!" Douglas yelled. "We've got a scenic flight to catch in twenty minutes. Didnae you read the itinerary?"

Hamish muttered as he pushed the covers back and got out of bed. He'd forgotten all about it. "I'm comin'," he mumbled when Douglas banged the wall again. He ran his hands down his face.

Ten minutes later, he and his brothers followed the path to the dock where the seaplane awaited them. Douglas had a literal skip in his step as he led the way, Hamish was in the middle and Angus dragged his feet behind them. He'd been in a sour mood since he woke up.

Settled on the seaplane, the pilot came back to talk to them. He was Polynesian and, unsurprisingly, similar in age to Taito and Krishneel.

Hamish noticed everyone seemed to be the same age here. Where were the families?

"I'm Ratu and I'm your pilot. Would someone like to join me at the front?"

All three hands shot up and Ratu chuckled. "Okay, everyone can have a turn. Who wants to go first?"

When no one put their hands down, the pilot pointed at Douglas and jabbed his thumb toward the cockpit. "You go first. Get up front and put your headset on."

Douglas smiled smugly as he stood and pushed past Ratu into the small cockpit.

"The flight will take an hour and a half. You two can figure out who's next. We'll be flying over Maritimo Island and other nearby islands."

Hamish nodded and Ratu joined Douglas at the front. Hamish moved to sit opposite Angus, who was slouched in his seat with arms folded.

"What's with you?" Hamish asked as the aeroplane revved up.

Angus huffed but said nothing.

"Come on, bro, stop bein' so immature. You're thirty, not thirteen. Talk to me. Ma wouldn't want you havin' a lousy time."

"Yeah well, I am," he admitted, his cheeks colouring. He lost all his attitude and his arms fell to his sides. "You and Dougie are havin' a grand ol' time, and I'm just along for the ride. Always ignored, left to fend for myself. It's bloody infuriatin'."

Hamish looked at him in surprise. "But you haven't been interested in many of the itinerary events. You like being by yourself and you're always lookin' for opportunities to escape and speak to Skye."

Angus tensed and turned to stare out the window, not bothering to answer. Something didn't quite ring true. There must've been more to it.

The plane sped along the water, then soared high into the air, giving them a perfect aerial view of the island.

The peak from up here was spectacular. They could also see the village where the locals lived, the resort, and the markets and shopping areas. It was a medium-sized island but had a small population. It was intriguing how an island like this survived and thrived without any of the usual things like hospitals, post offices, and major supermarkets.

Hamish turned to Angus. "Look, if that's how you feel I'm sorry. Dougie and I honestly thought it's what you wanted."

Angus sighed, then muttered, "Skye and I had an argument."

Hamish had to lean in to hear him, but he caught it. "Oh. I'm sorry. What happened?"

Angus' shoulders slackened as he turned to Hamish. "She's pregnant." He looked at Hamish with wide, scared puppy dog eyes.

Hamish's jaw dropped. This sounded eerily familiar. "Bro—" he shook his head, having no words, "—bloody hell."

"I know, right?" Angus paused. "I dinnae ken Da but I suddenly understood his reaction after Ma broke the news to him. When Skye told me last night, it took me by surprise, and I reacted without thinkin'."

"What exactly did you say?"

Angus' face turned red. "I told her I wasn't ready, that it wasn't what we'd planned. Then *she* thought I meant I didnae want the baby, and it all ended up bein' one big misunderstandin'."

"Dude," Hamish breathed out the word. "*Do* you want the baby?"

Angus nodded without hesitation, much to Hamish's relief. He wasn't equipped for a conversation about what to do if he'd said no.

"And she does too?"

Another nod.

"Alright, that's good. Then why dinnae you feel ready? What *was* the plan?"

"We wanted to marry first and have children a year or two later."

Hamish breathed out, nodding as the news sunk in. "You pretty much are married, you realise? You live together and share the bills, the only thing missin' is a piece of paper. This is great news. You do see that? It's what you both want. It's just been brought forward by a couple of years. That's how life goes sometimes."

Angus nodded and turned to glance out the window for a moment. When he turned back to Hamish, a slow smile spread across his face. He appeared lighter.

"I really am happy," he said, his eyes shimmering.

"Then you know what you have to do?"

"Of course I do. I'll call her once she's awake."

"No, you'll call once we land. I bet she's waitin' on you to fix this and she's probably not sleepin'. If she's pregnant, she needs to sleep and—"

"Alright, I see your point." His Adam's apple bobbed when he swallowed.

"Good. Embrace this, bro. Skye's a great lassie and what you two have is forever."

Chapter 13

♥

When the plane had landed and docked, Hamish removed his headset and turned to Ratu. "Cheers, mate. That was fantastic."

Ratu tipped his cap. "You're welcome. I remember taking your parents up all those years ago. She was a lovely woman, your mother. Left her mark on everyone." He smiled whimsically.

"What about our father?" Hamish couldn't waste this opportunity to ask.

Ratu's smile slipped and he shuffled in his seat. "I'm not supposed—"

"I'm not askin' you to reveal anythin' about this journey. I understand you cannae say anythin'. I just want to know what our father was like. As a person."

Ratu relaxed. "He was a good man. Larger-than-life type of personality. The life of the party. Doted on your mother, he did. You could see what they had was real."

This only fed Hamish's confusion about what could've gone wrong.

"That's all I can say, I'm sorry." Ratu reached into his jacket pocket and removed a familiar-looking envelope. "I've been instructed to give you this."

Hamish took it. "Cheers, mate. We're gettin' a collection now." He sent him a smile, then disembarked, finding Douglas waiting on the pier for him.

"I was wonderin' when we'd receive the next one." Douglas nodded at the envelope.

"Where's Angus?"

"Ringin' Skye. Said he'll meet us on the beach."

"Good. He told you the news?"

Douglas nodded. "I'm happy for them."

"Alright, let's grab him, then find some shade so we can read the letter."

Sweat dripped down Hamish's back, neck, face...*everywhere*. It was even more humid after last night's storm. He wasn't built for this heat, but he'd put up with it for a certain Fijian-Australian woman.

It didn't take them long to find Angus in a shady spot under some palms. He ended the call as they joined and smiled brightly. It was all the confirmation Hamish needed. Everything was okay.

Settled on the sand, Hamish ripped open the envelope and pulled out the letter.

My boys,

I hope Ratu let you all have a turn up front during the scenic flight. Your father and I fought over who'd get the front. Luckily, Ratu stepped in and suggested we share.

But in the end, your father let me stay up front for the whole flight. He was always so thoughtful like that. Even if he really wanted to do something, he'd give it up for me. And I knew he'd be the same with his future children.

But that's not a topic for now.

The rest of the day we enjoyed the markets, then after a relaxing afternoon, we attended the lovo feast in the evening. This is a must-do event as it's the lead up to the annual Tropical Harmony Festival, which will be held a couple of days before you go home.

At the lovo feast, your father and I had a long talk. About everything. The news of my pregnancy changed our relationship. We'd gone from being newlyweds to soon-to-be parents. We both had dreams, plans we wanted to fulfil while we were young. Your father wanted to open a distillery—

"What the?" Hamish said aloud.

The brothers looked at each other with wide eyes and open mouths.

The letter shook in Hamish's hands. He cleared his throat and continued reading.

It was a dream of his for as long as I remember. When you boys talked about wanting to do the same thing, it warmed my heart to know you were so much like him and didn't even know it.

But that aside, I had my own dreams too. I wanted to travel more, I wanted to start a business, I wanted to do everything. But things changed and our dreams seemed like such an impossible feat.

One thing that was certain was that we loved each other and when you love someone, you do anything to make it work. You jump all the hurdles together. You make new dreams together. Nothing should ever get in your way.

Enjoy the rest of your day. Until tomorrow.

Ma

"Then why the hell is Da not in our lives?" Douglas asked what everyone else thought.

A sense of foreboding hung over Hamish. Did his brothers feel it too? What did it mean? He locked it into the back of his mind for now.

While his brothers stared out over the ocean, Hamish reopened Ma's letter and reread the last paragraph. It was too early to even consider 'love' between him and Tenika, but something strong was growing. Something honest and *real*. When the time was right, he would talk to her and reveal the words his mother said. Make Tenika see that if they had something special, they couldn't lose it.

Tenika had left a note on the cupboard for Brenda last night, telling her not to wake her for a jog, that she needed to sleep. When she was finally up and about, she found a note from Brenda replacing hers saying she'd gone to look for Douglas.

Tenika didn't know what their itinerary held today and didn't want to know either. Last night proved one thing. She was in too deep with Hamish and it had to stop. She'd been so caught up in these new and exciting feelings, she'd forgotten all about the distillery plans Brenda told her about. When Hamish said it, she came crashing down to earth and it occurred to her they were such different people with their own dreams.

They couldn't work. Could they?

We won't know if we don't find out. Hamish's words flittered through her mind, making her doubt her determination. Was he right? Was she being too brash?

These thoughts played in her mind while she showered. Her heart longed to take a risk. Her head, ever practical and afraid of taking risks, overrode her heart. Stepping out of the shower, she wrapped a towel around herself and stared at her reflection in the steamed up mirror—glowing skin, hair hanging in tight curls past her shoulders, bright eyes.

She could thank the island for this transformation, but it wasn't just that. Hamish helped too. She felt things she was usually too afraid to. Confidence. Happiness. *Hope*. Turning away, she dried herself, then changed.

She needed a day of doing her own thing. Time to *think*. It'd been a whirlwind since she'd arrived.

Slipping on her sandals, she left her room to go for a walk and find some food. On the way down the stairs to the ground floor, her stomach grumbled. It was mid-morning and the buffet breakfast would be over, so she'd have to find something else.

Stepping out the door from the stairwell onto the ground floor, she walked past the archway leading to the pool and into the entry area. Opposite her was a large seating area with plush cushions and island-inspired décor. A place for guests to relax while they completed their check-in process or waited for their room to be ready. Beyond that was a terrace that spread across the western side of the building. She strode over and stepped out onto it. Her breath caught at the stunning view of the rainforest, the local village, and the sparkling ocean beyond it. The sky was blue with only a few white puffy clouds.

She turned to go back inside, her eyes drawn to the massive hand-carved reception desk. It gleamed with its rich dark wood, polished to perfection and adorned with fresh tropical flowers and Polynesian artwork. Adjacent to it was a concierge desk staffed by friendly attendants. Fijian music played softly in the background.

The restaurant was on her left where guests could enter from the terrace or the main entry area. Tenika strode in that direction, hoping there might be some food she could order.

A middle-aged Fijian woman looked up from reception as Tenika approached and smiled brightly. "May I help you?"

Tenika stumbled to a stop and blinked. Even though they hadn't officially met, she recognised her from the day she arrived. The same one who'd rushed up to greet Hamish and his brothers. The one she recognised. Litia. That was her name.

The woman cocked her head to the side, brow furrowing delicately as though she too recognised her.

"Tenika?" she asked, a large smile lighting up her face.

She nodded then bit by bit memories slotted into place. "Litia?" Now she remembered. "You have a son, don't you?"

If Litia's smile could grow any larger, it did. "Yes, Eroni. It is you, isn't it? You went to school with him."

Choked up and eyes filling with tears, Tenika inched forward as Litia came out from behind the desk. They met halfway and embraced.

"I can't believe it's you!" Tenika exclaimed as they pulled away. "It's been, what? Fifteen years?"

Litia's eyes shimmered as she nodded.

Tenika shook her head, unable to believe it. "I thought you moved back to Fiji?"

She'd gone to school with Eroni for about a year when Litia and Taito lived in Australia. Since she and Eroni shared Fijian heritage, they became instant friends. Unfortunately, it meant he too was often targeted by the bullies. She'd been so sad when they left without a goodbye. Eroni was the only one who *truly* understood her. She'd only overheard someone say that they were returning to Fiji.

"Oh no," Litia said. "We were always coming back here. I probably would've said we were flying back to Fiji because no one had heard of Maritimo Island." She chuckled, then reached out and clasped her hand between both of hers. "It's so lovely to see you. Eroni isn't here right now, but he'll be so happy to know you're here."

Tenika shook her head, trying to clear it. "What happened, Litia? One minute you're there, the next you're gone."

Of course, she knew the bullying would've been the trigger but that's all she knew.

A shadow passed over Litia's face. "We were only in Australia for a short time to learn new skills and save some money to help towards the resort. This is before we got the funding from Fiji that we get now. Then when things got bad at school for Eroni..." Her breath caught and Tenika nodded.

"I understand," she said, patting Litia's hand. "But Davina—" she shook her head, unsure what to say next.

"I don't like to hold on to resentment," Litia said. "When Davina reached out about the reunion, stating she was making amends, I couldn't refuse. It's good business, and after discussions with Taito and Eroni, we all agreed."

Making amends? Has Davina really changed that much?

"Wow," Tenika said, shocked at the revelation. "Um, is the restaurant still serving food?"

Litia took Tenika's elbow and led her to the restaurant. "Yes, of course. Tenika, I hope this is not too forward of me, but did you have a pleasant meeting with your family in Fiji?"

Tenika furrowed her brow. "Uh, how'd you know about that?"

"Oh." Her lovely laugh tinkled around the resort. "I apologise. Brenda mentioned you were coming but didn't say your name, which is why I didn't make the connection before."

"I see. Well, it was fine." She changed the subject. "Maritimo Island is such a beautiful place."

They stopped outside the door to the restaurant, Litia eying her curiously. "I know we haven't seen each other for a long time, Tenika, but you can always talk to me. For that year we were there, you were Eroni's closest friend and like a daughter to me and Taito."

Tenika smiled but didn't respond because Litia added, "And yes, we're very fortunate to live here. We rely on Fiji for many of our services, but we have a lovely little community. We always have one seaplane here in case of emergency, to fly us to Suva where the hospital is. We have a local doctor, and Taito is the equivalent of a Sherrif, but we don't get much riff raff here."

"Do you get many visitors?"

"We do now. Earlier this year we had a film crew run a documentary about the island, and it really gave us a boost. Our growth is a work in progress, but since our time in Australia we have come a long way! We're so small compared to other populated islands, and the resort only allows a certain number of people at any time. With the reunion attendees, plus some additional guests that needed to travel the same time, we're full for the first time."

"That's wonderful! And you mean the Scottish brothers, right?"

Litia beamed. "You've met them?"

Tenika couldn't stop the grin from spreading across her face. "We've been on a few outings together. They told Brenda and me about the journey they're following, one their mother took?"

The light in her eyes dimmed. "Yes, Isla McNeill, bless her soul. She was my best friend, and I couldn't say no to her request." She pursed her lips.

Sensing the topic was closed, Tenika changed tack again. "Tell me about the locals. Do many new people move here?"

Litia laughed heartily. "Oh no, dear. We're all like family. There is no one under fifty and everyone knows everyone."

A morbid thought crossed Tenika's mind and she blurted the next words without thinking, "But what happens when—?"

"We die out?" Litia finished with a sparkle in her eyes. "Don't think that hasn't crossed our minds. We're aware of our mortality and we have yet to figure out how to overcome that." Her smile was light and joking but Tenika didn't miss the worry in her eyes. "Anyone with children, those children have flown the nest and have no desire to return to such an isolated location. At least how it stands now. Who knows what will happen in the future, but we can't rely on them coming back."

Litia shook her head sadly but gestured for Tenika to follow her into the restaurant.

Their conversation stayed with Tenika though, whirring away, brewing with an idea. There was so much potential. An infusion of youth was so important to sustain its vitality and keep it growing. As in lots and lots of babies.

Tenika would put her hand up in a heartbeat...though she needed a man for that.

A certain red-headed Scotsman entered her mind, followed by the most adorable brown-skinned, red-headed child.

Tenika internally groaned. This was bad. This was very, very bad.

Litia excused herself, promising to catch up soon, and bustled off to work, leaving Tenika thinking about babies with red hair and suddenly having no appetite at all.

Chapter 14

♥

With thoughts of red-haired babies safely tucked away in her mind, Tenika finally found something to eat before walking towards the island's centre. She'd spent so much time on the beach, she hadn't taken time out to explore the local markets and residential areas.

She hadn't seen Brenda since last night, and with their phones still switched off because of their technology-free pact, there was no way to make contact. Tenika didn't mind though, enjoying the solitude. She and Brenda would have another chance to talk later. Hopefully before the lovo feast. She needed some Brenda wisdom before seeing Hamish.

Regret hovered like a rain cloud as she recalled their conversation from last night. He wanted to give them a chance and for a wonderful moment, she thought it could be possible. But then the feeling disappeared. Replaced by uncertainty. *Fear.*

Was it a hangover from her past? Ill-equipped for such a big commitment, fight or flight always resulted in the latter when faced with it.

But now...she wasn't so sure. What happened to taking a leap of faith? It was so easy to get caught up in the moment when they were swimming with dolphins. Everything was perfect. Anything was possible. But after revealing her past to Hamish, she was reminded yet again that life was never that easy.

Taking a leap of faith was *so* not her.

But it could be.

She continued walking, pushing the thoughts away for the time being, and enjoyed the warmth of the sun on her skin while breathing in the fresh, tropical air. It really was paradise. Even though the humidity was rife, for her it felt right. Natural, even.

Finding the markets, she explored the array of local delicacies, arts, crafts, jewellery, and clothing. She bought some island clothing, loving the colourful tropical patterns. Next she moved onto a jewellery stall.

"Tenika!"

Tenika froze as she inspected a necklace.

"Tenika! Over here!"

There was something familiar about it. Shrill. Perky. *Annoying*. Her hand trembled as she dropped a shark's tooth pendant. It fell back into place with the other necklaces. She turned, heart pounding, and spotted the blonde woman a few feet away, waving her arm.

"Tenika, hi!"

It was Davina.

Fight or flight kicked in and she was ready to leave Davina for dust. Until she remembered Litia's words. Then she recalled their kayaking expedition yesterday, and how different she seemed.

Davina ran up, smiling brightly. "Hi, thank you for stopping! I'm so glad I caught you. You're always so busy."

Davina laughed it off, but it sounded forced. She might be over the top bubbly and a little ditzy, but she wasn't dumb. In fact, even despite her bullying, she was one of the smartest girls in school. That's what stung the most. She had to endure so much crap from them *and* compete for grades too.

Not in the mood to be nice, Tenika settled for brutal honesty. "Davina, you and I both know I haven't been busy. I haven't wanted to talk to you." She drew in a breath to suppress the shudder threatening to rip through her body. "I thought you were arriving later, so your early arrival surprised me. I wasn't prepared to face one of the people who ruined my life."

Davina's mouth opened and closed but she pulled her shoulders back and stood up straight. "I appreciate your honesty, Tenika, and I'll return the favour."

Davina turned serious, transforming before her eyes.

"I get it. You're angry and if I were in your shoes, I would be too. I've got no excuses for what I did, and I'm not about to try and think of one. But I like to think I've grown and matured over the last ten years. Unlike my sister and brother-in-law."

Tenika's interest was piqued. What did that mean? She shouldn't want to know, but the curiosity killed her.

"All I want to do is apologise," Davina continued. "That's it. No hidden agenda. No tricks. Just a simple apology." She held out her hand, her bright smile back in place.

Tenika looked at it then back up at Davina. Was she genuine? Could she trust her?

It hung between them for a couple of beats before Tenika shook her head and stepped back. "It's going to take more than an apology to convince me you're not that person anymore."

Davina let her arm fall to her side. Nodding once, she offered a tight smile, then turned and walked away.

"**A**m I being too paranoid?" Tenika asked, glancing at Brenda through the mirror.

She'd just filled her friend in on everything that had happened last night and this morning while they got ready for the lovo feast.

Brenda leant against the bathroom doorframe. "Maybe a little, but you're protecting yourself and there's nothing wrong with that." She paused, then added, "But—"

Tenika froze and met Brenda's gaze through the mirror. "But what?"

"Well, you need to move on from this. You can't hold a grudge forever. If accepting an apology from Davina helps you move on, then do it. I honestly believe she's genuine."

Tenika shrugged and dropped her gaze.

"But that's just my opinion," Brenda continued. "Don't forget why you're here. These people don't deserve to stay in your memories forever. You're allowed to be happy and it's time to forget about them."

Tenika looked up and smiled. A weight lifted off her shoulders.

"And that means letting Hamish in too," Brenda added. "What if you guys have something special? You'll have massive regrets if you don't find out."

Nodding, Tenika sighed and let those words sink in. *That* had been on her mind all day too. She already had so many regrets but now she had the chance to find happiness. It was time to take that leap.

Scrunching up her curls, she smiled. "Damn, I'm *loving* this weather." The humidity did wonders for her hair. She'd never had this much success with taming them before.

"You're so weird," Brenda said. "Most people hate humidity."

"Yeah, well, I'm built for it. Seriously, look how great my hair is!"

Brenda chuckled and they both finished getting ready for the feast. Tenika changed into one of the new bula dresses she'd bought at the market. After slipping on some sandals, she checked out her reflection again. Nearly there, but something was missing. But what?

"Wait, I have an idea," Brenda said, holding up both hands.

"Huh?"

"Just wait." Then she dashed out of the room, the main door slamming after her.

Tenika shrugged and sat on her bed as she waited.

Five minutes later, Brenda returned, panting. "Here." She held out a red hibiscus flower. "It's great having a tropical garden on our doorstep!"

Tenika chuckled and took it. "This is perfect, thanks!"

She snapped off the stem, leaving enough to stick into her hair. She pulled her hair back then tucked the flower in. Her hair was so thick and springy, the flower didn't need any pins. Turning around, she held her arms out in a 'ta-da' gesture. "Well?"

"Perfect. You look stunning." Brenda's voice broke and her eyes filled with tears. "You look like one of them, Nika."

Tenika's heart filled with love and warmth. She *felt* like one of them. She finally belonged.

"Why the tears?" Tenika asked, taking hold of Brenda's shoulders.

Brenda sniffled. Her bottom lip trembled, and she wiped her eyes on the back of her hand. "Oh, I'm being stupid. I'm happy for you, Nika, really. You've come alive on this island. You've found a place you feel at peace, and I'm so, so happy, but I'm scared too because, well, I feel like I'm losing a best friend."

Tenika pulled her friend in for a hug. "Oh Brenda, we're always going to be friends, no matter where we end up." They pulled back.

"Hey, you could always live here with me. I was chatting to Litia before, and—"

Brenda shook her head. "As much as I love this place, I couldn't live here. I'm a city girl. I need the freedom to do whatever I want, lots of shopping places, and cooler weather." Brenda paused, then added in a whisper, "Maybe I'll end up in Scotland."

Tenika's jaw dropped. She'd only jokingly talked about Douglas and what could be. Now, something had changed.

"Wait, wait, wait." Tenika grabbed Brenda's hand and dragged her to the sofa where they both sat. "What the hell is going on? Last I heard you were still trying to get Douglas to kiss you."

"Oh, he kissed me alright," she said, her cheeks turning pink. "Last night under the stars, before the storm hit..." She shook her head and ran her hands down her face, breathing out deeply. "I know this is still so new and everything but...but...you know how sometimes you *just know*?"

Tenika nodded, her eyes wide. Isn't that exactly what *she* was experiencing?

"I just *know*," Brenda emphasised. "I won't do anything rash. All I'm saying is if, at the end of all this, he asked me to return to Edinburgh, I wouldn't even need to think."

Tenika flopped back in the sofa. "Wow. That's intense. And *quick*."

"I know. Crazy, huh? But you and Hamish—"

"I know." It came out in a whisper, but the words hung between them.

Tenika was all too aware of what she and Hamish had. The cliff's edge loomed right before her. If she wanted to take that leap, it was now or never.

It was all so overwhelming. Her brain was overloading and she needed a moment to talk about something neutral.

"Oh, hey, do you remember Eroni?" she asked the first thing that came to mind.

"Who?" Brenda grabbed the remote and turned the TV on.

"Eroni, that Fijian boy we went to school with, about fifteen years ago."

The weather channel appeared. It looked like more rain and storms were forecast.

"Not sure," Brenda said distractedly. "Oh crap!"

Tenika turned her attention to the TV where a cyclone warning was in place for the day before the reunion.

"Yikes, that looks bad." Her eyes widened. "Hey, do you think they'll cancel the reunion?"

Brenda switched off the TV. "I suppose it depends how bad it is. We should find out." She shook her head and turned the TV off. "Eroni did you say? That Fijian boy?"

Tenika nodded.

Brenda thought for a moment then shook her head. "No, I have no recollection. Was he in our friend group?"

"Sometimes, but I mainly hung out with him after school and got to know his parents, Litia and Taito, really well."

"Litia and—" Realisation dawned on her face. "As in the Litia and Taito who own and run this resort?"

"The one and only."

"What a small world! Sorry, I don't remember him." She checked the time. "We should get going. It's already six p.m."

A few minutes later, they stepped onto the beach where stones lined two lovo pits. Banana leaves rested over the mouth of the pits, concealing whatever was inside. Delicious aromas wafted in the air, making her stomach grumble.

Loud drums played as locals and guests turned up. Over the day, more school alumni arrived, so the crowd was bigger than previous nights. When she walked past Davina, she paid her no attention.

The bonfire burned like usual. Hamish and his brothers sat on a log on one side, partially obscured by the fire. With drinks in hand, they talked amongst themselves. She loved the family bond they shared and the fact they were on a journey for their mother was heartwarming.

"Don't wait for me," Brenda said in Tenika's ear, then disappeared to join Douglas.

Brenda's appearance by their side had Hamish looking up and around. It only took him a few seconds to seek her out and he raised his hand in a wave. She waved back but didn't move towards him, frozen to the spot. He didn't come to her either.

He respected her stance, and she appreciated it, but it meant *she* had to make the first move and she wasn't ready. That leap might have to wait.

She searched for Litia, eager to reconnect and learn more about the island. She found her sitting on the sand in front of the palms, a little way from the fire. "May I join you?"

Litia looked up with a bright smile. "Of course."

They sat in silence for a few moments as Taito and some locals tended the pits, moving food around from under the banana leaves. Each time the leaves moved, wafts of delicious aromas teased Tenika's senses.

Clouds rolled in overhead, and thunder rumbled. Remembering the earlier forecast, Tenika asked, "Should we be concerned about the cyclone?"

Litia waved a dismissive hand. "Don't you worry about it, love. We take cyclones seriously, and we'll keep all the guests updated. It's difficult to tell how bad it will be as they can be so unpredictable."

Tenika nodded, nerves fluttering in her belly. "Do you have emergency plans in place?"

"Yes, of course we do." Litia patted her arm. "You just enjoy your holiday and if anything changes, you'll be notified."

That wasn't the answer she'd hoped for, but she should've expected it. She released a slow breath as a few drops of rain landed on her skin, her nerves drifting away on the breeze, She held her hands palms up as she glanced up at the darkening sky.

"God I love this place," she said aloud.

Next to her, Litia said, "You know you'd be welcome if you were to stay."

Those words stayed with Tenika. Planted by Brenda, Litia gave it some water and the idea grew. There was no way it would budge any time soon.

Chapter 15

H amish lost sight of Tenika but eventually found her sitting on the sand in front of the palm trees next to Litia, deep in conversation. She looked completely in her element. So stunningly dressed in Polynesian style clothing, complete with a hibiscus in her hair. Just when he thought she couldn't get more beautiful.

He desperately wanted to talk to her, suggest they go for a walk along the beach, but he respected she needed space. He wasn't ready to give up yet, but he'd wait. Maybe tomorrow he'd seek her out. He witnessed her hesitation last night but he was certain she didn't mean what she said. She was scared and he understood that, but he had to prove he wasn't the same as the people from her past.

While the drumming continued, the bonfire crackled. Even though the rain came and went, it kept burning. Never enough to douse the flames.

Over the last day or two, the guests had easily doubled, if not more. Now there were guests and locals alike seated in a large circle around the fire. One big community. Hamish had Angus on one side, and a man he didn't recognise on the other. Probably another reunion attendee. They chatted on and off but never introduced themselves. Douglas was with Brenda somewhere, but Hamish lost sight of them.

The drumming stopped while they ate off banana leaves. Delicious pork and fish with vegetables perfectly smoked from the lovo pit.

Once everyone had eaten, the drums started again and Taito told one of his epic stories about a magical coral reef. While he spoke, individual wooden cups of kava, a milky but watery type of drink made from the root of the kava plant, were handed out to everyone. Hamish didn't like the earthy flavour but appreciated the opportunity to try it.

By the time drinks were drunk, all the locals got up to dance their local dance around the fire, sand kicking up under their feet. Men and women would approach the guests and encourage them to dance. If they refused, they would take their hand and pull them to their feet, not taking no for an answer. When one came over to Angus, and he got up willingly, Hamish nearly fell over from shock.

Someone came over to him, and not about to be outdone by his introverted brother, he joined in without hesitation. He wasn't much of a dancer, had never been into the clubbing scene, so moving around a fire, stomping and shuffling his feet was awkward and clumsy, yet he had fun.

The drumming stopped but the dancing continued after someone set up Bluetooth speakers and the party raged with a mix of modern and older dance music.

There were many people, most of them Hamish didn't know, but some locals he recognised. Then an all-too-familiar exotic face danced into his line of vision, moving to the beat with her arms up in the air, showing off her magnificent figure.

Before he knew it, Tenika was in front of him and they stopped for a moment, breathing heavily from the exertion. The only sign of surprise from her was the widening of her eyes, but neither of them spoke. The song changed to another dance number, and they started moving slowly together. His hands instinctively settled on her hips while her arms wrapped loosely around his neck. They were so close he could smell her intoxicating coconut scent, mixed with the natural scents around them of bonfire smoke, rain, ocean, and sand.

The crowd laughed, danced, and cheered, losing themselves in the music and the tranquil environment. The area vibrated with energy, rain falling in a fine mist, occasional flashes of sheet lightning stretching across the sky. Bodies bumped into them, but they remain rooted to the spot, swaying, eyes connected, caught up in their own world. Hamish lifted one hand up to brush his fingers across the smooth skin of her cheek, tucking a stray curl behind her ear.

He leant in without thinking, desperately needing to kiss her but then stopped. Remembered what happened last night. She tightened her hold around his neck and pulled him down to meet her lips in a short but heated kiss. The type that drowned out their surrounds. The only thing seeping through was the gentle rain coating his skin and her delicious lips tasting of rainwater, salt and smokiness from the fire.

Cheers and whistles interrupted them. Tenika was whisked one way by a dancing crowd and Hamish was pulled the other way. His head spun, the moment feeling like a dream but the tingling in his lips reminded him it wasn't. He broke free from the crowd and stumbled into a heap on the sand, breathing heavily, bewildered by what just happened.

He raked his hands through his hair.

"You want to rethink that distillery plan, bro?"

Startled, Hamish looked up with wide eyes. Angus stood in front of him, sweating and breathing heavily, but looking so mature all of a sudden. It was like finding out he was going to be a father had changed him.

How could he answer his question?

Angus smiled sympathetically before squeezing Hamish's shoulder then walked away, through the trees.

Honestly, Hamish was rethinking his entire life.

Hamish tossed and turned all night. When he slept, he dreamt of that kiss. When he was awake, his mind was in turmoil and his emotions were all over the place. All he wanted was Tenika. To talk to her. Hold her. Figure out together what they could do. How they could traverse this new relationship.

He knew one thing. He didn't want to give up on his distillery dreams. It'd been a part of their lives for years, and after learning their father had the same dream, it seemed like the right thing to do in his memory. It was nice to have a connection, even if they never knew him. But what did that mean for him and Tenika?

It was still dark when he gave up on sleep. Sunrise wasn't far off. He'd go for a jog and hopefully run into Tenika too. Their kiss last night *had* to mean something. She'd taken the initiative in the end and kissed him first.

He'd find her today. If he remembered correctly, their itinerary was light on. The morning at least. If he didn't find her on the jog, he'd search for her after breakfast.

Once ready, he checked to see if Douglas wanted to join him, but while Angus snored away, Douglas' bed was empty. A shiver of trepidation traipsed along his arms. It wasn't like Douglas to stay out without a message but shoved the worry aside. He was probably with Brenda.

As luck would have it, Douglas came up the jetty whistling a happy tune while Hamish stretched. It didn't require rocket science to figure out they'd spent the night together.

"I wondered where you were," Hamish said nonchalantly as he changed legs.

"Brenda and I stayed out for the night." Douglas said, a grin spreading across his face.

"Things are serious then, huh?"

Douglas narrowed his eyes. "If you're gonna give me the third degree—"

Stretches done, Hamish stood straight with his hands on his hips. "I wouldn't do that. I'm happy for you, bro. I just dinnae want you to get hurt."

"I won't," Douglas stepped past Hamish and slapped his arm. "Dinnae stress, I can look after myself."

"You want to join me for a jog?"

Douglas stopped at the door and turned. "Not this mornin', I'm spent. Our first activity isn't until after lunch so I'm goin' to get some shuteye."

Hamish nodded and Douglas went inside. When the door clicked shut, Hamish started off on his jog. The air was damp, and the ground was wet from last night's storm. As the sky grew lighter, he could make out the palm fronds waving in the breeze, the clouds racing across the sky.

His feet pounded the ground as he breathed in the pungent tropical air that strangely rejuvenated him. The intense heat and the heaviness of humidity during the day was no fun, but mornings and evenings were bliss. He felt so alive when he was here.

He picked up his pace as the sky changed quicker now, the eastern horizon taking on a yellow, orange, and pink glow. As he approached the point where he first ran into Tenika and Brenda on their first morning, he stumbled to a stop, breathing heavily. Sweat formed a V on his tank top and he wiped his arm across his brow.

There, a few metres away, was Tenika. Sitting on the sand, arms behind her, legs outstretched as she watched the horizon.

Reminded of their kiss the night before, his heart flipped, and he moved towards her.

Now or never.

Transfixed by the sunrise, she was oblivious to his presence. He approached and stood beside her. "I was hopin' I'd find you here."

Her head whipped around, and she looked up, eyes wide. A slow smile spread across her face. *So far so good.*

"Good morning," she said. "Would you like to join me?" She patted the space on the sand next to her.

Hamish sat so their shoulders touched, setting his insides alight. His breath caught in his throat, and he had to take a slow, deep breath to regulate it again.

For a few seconds they sat in silence. Watching. Listening. Waves lapped at the shore. The wind rustled the large palm fronds. The chirp of birds and squawks of seagulls disturbed the early morning as they woke up with the sun. Thunder rumbled in the distance as the clouds drifted away. But no traffic. No horns. No mayhem.

Total bliss.

Hamish saw what Tenika did. Why she wanted to stay here. Life was pretty darn good.

"I wasn't sure if you'd want to see me," he said softly as their eyes remained glued to the horizon painted in gold as the sun peeked above it.

"Even after last night?" she asked, glancing across with a small smile.

The memory of their kiss once again flashed up in his mind. "May I remind you, it was *you* who kissed me first."

Tenika's smile grew wider as her gaze returned to the horizon. "Yeah, sorry about that. But I could see you wanted to and were holding back because of me, so consider it an apology kiss."

He chuckled lightly. "I'll take an apology kiss any day. You dinnae regret it...do you?"

To his relief, she shook her head. She folded her hands on her lap. "If I gave off the impression I don't want to see you, it's because I *always* want to see you."

He frowned, his stomach twisting. They were words he'd hoped so much to hear, yet—

"That makes no sense," he said.

She shrugged. "I know. I guess it's fear taking over again. Fear of the unknown. Fear of not wanting to hurt you. Of not wanting to *get* hurt."

Those words hung in the air as they turned back to the horizon, the sun fully rising above it and painting the area in a rich golden glow.

"I dinnae want that either," Hamish finally said.

When the sun got too bright, they turned to each other. With nowhere to hide, it was time to be entirely truthful.

"Then how do we stop it?" she asked. "We both have such different goals in life, it seems inevitable."

He cocked his head to the side, his eyes searching her face. Ma's letter from yesterday popped into his mind. "If we want this, we both do what we can to make it work. We jump hurdles together. Make new dreams. Dinnae let anythin' stand in our way."

She stared at him, mouth agape. "They're very wise words."

"You can thank Ma for them. She said somethin' along those lines in a letter we received yesterday." He stared at her intently, trying but failing to gauge her thoughts. "What do you think? Are you ready to take a leap of faith?"

"You sound like Brenda. She's always on at me about that."

"She's a wise woman. By the way what's with her and Dougie, huh? I never thought he'd find a woman here of all places. Neither did I for that matter."

They shared a smile and Tenika shrugged. "I think Brenda and Douglas just found the one they were looking for."

This was his opening. "Yet *they're* not afraid of leapin'."

She huffed out a laugh. "Damn it, I thought we'd changed the topic."

"No, Tenika. I want to talk about this. I dinnae want to leave this island with any 'what if's'. I'm not askin' for a no strings attached fling. All I'm askin' is to see what we can have, where this might lead. Things have a habit of workin' out when they're meant to."

She released a slow, shaky breath. "You make a very compelling argument there, Hamish. Anyone would think you were a lawyer."

He chuckled. "Far from it, but I know when I want to get to know a bonny lassie." This time he didn't even hesitate when he leant in and planted a soft kiss on her lips. When they pulled apart, he asked, "So how about it? Will you take that leap with me?" He held out his hand to her.

She looked at it, then at him. She swallowed but when she took it and nodded, he could've sworn the sun shone brighter.

He stood and helped her to her feet. "I'm free this mornin'. How about we have breakfast together and find somethin' fun to do?"

"I'd like that but let me change first. How about I meet you at the restaurant in about half an hour?"

He agreed, then they went their separate ways. Hamish had a skip in his step as he saw all the possibilities laid out before them.

Anything was possible and he intended to embrace it.

Chapter 16

♥

Tenika floated back to her room. She didn't get an ounce of sleep last night, too wired with memories flittering across her mind. Of dancing with Hamish. Kissing him while the music vibrated around them. The rain on their skin. She'd never be the same person again.

The island changed her.

Hamish changed her.

She was learning who *she* was. Her past no longer dictated her future. With the reunion two days away, the anxiety had all but disappeared. There were some lingering nerves but that was to be expected. Compared to a few days ago, she was a new woman. Life was good. Great even. Now that she and Hamish had talked, she wanted to ask if he'd attend as her plus one. While they hadn't discussed it, Tenika assumed Brenda would invite Douglas.

As she approached the room, she heard off key singing coming from inside. Brenda didn't come home last night. When Tenika had returned after midnight, there'd been a note from Brenda telling her not to wait up and they'd talk in the morning.

Tenika grinned as she opened the door and stepped inside. Brenda had earbuds in as she danced around the room, singing at the top of her lungs. She was standing on the sofa, arms outstretched, torturing the chorus to *Can't Help Falling in Love*. Halfway through, she opened her eyes and spotted Tenika. She shrieked and held a hand over her heart.

"Holy crap, you scared me half to death," she said as she stepped off the sofa and removed her earbuds.

"Don't quit your day job," Tenika quipped.

Brenda laughed and slipped the earbuds into a pocket of her track pants. "Are you coming back from your jog?"

Tenika nodded.

Brenda's eyes searched her face. "Did you run into Hamish?"

She nodded again. "No Douglas though." She smirked at Brenda's reddening cheeks.

"He's probably sleeping since—" She bit her lip, her cheeks turning even redder. "Did you and Hamish talk?"

"Nuh uh." Tenika stepped further into the room. "We're talking about you. I'll fill you in later."

Brenda looked like a kangaroo caught in headlights, but a smile blossomed on her face. "Oh. My. God." She fell back onto the sofa, resting the back of her hand on her forehead. "Nika, I think I'm in love."

Tenika sat next to her, frowning.

Brenda glanced over and grimaced. "Don't give me that look. I know how it sounds, okay? But you gotta trust me on this. Last night was..." she sighed and covered her face with her hands.

"You had sex then?"

Brenda nodded, letting her hands fall to her lap. "We snuck away when everyone was dancing. We planned to go back to the bungalow, but Hamish or Angus could've walked in on us."

"That would've been awkward."

"Exactly. Anyway, in the end we stumbled across a secluded spot in this beautiful cove, like a hidden beach. It was perfect."

Tenika wrinkled her nose. "Wait, you had sex on the *sand*?"

Brenda nodded, then giggled. "It was as messy as it sounds. I swear I'll be finding sand for days."

Tenika shook her head, ridding the image from her mind. That was *not* on her bucket list.

"Thanks for the warning though, I guess," Tenika said as an afterthought. "You were...safe, right?"

"Of *course* we were." She rolled her eyes but her smile showed her thanks. "But zero out of ten, would not recommend getting intimate on the sand. It wasn't *just* sex though." Brenda went all dreamy-eyed as she stared vacantly at nothing, obviously reliving her night of passion. "We *made love*."

"Oh my God, that's so corny," Tenika said with a snort, and they collapsed into giggles.

She trusted Brenda, and she sort of trusted Douglas too, but she didn't know him well enough. Then again, if he was anything like Hamish, he couldn't be all bad.

"I know it's corny." Brenda said between giggles, wiping her eyes. "But I don't know how else to put it. Sex is sex, but making love is all about *feelings*. It's a level I've never experienced."

Her eyes grew wide again, and she gulped.

"You're serious, aren't you?" Tenika asked.

Brenda nodded. "It's scary, Nika, but it's right. I know it. There have been no declarations, and everything I'm telling you stays between us. I just needed to get it off my chest. Now to figure out how to deal with everything and not scare him off." She blinked, a hopeful look filling her eyes. "How about a girl's day? I could really do with a distraction."

Aware of time slipping by, Tenika glanced at her watch. *Crap*! She had to meet Hamish in ten minutes.

"I'm sorry, I'm meeting Hamish for breakfast. How about this afternoon? I'm pretty sure the boys have other plans then."

Brenda nodded and got to her feet when Tenika did. "Sounds perfect."

Tenika rushed to her room and changed into sandals and a summer dress. Brenda stood in the doorway, looking expectant. "Sooo, you and Hamish?"

Turning to the mirror, Tenika tamed her curls. She caught Brenda's gaze and shrugged. "We talked about things and I suppose we're going to see where this leads."

Brenda yelped in excitement and ran forwards, embracing Tenika from behind in a tight hug. "Oh my god, we're both getting lucky! Wait, are you actually getting lucky, *lucky*?"

Writhing free from Brenda's grasp, Tenika turned to face her and shook her head.

"We're not at that point. There's no rush though, right?"

"Of course not," Brenda said, though she had a look in her eyes that said the conversation was far from over.

"We'll talk more later. For now, I really must go."

Leaving a dreamy-eyed Brenda, Tenika rushed downstairs to the restaurant. She stopped outside the main doors, taking a moment to pull herself together. Her mind was so consumed with what could be with Hamish.

In such a short time he'd invaded her mind and her dreams. It was impossible not to think about what it would be like to experience *all* of him. The thought alone sent a shudder along her spine. But that was a big step. One that meant the relationship was serious, and once they crossed that line, heartbreak was inevitable if it didn't work out.

·❤·❤·❤·❤·❤·

WW hen she stopped outside the entrance of the resort with
Hamish an hour later, the sun shone brightly, not a single
cloud in her sight. She thought of the cyclone warning and wondered
if it had moved away? She'd have to check later.

"I thought we could walk up to the peak," Hamish said. "Except
those shoes might not be any good."

Tenika glanced down at her sandaled feet and grimaced. "I can duck
upstairs and change them. If you're sure you've got time, I'd love to see
it."

Hamish checked his watch. "As long as I'm back in three hours, I'll
have time. It's about an hour there and a little less back."

"Okay, I'll be back in five."

Five minutes later, Tenika grabbed his hand and tugged on it as she
tried to bound ahead. "Come on, let's go!"

She'd been wanting to visit the peak since Hamish first told her
about it. They chatted while they hiked, seeming to have endless things
to say. Now they'd pushed past the uncertainties and agreed to see
what happened, they could be open about everything. She asked about
the distillery and the whiskey making process. He asked about the
Fijian heritage and lifestyle. She'd done lots of research before and was
more than happy to educate.

When they were nearly at the peak, Tenika realised in all their
talking she hadn't asked him to the reunion.

"Hey," she said between pants, "how would you like to come to the
reunion with me?"

In her periphery, Hamish glanced at her in surprise.

"Brenda hasn't said anything yet, but I'm sure she'll ask Douglas. It won't be total torture for you."

He came to a stop and took her hand, forcing her to stop too.

"Are you sure you want me there?" he asked, his brow furrowed. "I know the history now, and I cannae guarantee I'll be able to keep my hands to myself if anyone does anythin' to hurt you or Brenda."

Tenika squeezed his hand, appreciating his concern. "That's even more reason to have you there. You're the perfect bodyguard."

"Ouch!" He clutched his chest. "I'm wounded."

She chuckled. "Seriously, it'll be nice to share a new chapter of my life with you."

He stared at her for a long moment, then he leant in, tilted her chin, and kissed her oh-so-sweetly on her lips. Such a small gesture but with a big impact. It lifted her off the ground and onto cloud nine.

"Then I'd love to," he said when he pulled away. He took her hand again. "Come on, we're nearly there."

A few minutes later, they reached the peak, panting from the exertion of the final steep climb and the talking. She did a slow three-sixty turn, admiring the entire island and beyond. She saw a seaplane arriving and wondered if it carried more people for the reunion. Who was still to come?

She turned back to Hamish and beamed at him. "This is perfect, thank you." She stood on her tiptoes and pressed her lips to his.

He placed his hands on her hips as he returned with fervour, making unspoken declarations and promises. This kiss showed her all the possibilities before them. She could see a future together. Not just on this island. But in Scotland too. She wanted to experience both. Somehow.

What if we could?

Stricken by the thought, she pulled away with a gasp and stared at him. It was all so clear!

Hamish stared into her eyes, brow furrowed. "Are you alright?"

"Everything's perfect. I just—"

There was a rustling sound behind them, followed by a curse. "I didn't think you were coming up here today."

They spun around. A tall and skinny man stood only a few feet away. He wasn't there when they arrived, but by the looks of it he'd exited from a space hidden behind foliage.

"Scott, hi," Hamish said, confusion written across his features. "I didnae think we needed permission to come up here."

The man, Scott, lifted his wide-brimmed hat and scratched his head. "Oh, uh, you don't. But, um," his face crumpled, and he tried to shift the foliage back into place inconspicuously without success, "please pretend you didn't see me or...or...this. *Please*."

He shot past them and disappeared down the path they came up. Tenika glanced back at Hamish and his gaze zeroed in on the spot Scott had emerged from.

"I didnae notice that last time," he moved away to investigate.

"Hamish," Tenika hissed, following him. "You heard what he said."

"That's like tellin' someone not to press the red button." He turned his head and gave her a dazzling grin. "Come on, what harm could it do? We'll take a brief look, and it'll be our little secret. We won't tell a soul." He crossed his heart.

She stared at him, torn, but then looked at the gap in the foliage and understood the temptation. How could they *not* look?

"Fine," she relented, "but it's *our* secret."

Hamish winked then turned to push the foliage aside. He ducked, then slipped through. She prayed she wouldn't regret this. When she came out the other side and saw what Hamish was looking at, she gasped.

Chapter 17

♥

Hamish heard the foliage rustle behind him, followed by Tenika's gasp, but he couldn't move. Couldn't talk. Couldn't do anything but stare, his heart in his throat.

His knees gave way. He fell on the soft, moist ground as his heart pounded inside his chest. He read and reread the inscription. *In loving memory.* Three simple words that explained everything Hamish had ever questioned.

Someone had taken good care of the marble headstone, and it gleamed in the late-morning sun. Was that what Scott had been doing? Tending the grave? There were even some fresh flowers leaning against it, a nice floral arrangement with a variety of colours of hibiscus and some other tropical greenery, a piece of string wrapped around the stems.

He reached out and ran his fingers over the letters of his father's name. A strange sensation surged up his arm. He never knew his father, yet his heart was heavy. Emptiness consumed him. A similar feeling to when his ma died. Grief. But on a lesser scale. How could he grieve for someone he'd never known? Or was that it? Did the grief stem from never having the opportunity to know his biological father?

The years of wanting to know about his father surfaced. Memories of the few times he or his brothers asked their ma about him, but she'd brush them off. Told them she didn't want to talk about it. They'd complain to each other, but not for long. Always worried she'd find out and tell them off.

Now things began to make sense. Ma was heartbroken. She'd lost the love of her life and had to raise her three sons alone.

"Oh Ma," he murmured, "I'm so sorry."

Yet his emotions were still so mixed. Hurt. Sadness. Grief. Anger. It formed a ball in his stomach and settled like lead. It must've been so difficult for her, and she coped the only way she knew how. But did that make it right to keep it a secret? That was a question he couldn't answer. Not right now. Maybe never.

Behind him, Tenika rested a hand on his shoulder. He'd forgotten for a moment she was there, too caught up in this revelation. He placed a hand over hers, thankful she was. She was a comfort he needed right now.

Dropping his head, his gaze landed on a small, framed photo leaning against the bottom of the headstone on the right. He picked it up and his heart shattered. It was a photo of Ma and Da on their wedding day. They looked so happy. So in love. So *young*.

As he looked closer at his father, it was like looking in a mirror.

"You look just like him," Tenika observed.

He nodded, a shiver running down his spine as he dropped his hand covering Tenika's and put the photo back. Their resemblances were uncanny. Seeing Ma and Da together, he also saw his two brothers shared resemblances to both.

He cast his eyes over the dates under the inscription and everything slotted into place. The journey. Ma's cryptic letters. In three days, the day after the reunion, it would be thirty-one years since their father died. He was only twenty-one years old.

This was why Ma had wanted them to travel now.

"Did you know anything about it?" Tenika asked, kneeling beside him.

He shook his head and swiped away an unexpected tear. "Ma never talked about him. There were no photos of him either. We're learnin' everythin' while we're here. I assume by Scott's reaction we weren't supposed to see this yet."

"This is why red buttons shouldn't be pressed," Tenika said gently.

Hamish glanced across at her and smiled weakly. He deserved that. He'd always been too spontaneous for his own good.

Hamish took in the surrounds of tropical foliage on their sides and behind the headstone, likely planted to protect the gravesite and keep it hidden. In front was a fenced off cliff. The view of the ocean and multiple islands dotted around was breathtaking, a stunning setting that looked like it once might've been a lookout open to the public.

Why was it hidden from view like this? He supposed he'd learn about that in one of Ma's letters.

"Are you going to tell your brothers?" Tenika asked.

He sat back and breathed out slowly. That was the million-dollar question. Ma clearly intended for them to find out the truth on this journey, and most likely on the anniversary of his death. He'd ruined it for himself. How could he also ruin it for his brothers?

"No," he said with a firm shake of his head. "They should find out the way Ma intended."

He was content with his decision. For now. He still needed to come to terms with it. Who knows what could change after a day or two.

"How much longer do you have on your journey?" Tenika asked.

It was at this moment he realised they'd never talked about how long either of them was there for. It didn't seem relevant before now.

"We go home a couple of days after your reunion."

Saying the words out loud added a heaviness to his shoulders, which only made the surrounding humidity more suffocating. They turned to each other. He saw the unwritten question in her eyes. *What will happen to us*? In the blink of an eye, the end steamrolled towards them. He'd convinced her they'd figure it out, but he was no closer to doing so.

"Oh." Her brow furrowed delicately but she nodded.

He reached out to stroke her cheek, wanting to tell her everything would be okay but how could he say that when he didn't know? He'd been so confident everything would fall into place, but now he wasn't sure.

This revelation had changed his perspective on everything. His parents had been young, carefree, *in love*. But his father had died. *On their honeymoon*. Hamish still didn't know how, but the specifics didn't matter. What *did* matter was the fact that things could change so quickly. Was this a sign to dive in headfirst with Tenika? Throw caution to the wind?

He couldn't make sense of anything and his whole world was off kilter. Perhaps he needed time to digest this before making any rash decisions.

Dropping his hand, he got to his feet, brushing moist dirt off his knees. He checked the time on his phone.

"I need to get back," he said. "Are you ready?"

He still had some time before their first itinerary item for the day, but he needed to gather his bearings if he was going to keep this a secret for three days.

Tenika nodded and got to her feet.

Neither of them talked on the way back and he appreciated she gave him time to think. God alone knew he needed it. When they reached the bottom, he stopped and turned to her.

"I'll leave you here. I have to go that way." He pointed to the west.

She nodded and smiled, standing on her tiptoes to kiss him. He returned it with an unspoken promise they'd see each other again soon and that everything would be fine.

Or so he hoped.

"Please dinnae mention this to my brothers," he added. "Or Brenda. Not yet."

She opened her mouth as though to talk, then closed it again. After a breath, she nodded.

"Thanks," he said, planting a kiss on her forehead. "I'll see you later." With a squeeze of her hand, he turned and left.

Hamish had spent his entire life locking away the desperation to learn about his father. The urge to find out more had always been there, but out of respect for Ma he kept it hidden. But he'd been riddled with 'what ifs'. What if their father chose not to be a parent? What if he had to go away and would be back any day? Douglas lived in bitterness and assumed the worst. Angus, too afraid to make waves, didn't seem to think about it at all.

All of Hamish's 'what ifs' were gone. Their father was dead.

He wasn't completely oblivious. The possibility *had* crossed his mind before but he dismissed it, not wanting it to be an option. But now, it had become a horrible reality.

Today Angus and Douglas walked ahead while Hamish lagged. Their itinerary directed them to a hidden beach called Serenity Bay. This was a spot Ma and Da had spent an afternoon together followed by a sunset cruise.

It was all very romantic, but everything was tainted now.

When they rounded the island and the bay came into view, Douglas let out a loud 'whoop' and fist-pumped the air.

"I knew this place was special!" he cheered. "This is where Brenda and I ended up last night." He hollered a laugh and stripped down to his board shorts before running across the sand and into the secluded beach.

Douglas acted like a different person since last night and while Hamish was happy for him, his heart still wasn't in it. He sat on the sand next to a basket of snacks and drinks. Angus joined him a moment later.

"You're very quiet," Angus observed. "Are you still recoverin' from last night?"

"Yeah, somethin' like that," he lied. Because while last night had changed things between him and Tenika, today *had* changed him for another reason.

"You'll figure it out," Angus said, pulling his knees up and resting his arms over them. "So, what do you think happened to Da?"

Hamish kept his eyes on the horizon and focused on breathing. Angus the non-talker suddenly wanted to talk. Hamish didn't want to discourage it, but why now?

"No idea," Hamish said. At least this was partially true. He *didn't* know how he died. "I guess we'll find out in a few days. What do *you* think happened?"

Angus shrugged. "He probably didnae want to be a father. Isn't that usually the case with absent parents? But for some reason it's important to Ma, so it's important to me."

Hamish smiled. "I agree."

Angus dragged the basket over and opened it. "Hey, here's today's letter." He whipped out the envelope and handed it to Hamish.

It trembled in his hands. He couldn't bring himself to read it, so he shoved it against Angus' chest. "You open it."

"Hey Dougie!" Angus called. "Get your arse over here!"

Douglas waved to show he heard them, then strode through the water, onto the shore and came over, plopping down beside Hamish cross-legged. After drying his hands, he reached across to snatch the letter from Angus. "I'll read it."

He ripped it open without a thought and pulled out the A5 piece of paper.

My boys,

By the time you read this, you'll be in the most magical place on this island—Serenity Bay. Though your father would disagree. He preferred the lookout at the peak.

Hamish tensed. It'd been the first time she mentioned it and if he hadn't stumbled across it today, he wouldn't be any wiser now.

Douglas lowered the letter and frowned. "Did either of you see a lookout?"

Angus shook his head and so did Hamish, though guilt overwhelmed him as he did so.

Douglas continued reading.

But that's a story for another day. Today is all about the love between a couple. Serenity Bay is a great place to stop, talk, and connect. Angus, I know you're probably missing Skye but take a moment to reflect on the relationship you have. I can see in you two what your father and I once had.

Douglas pretended to gag but Angus only grinned and punched his shoulder. "Maybe you can reflect on your blossomin' relationship with Brenda," he said in a teasing voice.

Even Hamish couldn't stop the smile when Douglas' cheeks turned bright red.

Hamish and Douglas, I hope this place sows a seed in your hearts. I want nothing more than for you two to settle down with your special someone, whoever they may be.

Then tonight, enjoy a lovely sunset cruise and a seafood dinner. Taito will join you and tell you the legend of the Maritimo Lovers.

With love, Ma

Douglas scoffed and put the letter and envelope back in the basket. "Taito's stories are certainly somethin'. Mermaid guardians, dancing coral, and now a legend of lovers? What a load of rubbish."

"I like them," Angus said, pulling out the food and drinks.

"Yeah, you would, you sappy romantic." Douglas picked up a grape and threw it at Angus' head. It bounced off and they all laughed.

"Skye doesn't complain." Angus smiled smugly and this time caught the grape Douglas threw at him and ate it. "By the way, is it weird that it feels like Ma is here? It's like I can sense her presence somehow."

To Hamish's surprise, Douglas didn't joke about this. When he looked at him, he had a wistful expression on his face.

"She is," Hamish said. He almost added, "So is Da," but stopped in time.

Chapter 18

♥

After an afternoon of food, swimming, and beach sports, Hamish joined his brothers on a catamaran, gliding through the water away from Maritimo Island as day turned to night. The once clear day had now become overcast with heavy grey clouds. The air had a stormy feel to it. Hamish had overheard Taito and Krishneel talking about the cyclone but missed any specifics when they switched to talking in Fijian.

The clouds thinned closer to the horizon and the sun peeked out beneath them as it dipped lower in the sky. It slowly sunk behind the palms and hills of the island, casting it in a silhouette.

While Hamish sat on a bench facing the island with Douglas in the middle and Angus next to him, Taito stood in front of them appearing larger than life. His voice was a loud baritone as he told a tale of love and loss, recounting the legend of the Maritimo Lovers. Two people with a deep and real love who died in each other's arms during a terrible storm.

As the story continued, the sky turned vibrant shades of red, orange, and yellow with the island a silhouette, the shapes of hills and palm trees prominent. Hamish sat forward with his gaze glued to the horizon as the colours only seemed to grow brighter before his eyes.

Taito finished his story and the boat came to a stop, bobbing on the water. Silence fell upon them as they stared transfixed at the tropical sunset.

Now that he'd seen a photo of his parents, Hamish could envisage them here. In each other's arms, watching a spectacular sunset.

Emotion rose in his throat, and he wished he knew exactly what had happened to his father. Was it unexpected, like a freak accident? Was he sick? So many questions and no answers. Knowing his parents were so in love made the reality of it even more painful.

Closing his eyes, he thought back to his beloved ma. He absentmindedly rubbed his chest as the emotion intensified. He missed her like crazy. Would never forget her. She was so kind. Giving. Calm. Always so happy and had given so much of herself for others...until she couldn't.

When a hand took his, his eyes flew open. He glanced at Douglas in surprise and noticed Angus had taken Douglas' other hand. They'd never been the touchy-feely type of brothers yet somehow, in this moment, it felt right. Natural. Not at all weird. They were all thinking about Ma.

They stared at the sunset in silence as it faded, and Hamish relished in this closeness with them.

"It's almost like she's here," Angus said.

Hamish glanced across at him. The cool breeze off the water ruffled his hair as his bottom lip wobbled and a tear streaked down his cheek.

To Hamish's surprise, a tear also slid down Douglas' cheek too, followed by another and another until the dam burst. Soon Douglas was sobbing into the breeze as the three of them continued to hold hands and say their last goodbye.

Hamish couldn't remember Douglas ever crying in their presence when Ma died, or at her funeral. Possibly he did in private, but the way he sobbed now, it was as though he'd never properly grieved.

Thank you, Ma, Hamish thought with the realisation she knew they needed this, to learn more about her, their father, and their relationship. Especially Douglas.

Hamish breathed out as his eyes stung with his own tears, releasing pent-up emotion he didn't realise he'd stored. He'd forever miss Ma, but he was so happy to have his brothers. No matter what happened, they would always have an unbreakable bond.

He wondered, yet again, if he should tell them the truth. He'd never kept secrets from them, and it felt wrong. They'd always confided in each other about everything. Usually before telling Ma, too. Especially about things they needed a father for—the ups and downs of puberty, sexual experiences, and the general angst of growing up. They'd always talked freely. So why couldn't he now?

As the sky lost its vibrance, the motor spluttered to life and Krishneel began the short trip back to the island. Angus and Douglas had recovered and were talking, so Hamish left them to it and got to his feet, joining Taito at the starboard railing. He rested his arm on the rail, facing the front.

"Cheers, mate," Hamish said. "That was some sunset."

Taito nodded once but didn't smile. "How much do you know?" His tone was sad. He turned to Hamish and his eyes lacked their usual shine.

Hamish didn't have to ask what he meant. Scott had obviously gone back and explained what happened. Hamish felt bad about it. The timing couldn't have been worse.

He considered lying. Tell him he'd heeded Scott's advice and didn't snoop. But lying never sat well with him, and he sucked at it. In the end, he shrugged and offered an apologetic smile. "I'm afraid I saw the gravesite." He kept his voice low.

Taito jabbed his thumb in Angus and Douglas' direction. "They don't know then?"

"Not yet."

"Can I trust you not to say anything?"

Hamish sighed and nodded. As much as he hated the secrecy, for the sake of Taito's sanity, he'd keep up the façade. He didn't like it one bit, but he'd already decided to keep it to himself.

"Look, Taito, I didnae go out of my way to find out. I didnae want to ruin anythin'. I respect Ma had her way of wantin' to do this and I was willin' to follow it. But when an Australian man stumbles out of the foliage lookin' guilty as sin, what's a red-blooded Scotsman meant to do?"

"Keep walking," Taito said, his tone a little lighter.

"Perhaps a wimpy Scotsman might have. As I'm not, when I see a metaphorical red button, I'm goin' to press it."

This time Taito smiled. "One day pressing red buttons is going to get you in a whole lotta trouble."

"If it's any consolation, I didnae particularly like findin' out that way. Now I have even more questions." He ran a hand through his hair. "I really am sorry. But nothin' has changed. There's still a lot to learn."

Taito nodded. "I suppose you're right."

"No hard feelings?"

Taito slapped his shoulder hard, making Hamish flinch. "No, but next time you see a red button I highly suggest you avoid pressing it."

Hamish mock saluted. "Aye, aye captain."

Taito grinned, then joined Angus and Douglas. Hamish stayed put, watching Maritimo Island draw closer. So close now he saw locals and visitors sitting on the shore, but no one swam.

He turned to glance out at the ocean behind him and saw large, dark grey storm clouds rolling towards them. His stomach twisted into a knot. Storms in Scotland were one thing, storms buffeting a small island...he couldn't even imagine. He trusted the locals knew what they were doing, and he'd follow their instructions.

After Krishneel docked the catamaran, then got off to moor it, Taito announced, "I hope you're hungry. Tonight, I'll show you how to cook a delicious seafood feast on the lovo pit."

Douglas exaggerated a groan. "You mean we have to *cook*? This is supposed to be a holiday."

Taito stepped onto the pier once Krishneel gave the all-clear. "Or you can go hungry," he called out with a shrug.

This silenced Douglas.

"Thought so," Taito added with a chuckle. "See you boys in half an hour."

"Why do we do this to ourselves?" Tenika whined, holding a hand against her overfull stomach.

They'd ordered an overabundance of delicious food and snacks through room service and ate every morsel over the afternoon. It truly was a delicious feast, but she had big regrets.

"Because it's a girl's afternoon," Brenda responded, reaching for a spoon and the chocolate ice cream. "It's *law* that we stuff ourselves stupid."

She took a large spoonful, then held the ice cream out to Tenika, who groaned and pushed it away. "If I eat another bite, I'm going to throw up all over you."

Brenda snatched the ice cream back with narrowed eyes. "So, what's up with you anyway? You've been quiet since you got back."

Tenika turned to the TV where the movie showed a couple finally getting back together after their breakup. "Nothing," she lied.

As much as she wanted to tell Brenda everything, she respected Hamish's privacy. That was a doozy of a secret and finding out like that...wow. She was certain their mother would've revealed it in a more tactful way through her letters.

Tenika understood the feeling all too well. Although in a way she wished she *had* seen her parents' gravesites. Maybe it'd make coming to terms with their deaths easier.

When Brenda continued to stare, not believing her, Tenika had to say *something*. She sighed for effect then shrugged. "I'm nervous about the reunion, I guess."

This seemed to work, and Brenda nodded, her face clouding with sympathy. "I understand, Nika." She placed a hand on Tenika's arm and squeezed. "But it'll be over before you know it. Two more days, then it'll be done and you'll have a week of relaxing."

"That sounds nice, but what'll be nicer is if the cyclone comes, we're evacuated, and the reunion is cancelled."

Brenda tsked and rolled her eyes as she took another spoonful of ice cream. "You wish. Last time I checked, the worst of the cyclone would miss the island but we'll still get some bad weather. I'm sure it won't be enough to cancel the reunion."

"Shame." She smiled slyly. "Anyway." She got to her feet. "I think I'm going to walk off some of this food. There's no way I'll be sleeping while I'm this full."

She checked the time on the wall—seven-thirty p.m. Plenty of time before bed and a walk sounded ideal.

"You want to come?" she added.

Brenda shook her head. "No thanks. I'll be in a food coma soon and I'll sleep it off."

Tenika went to change and said from her room, "I don't know how you can sleep with a full stomach."

"I don't know how you *can't*."

Tenika chuckled. "Are you asking Douglas to the reunion?"

"Already done. And you with Hamish?"

"Of course."

Brenda squealed, then she rushed into Tenika's bedroom, grinning widely. "You mean this is our first double date?"

Tenika grabbed a change of clothes, then stepped out of her track pants and t-shirt, donning a dress and sandals instead. "I suppose it is. Alright, I'm off. See you later."

She waved a goodbye, then left.

So overfull, even walking was difficult, so she took it slow and headed downstairs to the terrace. She'd walk further once her food had digested some more.

When she reached the ground floor, she stepped outside first to check the weather. The cyclone was forefront of her mind and after the clear morning, she wondered if it was still that way now. Her heart stuttered when she looked up at the night sky and noticed clouds rolling in thick and fast, promising the expected storm.

Glancing down the path, she spotted three familiar red-headed figures approaching. Goosebumps broke out on her skin when she spotted Hamish. He and his brothers were talking and laughing, oblivious to their surrounds.

Hamish was the first to look up and their eyes met. He was talking but stopped mid-sentence, said something to Douglas and Angus, then approached her. The two brothers waved as they passed, and she waved back.

"Hi," Hamish said with a smile, wrapping his arms around her.

"Hi back." She hung her arms around his neck and pulled him down for a swift kiss that ignited her nerve endings.

When they pulled away, her heart raced. She could stay like this forever.

"Did you have a good afternoon?" he asked.

"It was great." She searched his eyes looking for any evidence he was struggling from the events of the morning. "How are you feeling? About everything..."

When he smiled, his eyes were bright. "I'm good. Better now you're here."

He pressed his lips to hers once more, the cool breeze whistling around them. He tasted of salt and sunshine. Something had changed between them today. Even at this moment everything felt different. She was high on life with a whole future ahead of her. There were so many possibilities...ones she wanted to share with Hamish.

"Are you free this evening?" she asked when they pulled away. Maybe this was the moment she could share her epiphany with him. She was confident together they could work something out.

Disappointment surged through her when he shook his head. "Afraid not, and we're busy all day tomorrow too." He frowned and stared deep into her eyes, as though searching their depths. "This holiday is goin' way too fast. We need time to talk about us."

"I agree. How about Saturday? After the reunion?"

"Perfect."

She forgot how to breathe as all these crazy thoughts came to life in her mind. *Stay with me. The night that is. Stay the night. Let's take this to the next level.* Was she brave enough to say them out loud?

She opened her mouth to speak, but no words came out. Clearing her throat, she tried again, "Um..." she rubbed her nose. *Come on, you can do this.* "Um...do...do you...would you, I mean...like to stay over Saturday night?"

Get a grip woman. Think straight.

Her stomach flipped. "Uh...I could get Brenda to stay out for the night with Douglas. You...you could come back to my room."

She cringed and looked away, her heart racing. At least she wouldn't have to tell him she was out of practice. It was pretty damn obvious.

Hamish lifted her chin, so she stared into his sparkling eyes. There was no mockery in them, just genuine happiness. She smiled and breathed easier.

"You're cute when you're nervous," he said, then pressed his lips against hers in an urgent kiss that gave her the answer she'd hoped for. He pulled away and rested his forehead on hers. "In case I didnae make myself clear, that was a yes."

She breathed out a laugh. "I couldn't have botched that up more if I tried."

He kissed her once more, slow and sensual this time. "It was perfect. I've got to go. If we finish early tomorrow night, I'll drop by."

One more kiss and he was gone, leaving her staring after him with a silly grin on her face. It was in that moment she fell. Well into the depths of whatever their relationship was. Down, down into the overwhelming and wonderful feeling that this was it. She was gone. Head over heels in love with this beautiful Scotsman.

And she was okay with it. More than, in fact.

Chapter 19

♥

Tenika stepped into the entry area of the resort and stopped. Staff flitted around like it was the peak of the day with new guests arriving. But it was after seven-thirty in the evening and with the reunion so close now, she was certain all the alumni had arrived.

She spotted Litia behind the reception desk talking to a young Fijian man around Tenika's age. Even though she hadn't met everyone on the island, she'd seen a lot of the locals, and this one stood out. Was he new?

Tenika strode up to reception and as she drew closer, she stopped and gasped. "*Eroni*? Is that really you?"

The man spun around and he stared at her, mouth agape, then he grinned. "Tenika!"

He rushed out from behind the desk and they embraced. He was all man now, yet still *so* familiar. Tears pricked her eyes as she reunited with her friend once again. They'd kept in touch on and off after he left, but as the years passed and they got busy in their adult lives, their communication waned.

"Mum told me you were here," Eroni said when he stepped back, his smile blinding and his eyes shimmering.

Tenika took a good look at him, shaking her head in admiration. She'd forever only have eyes for Hamish, but she was a woman who appreciated a good-looking man and Eroni was *hot*. Brown skin, deep chocolate brown eyes, short black hair, rugged and defined. A younger version of Taito.

"Look at you," she said. "You look great!"

"So do you." He turned serious and she knew what was coming. "How *are* you? Really?"

When they kept in contact, she'd tell him bits and pieces but never everything. He knew enough to understand her school life was bad. He was fortunate to have escaped and she always slightly envied him.

"I'm good," she said, reaching out to squeeze his arm. "Honestly."

She wasn't sure how much Litia and Taito knew. She'd grown close to them the year they were in Australia, but they were an escape. A place to forget about school, not talk about it. They knew she was bullied too, but not how bad it got.

He smiled in relief and hugged her again. "It's good to see you."

"When did you arrive?"

Litia came over at that moment and looped her arm through Eroni's. "Tenika, *bula*! He arrived today," she answered for him.

That must've been the seaplane Tenika had seen earlier.

"He's been in Australia the last ten years," Litia explained. "But he's been kind enough to come over and help us as the resort grows."

Tenika stared at Eroni in surprise. "You never said you returned to Australia. I wish I'd known."

She furrowed her brow as she thought about it. They lost contact after they graduated, which would've been around the time he returned. Was there a story there?

Eroni smiled in apology. "I'm sorry. Life just sort of took over, you know?"

He shrugged and she nodded but she still suspected there was more to it.

"Now I'm between jobs," he added, "and I'm at, shall we say, a crossroads in life."

She didn't miss the pained look mother and son exchanged but neither elaborated and Tenika didn't push, though it *did* confirm her suspicions. As much as she wished he'd reached out, she understood how life could take you on a journey you least expected.

"Since I'm not sure what I want to do," Eroni continued, "and knowing Mum and Dad are expanding and bringing in more business, I thought I'd help. It seems I came at the right time, with the storm and everything."

"Eroni," Litia hissed.

Tenika's ears pricked up. Now *this* she could prod. She leant in closer. "I've heard whispers. I promise I'll keep it quiet. You can trust me. Can I help somehow?"

"You're on holiday," Litia said with a tut.

"*Actually*," Eroni smiled good-naturedly at Litia, "as much as we don't want to intrude on your holiday, we'd love some help."

"Then count me in. What's going on and what do I need to do?"

"Tenika." Litia's brow furrowed. "It's such a big ask."

"It's really not." She reached out and gently patted her arm.

Litia pursed her lips but nodded and looked at Eroni. They appeared to have a silent conversation before Eroni nodded, then went to the end of the reception desk and lifted the top, gesturing for Tenika to come through.

Litia raced up and embraced her tightly. "I appreciate your help," she said when she pulled away. "Thank you. Storms are not uncommon around here, but the weather they're forecasting, it looks like it'll be a bad one. We're prepared but there's a lot to do."

Tenika nodded. "We've got this. Eroni, tell me what I can do."

He nodded and led her through a door into a small office. He sat on one side in front of a computer and indicated Tenika sit on a chair opposite. She did so and drew in a deep breath. She wanted to help, but the confirmation about the bad weather concerned her.

Would she get her wish of the reunion being cancelled?

As if reading her thoughts, Eroni said, "We're on the 'prepare to act' alert." He turned the screen to her.

A large weather map was centred on their location and the surrounding Fijian islands. In the east, a large cyclonic cloud with various shades of blue, yellow, orange, and red moved on the page as it showed a ninety-minute forecast. It appeared to be moving towards the island but slightly north, which meant the eye would miss them, but the edges would hit.

"What happens if we're told to act?" she asked.

"We evacuate." His serious gaze met hers. "Because of how many people we have here, there are additional planes on standby."

She swallowed. "What's the likelihood that will happen? It looks like it's still a fair way away."

"You're right and if it keeps moving the in direction it's going, we'll be able to withstand it. We'll get buffeted around a bit but there won't be any need to act. While large storms like this are rare, the island is prepared for them."

"You know a lot for someone who hasn't been here for ten years."

He sat back with a smile, eyeing her curiously. "I moved back to Australia after I graduated. I studied in Sydney, got a job, but Mum and Dad always kept me updated and I'd watch the weather patterns."

"You can take the boy off the island..."

"...but not the island out of the boy." He grinned and it was like the sun warmed her from the inside out. He'd grown into such a handsome man. "Exactly. I vowed I'd never come back. I felt so suffocated after we moved back here. I really loved life in Australia, apart from the issues in school, that is." He winced. "But after graduation, it was like I had a whole new lease on life, which is why I went back."

"Now here you are."

"Here I am." He sighed and shrugged. "It's been less than a day, but it feels different somehow. Less suffocating."

"Or maybe *you're* different. Older and wiser and all that."

He chuckled lightly. "You're probably right."

Silence overcame them and Tenika couldn't hold her tongue. "What happened, Eroni?"

When he looked at her, his eyes were large and sad. She felt his sadness deep in her soul. All she wanted to do was hug him until he smiled that brilliant smile again.

"Fell in love, got married, had a kid." He shrugged and managed a sad, wobbly smile. "But life doesn't always pan out how you expect, hey?"

She had so many questions—where was the wife and kid now? What happened? But a shutter came down over his features and the subject was closed. She reached out to squeeze his hand, then cleared her throat and gestured to the map on the screen. "So, what's the plan?"

"Right now, we're monitoring the weather. We're intending for the reunion to go ahead but if the weather's bad on the day, we can reassess. The storm should hit tomorrow around midday and should clear by Saturday late morning or early afternoon. We all know how unpredictable cyclones can be though. They can change direction any time."

"What do you need me to do?"

"We're going to be encouraging everyone to stay in their rooms. The restaurant is preparing hampers, so no one has to go out. Not just for resort guests, but we're helping the locals too. The cleaning services will make sure guests have fresh towels, toiletries and the like. Things are under control, but most of our staff will be busy delivering hampers, making sure everyone has up-to-date information, and are equipped with everything they need. If you can man the desk here, answering phones, placating any nervous guests, that sort of thing, it'd be much appreciated."

Tenika nodded. "Do you need me tonight?"

"No, but early tomorrow morning will be great. Everyone will be notified of the prepare to act notice this evening and we will deliver everything in the morning. We want people to be safe in their rooms when it hits."

"Is eight in the morning too late?"

"No, that's perfect." When he stood, she did too, and he came around to embrace her. "Thank you, Tenika, I...*we*...appreciate your help."

She said goodbye, then left the resort. She'd long forgotten being overfull and was running on adrenalin. Before returning to Brenda in their room, she took a cart and drove it to the eastern side of the island. Normally she'd walk, but with the weather changing she wasn't about to take any risks.

Stopping the cart, she stepped off it and walked over to the water. It was dark now, the sky covered with clouds. Apart from the solar lights, there was no other natural light from the moon or stars. The blackness was strangely eerie.

As she stared out over the horizon, she could make out the shapes and movement of the clouds but couldn't see how bad it was. The hair on her arms stood on end and she breathed out a shaky breath as nerves consumed her. This was *real*.

She needed to get back and fill Brenda in. On the drive back, despite her nerves a thrill traipsed along her spine. To be in the thick of it. Helping at the resort. Being a part of the island. *This* was what she wanted.

Chapter 20

♥

"I've got to leave in a minute," Tenika called out to Brenda the next morning.

Wanting to fit in with the staff and *not* look like a tourist, she wore her bula dress with her curls hanging loose below her shoulders, looking extra springy thanks to the hair product she'd applied. It was like starting a new job. A thrum of excitement skirted along her skin. What if this could be her job?

Brenda came out of her room yawning and rubbing her eyes. She grabbed the TV remote and switched it on. It was still on the weather channel as they'd been watching the forecast. "Yikes, look at that thing coming straight for us."

Tenika glanced at the screen and her stomach flipped. The storm was closer than last night. The eye looked like it would still miss them, but the edge of the cyclone coming for them had a lot of yellow and red. They were in for some wild weather.

"You're not going out in that, are you?" Brenda asked, turning to Tenika with a frown.

"Of course not. I'm only needed at reception." Tenika went to the balcony doors and pulled the curtains apart.

On the fourth storey of the resort, they had a lovely view of the eastern side of the island. Below them was a beautiful tropical garden and beyond that she could see the ocean. The fishing boats that usually bobbed on the water in a small marina were gone, most likely secured somewhere safe. It was a precautionary measure, but nerves fluttered in her stomach as the reality came crashing down.

Opening the doors, she stepped onto the balcony. A strong gusty breeze whooshed past and ruffled her hair. Resting her hands on the stone barrier, she breathed in the salty air still tinged with warmth. The dark, heavy cloud cover from last night had spread over the entire island, giving it an eerie feel. Light sprinkles of rain touched the back of her hands as palms swayed with the breeze. She hadn't spent enough time out here.

Spotting some golf carts heading towards the resort snapped her into action. She had to go! When she stepped back into the room, Brenda had settled herself on the sofa in front of the TV. She sat with her back against the armrest, her legs stretched out in front of her, and a plate of selected pastries on her lap from the breakfast tray that had arrived earlier. The TV had been switched to the movie channel.

"Comfy?" Tenika quipped.

Brenda smiled and nodded. "Not much else to do, is there? When are the hampers being delivered?"

"Sometime this morning. I've got to run. See you later."

With a wave, she dashed out of the room. She took the elevator to the ground floor and was in the foyer a few minutes before eight. Through the main doors she saw golf carts lining the drive with hampers anywhere they would fit. Inside, it buzzed with activity—guests darting to and from the restaurant for breakfast, and staff and locals working to complete tasks. She admired how they all banded together to help.

"Tenika, good morning!"

She turned to the reception desk where Eroni waved at her. He gestured for her to join him behind the desk.

"Thank you so much," Eroni said when Tenika sidled up beside him. "Your timing is perfect. We're about to get started now. All we need you to do is answer phones, take any messages, and help anyone with enquiries. I'm sorry to dump you in at the deep end, so don't bother learning the computer system. Make notes and take messages and I'll sort it out when I get back."

"I've got you covered."

He gave her a brief rundown on the phones, including advising her of the two distinct tones—one for guests calling reception, the other for incoming calls.

Within a matter of minutes, the buzzing stopped as everyone left with something to do. Delivering hampers, bathroom essentials, or any messages that weren't delivered the night before kept them busy.

The first few minutes were quiet before her first call came through. It was a simple enquiry asking about rates and availability, which she couldn't answer. A ripple of excitement shot through her as she took a message.

Another call came through about ten minutes later.

It continued like this for the next hour. A few more calls came through, some questions she answered, others she took messages for. It was such a simple job, but being a part of it all thrilled her. This was where she needed to be. What she wanted to do. And she couldn't wait to talk to Hamish tomorrow about how they could make it work. The more she thought about it, the more confident she became. She only needed Hamish to agree.

Another hour passed. Some people came back for more hampers and left again. Now, Tenika stood in silence and shuffled from foot to foot, growing restless. It'd been quiet for over half an hour. She left the desk and went out onto the terrace. She followed it to the northern end, which passed the restaurant and gave a better view of the ocean. The water, usually so calm, was choppy as the wind picked up. The beach deserted of any guests.

When the phone rang, she ran back to answer it. As she said goodbye, she looked up and her heart rate spiked. She dropped the receiver. Standing at the desk, all calm and confident, was Davina. Tenika's hands shook and her heart raced as she fumbled to put the receiver back in place.

Breathe, don't show your fear. You're not the same person you were a week ago.

She swallowed and cleared her throat. "Davina, can I help you?"

Davina's delicate brow creased as she took in the scene before her. "You...you work here now?"

"No. I'm just helping while they finish preparing for the storm."

She nodded once, a small smile tugging at her lips. "You haven't changed a bit, have you? You were always the one helping the teachers."

There was no malice in her words, but Tenika's spine stiffened as memories of her primary school years flooded her mind. The taunts she'd tried so hard to forget came back to life in her mind. She'd rather taunts over how bad it got in high school, but the harsh words never left her.

Davina's eyes widened as though she remembered the same thing. "I-I didn't mean anything by that," she rushed to explain. "I think it's great. You really fit in."

Tenika shuffled from foot to foot. "Thanks." She rubbed her nose, willing the floor to swallow her whole. "Uh, so *can* I help?"

Davina's shoulders sagged. When her gaze met Tenika's, there was resignation in her eyes. "Why do you even care? You're volunteering, you don't have to help me. You've made it clear you won't accept my apology so if you're out for some petty revenge or whatever, I don't want to deal with it right now."

Tenika pulled her shoulders back and held her head high. "I'm not out for revenge, Davina, though it is tempting." Davina winced, but this only spurred Tenika on. "It's not always about you, you know? It's difficult for me to be here, facing a past that still haunts me. The last thing I want to do is help you, but I'm doing the lovely people here a favour, so if I can make *their* life easier, I will."

Davina's mouth opened and closed. "Fair enough." She pulled her shoulders back and lifted her chin. "I hoped I could get an update on whether the reunion was going ahead tomorrow. Everyone is asking me, and I don't know what to tell them."

This at least Tenika could answer. "If the worst of the storm has passed, it'll go ahead. But they won't know until tomorrow. There's no controlling what the weather does, especially a cyclone."

Davina smiled. "Thank you. I guess we just have to hope."

"I guess so."

The phone rang again, and Tenika answered it. It was an enquiry, which Tenika could help with. When she hung up, Davina still hovered.

"I have many regrets, Tenika. What happened in school is my biggest one. It haunts me too." Their gazes met and Tenika shivered at the hollowness in Davina's eyes. "I have nightmares most nights..." She breathed out a shaky breath and swiped away a tear. Her laugh was humourless. "I'm not trying to make this about me."

Another tear dripped down Davina's cheek. Tenika located a box of tissues behind the reception desk and held them out. Davina took one with a grateful smile.

"I realised too late that Zach was the problem," Davina said after she'd composed herself. "Belinda and I thought we were so cool because everyone feared us. It was some sick teenage power trip." She pulled a face and shook her head in disgust. "Then when we graduated—the night of the formal, you remember that night don't you?"

Tenika frowned in reflection. There were some memories she'd successfully locked away. For good reason. As she focused on that specific night, visions came back with force, one by one, almost knocking her off her feet.

Dizziness had her grappling for the desk, and she had to breathe slowly and deeply to stop the rising panic from overwhelming her. She *had* forgotten for a very good reason.

Davina paled and cleared her throat, averting her gaze. *She* hadn't forgotten either, it seemed.

Tenika's insides trembled and icy fear spread across her skin. Zach's failed attempt to force himself on her in a drunken state may have been locked away for years, but they were going nowhere now. Now she understood *why* her past had such a hold on her. Why trusting Hamish in the beginning was difficult.

If it wasn't for Travis showing up, Tenika hated to think what would've happened next.

"After what happened," Davina said, "I knew he wasn't worth it. It was like seeing him in a new light. One I despised." She frowned as though confused. "He disappeared afterwards and when I searched for him to end it for good, I found him with Belinda. They were having sex in the back of his car. Turns out they'd had a thing for each other for ages and had been sleeping around since year eleven."

Tenika folded her arms and rubbed them as the chill intensified. Her heart raced. They'd had sex after he'd tried to—

Bile rose in her throat and nausea rolled in her stomach. Where was Eroni? Or Litia? She needed to leave. *Now*, preferably.

"I'm sorry," Davina said, noticing Tenika's reaction. "I didn't even think." She shook her head and raised her eyes heavenward. Her lips moved as she muttered something under her breath. "I'm really botching this up, aren't I? I'm not trying to make this uncomfortable." She huffed out a breath. "All I'm trying to say is that night changed my life too. I saw who I'd become. Who Zach and Belinda really were. They both betrayed me. My boyfriend. My own *twin* sister."

Tenika stared at her hard, and hopefully with no empathy. She had none left. "Look, I get it, it sucks. But if you expect me to cry you a river and have sympathy for you—"

"No, no, that's not it at all." She shook her head. "I need you to see how it changed my life. How it changed *me*." A look of urgency passed across her face. She stepped closer but Tenika stayed put. "I had a huge reality check that night. I went to my parents who'd always tried so hard, but Belinda and I made their lives difficult. They didn't like Zach either. They always called us their 'problem children'. I thought *they* were the problem...until I realised they weren't. I blocked my sister and ex on all social media, cut all contact, started a new life, and learnt how to be a decent human again." She smiled. "It was invigorating, actually."

She appeared to drift off into another world for a moment. Then she blinked and said, "It wasn't easy facing head on who I'd become, but in time I did it with my parents' support and some new friends I'd made. About two years ago I was finally happy with who I'd become.

Almost. And that's when I had the idea of organising the school reunion. It was a means to make amends. To you, and the many others I treated badly too."

"But Belinda and Zachary aren't here."

"I didn't invite them. As far as I know, no one from school has kept in contact with them so they probably didn't hear about it. My parents only speak to Belinda once or twice a year, so they'd never tell her. Besides, it's not up to me to apologise for *their* mistakes. If they had an attack of conscience, it's on them to sort it out. I'm only accountable for my actions."

Tenika couldn't argue this. The phone rang again, and she excused herself to answer it. When she hung up, Davina had moved to the main doors leading outside.

She turned back to Tenika. "Would you mind letting Litia know I need to speak to her? Since it's full steam ahead for now, I need to confirm some things."

"Sure, I'll leave her a message."

Davina smiled tightly, then with a wave, turned and left. Tenika had the urge to remind her not to go outdoors but stopped herself. If she got caught in the storm, it wasn't *her* problem. Petty? Sure, but did she care? Hell, no. Davina might've been genuine, but Tenika still wasn't convinced. What if she was just after attention? Putting on an act as the hard done by bully who'd turned her life around? Tenika didn't buy it.

She leant against the desk and blew out a long breath. Her heart rate began to slow, but she was all out of sorts. That was *not* what she'd expected this morning.

Chapter 21

♥

Paddle boarding was the first event of the day, but it had been cancelled due to bad weather.

That morning they had moved into the main resort building for their safety. Their suite was smaller than the bungalow, and they felt caged in the moment they dropped off their things. Needing to get as much air and freedom as possible, they went for a late-morning walk before the storm hit.

They were only walking for a few minutes when they stopped again, standing on the sand. Hamish looked at his brothers, all sharing the same startled expression when they noticed the sudden drop in temperature. The cool breeze was a welcome relief, but it was stronger than before. White caps formed on the waves. The palms bent and swayed like they weighed nothing.

"What now?" Angus asked.

"Go back to our room and veg out I suppose," Hamish said.

Douglas groaned and gripped his hair. "I'm gonna go stir crazy!"

"You'll have to deal with it, bro." Hamish slapped Douglas' arm. "We can bond over our hamper of scran and sit around singin' *Kumbaya* until this thing is over."

"Funny." Douglas rolled his eyes, but there was no missing the smile on his lips. He'd been smiling a lot lately.

Brenda had done him good, and Hamish wondered what would happen at the end of the holiday. It reminded him of their looming departure and heaviness rested in his chest. Disappointed he wouldn't see Tenika at all now, tomorrow night couldn't come soon enough. A smile tugged at his lips as images of what was to come flashed through his mind.

The strong breeze whistled through the palms and Hamish glanced up at the sky. The dark clouds rolled. The drizzling rain turned into larger drops.

"Hey, earth to Hamish."

He blinked and winced when someone hit his arm. "Ow." He rubbed the sore spot. "What was that for?"

"We were talkin' to you," Douglas said. "You were off with the bloody fairies. We're headin' back to the resort, the weather's crap. You comin'?"

"Yeah, I'm comin'. Let's go."

They walked off the sand through the trees and onto the path, following it to the resort. Within minutes, the rain turned heavy and horizontal as the wind grew even stronger. The three of them broke into a sprint and dashed to the main entrance of the resort, managing not to get too soaked.

Golf carts arrived and were secured while people ran for shelter as they returned from delivering hampers.

When they entered through the main doors, Hamish stumbled to a stop when he saw Tenika standing behind reception talking to a young, good-looking Fijian man. He said something that made her laugh and Hamish saw how well she fit in. She was one of them.

For a split second, an unexpected wave of uncertainty washed over him. Why would she want to be with him when she could have someone who understood her culture? As he watched them talk with ease, not flirting, but comfortable around each other, the uncertainties grew. This was not like him at all!

Tenika stopped talking and looked up. Straight at him. A wide, beaming smile spread across her face and turned him into a puddle. That smile was all for him. His heart felt lighter and filled with love. Yes *love*. His uncertainties dissipated to nothing. What had he been so worried about?

"If you dinnae do somethin' about this soon, I will," Angus murmured beside him.

Hamish broke his gaze with Tenika for a second to turn to his brother. "I've got this, trust me."

Angus slapped his shoulder. "Good because she's worth it. We can work out the distillery details wherever you are."

He walked off and Douglas followed, winking at Hamish but saying nothing. He didn't need to. Deep down he realised he'd needed some sort of confirmation, or permission, that they were okay with this. Now that he had it, he knew what he had to do.

Pulling his shoulders back, he strode across to the reception desk towards Tenika. She smiled at the man and excused herself. She came out from behind it as he approached. The man looked at him curiously, so Hamish held out his hand.

"Hi, I'm Hamish."

The man took his hand and shook it, a kind smile on his face. "Eroni. I'm Litia and Taito's son."

Hamish took his hand back. When Tenika came up to him, he slung his arm across her shoulders and kissed her temple.

"Hamish is visiting with his brothers," Tenika explained. "They're following the same journey their parents did thirty-one years ago."

Eroni's eyes widened. "Mum told me about that. It's quite the story."

Litia popped her head out of the office and spotting Hamish, smiled broadly. "Hello, Hamish. Are you all settled into your suite?"

"Aye, all good, thank you. I appreciate you findin' room for us."

"Think nothing of it. Eroni, can I borrow you please?"

Eroni nodded, excused himself and followed Litia into the office. Hamish turned to Tenika, who looked at him quizzically.

"What?" he asked.

"What was that all about?"

He stared at her, baffled. "What are you talkin' about?"

A smile played at her lips. "Were you staking your claim or something? Putting your arm over my shoulder like that."

He laughed but tightened his hold as he steered her towards the doorway leading to the outdoor pool area, elevators, and ground-floor rooms.

That thought hadn't even crossed his mind, but now that she'd mentioned it, maybe it *had* been an unconscious action. "Not intentionally! I just want everyone to know you're mine, not just good lookin'', presumably single, Fijian men."

Tenika giggled but stopped for a moment to kiss his cheek, then continued walking. A silly grin remained fixed to his face.

"He's actually an old friend," Tenika said, then explained the connection.

"What a small world," Hamish said as they stopped at the doors leading to the pool area. They had been closed, but the steel shutters hadn't been brought down yet so they could see outside. People rushed around, going to each window and securing the shutters.

"There's something else you should know," Tenika said, shifting from foot to foot.

He turned his full attention to her, noticing a catch in her voice. When she explained the memory of what the bastard Zachary had done, it took every ounce of strength he had not to lose it. The thought of someone hurting his girl *like that* sent him raging mad.

"Are you okay?" Tenika asked, her brow furrowed.

He breathed in slowly through his nose and forced a nod. "I will be." He pulled her into his arms and held her tight. It cooled his simmering anger. "I appreciate you tellin' me. I'm only angry at *him* for hurtin' you. I would never be angry at you."

He let her go and she smiled up at him. "I'm okay now. It shook me when the memory came back, but I've recovered well. I think that proves I'm finally moving on."

A loud *bang* had them glancing out the window. A shutter had come down on a window next to the one where they stood. Palms swayed and horizontal rain pelted the ground. That was the last thing he saw before the shutters came down in front of him.

"I've never seen weather like this," Hamish murmured.

"Me either. What's the weather like in Scotland?" Tenika looked up at him.

"Nothin' like here." He grinned at her. "Fairly mild and we get lots of rain and snow but never severe like this."

She nodded. After a pause, she asked, "So you're staying in the resort now?"

"Just until the worst of the storm passes." He turned to her and took her hands, relishing in those familiar zaps of electricity shooting up his arms. "I hadn't expected to see you at all while we bunkered down so I want to relish bein' close to you."

Her gaze met his and her smile warmed him from the inside out. "Me too, but even though we're safe here, we're still encouraged to stay in our rooms this afternoon and this evening. I'm sure we can spare five minutes now." Her eyes glinted with mischief.

He held a hand over his heart and groaned. "Only five minutes? You're killin' me!"

She reached up to caress his cheek. "I wish it was longer. I'm looking forward to tomorrow night." Her smile wavered as her cheeks turned red, and she averted her gaze.

"Dinnae hide," he said, lifting her chin with his index finger. When he'd captured her gaze again, he ran his thumb across her bottom lip, loving the way she shuddered. "I'm lookin' forward to it too." He held her by the tops of her arms, admiring her appreciatively. "Have I told you how stunnin' you look? You really fit in here."

She smiled shyly. "Thanks. They asked me to help while they delivered the hampers. I didn't want to look touristy so—" She shrugged and ran her hands over the dress.

She looked back up at him as she worried her bottom lip, unanswered questions in her eyes. Tomorrow night was too far away, he had to at least tell her his thoughts. They could discuss the details tomorrow.

"I know you dinnae want to leave here," he said, running his hands down her arms to take her hands. "And if you dinnae mind, I wouldn't mind stayin' for a little longer too."

Her eyes widened as she released her lip. It was red and lightly swollen. He couldn't stop himself from leaning in to kiss it. She turned into it, and he held her tight as the wind whooshed past the building and rain pelted the roof, shutters, and ground.

"Are you serious?" Tenika asked when they pulled apart.

Her heart beat against his chest in time with his. "I'm not ready to leave you. I may never be."

She drew in a breath and smiled so brightly it was as though the clouds had parted for a second and the sun shone through. "I feel the same, but I actually had an idea—"

A large gust of wind rattled the windows. Despite the shutters being down, they took an instinctive step away.

"It's really ramping up out there," she said. "We should go to our rooms. We can talk tomorrow. Where's your room?"

"First floor, I'll take the stairs." He pressed his lips against hers once more, pouring all his unspoken emotions into it. When he pulled back, he said, "I'll see you tomorrow," then squeezed her hand and left.

When he entered their suite a couple of moments later, he found Douglas standing over the hamper as Angus emptied it.

"I know there are three of us," Douglas said, "but that's a ton of scran. I hope that doesn't mean we'll be stuck indoors longer than they said."

Hamish strode over and peered over their shoulders. They'd been provided an array of food that could be left on the bench top or in the fridge. Two loaves of freshly baked bread, loads of condiments, containers of food that could be eaten cold, bottles of juice and extra bottles of water, and a variety of snacks.

"They're takin' precautions, I guess. Cyclones are unpredictable." Angus removed an envelope. "Here's Ma's letter."

It was nearly lunchtime, so they left some food out and ate while Hamish read the letter.

My dear boys,

I hope you have a better time paddle boarding than I did. I couldn't stand up on the thing and your father laughed at me the entire time.

At this stage of the holiday, your father had accepted the pregnancy and was excited at the idea of being a father. It was so endearing to see. We were talking about names and we both loved the name Hamish, which is why you, Hamish, were named that as the oldest.

"See?" Hamish joked. "I'm special."

"Very," Douglas joked back, pulling a face.

Hamish chuckled and kicked his leg under the table.

Of course, we didn't know we were going to have three so since I was alone, I had to name the other two. Douglas was the second choice after Hamish, and Angus was your father's middle name.

Angus puffed out his chest and grinned. "Well, I think *I'm* the special one now."

They laughed and Hamish continued reading.

We never could decide on a girl's name, so I can't deny I was relieved when I found out the gender. But I'm rambling...

After paddle boarding you'll enjoy some local caves and later on this evening will be the Tropical Harmony Festival. So long as the weather is good of course. If it's too stormy, they will cancel it. It's a festival where all the locals sell their wares and everyone celebrates life on the island.

We had such a wonderful time and made even more friends. You will never find truer friends than those on the island. They're so kind.

Now, I know there are a couple of days left of your holiday and I'm sure you still have so many questions. In this envelope you'll find a photograph of your father and me on our wedding day. I think it's time you saw him. Hamish, you might get a surprise.

Hamish stopped reading and closed his eyes, focusing on breathing. He wasn't ready for this. Had hoped he'd have more time. The last thing he wanted to do was lie to his brothers, but he didn't think he could pull off a look of surprise when he saw the photo.

Angus grabbed the envelope and pulled out the photo.

"Holy crap," Douglas and Angus said.

The photo appeared in Hamish's vision, and he took it automatically, staring at it without emotion. Yep, it was the same one, just better quality.

He sighed. There was no saving this. It was time to be honest. "Look, guys there's somethin' you need to know."

Angus and Douglas both looked at him in surprise.

It was Angus who figured it out first. "You've seen this before, haven't you?"

Hamish ran a hand down his face. "Yes."

"How? Where?" Douglas demanded.

"Let me finish the letter," Hamish said, "then I'll explain everythin'."

Douglas stared at him hard, but he nodded once and folded his arms over his chest. Tension radiated off him and Hamish hated being the cause, but there was also an element of relief knowing he could finally get rid of the burden.

Hamish swallowed his guilt, placed the photo on the table, then continued reading.

I'm sorry I never showed you a photo before now. I missed your father so much and Hamish, every time I saw you, it was like looking at him. I love you, my son, but it always hurt so much to look at you. It was a stab to my heart every single day. I feared if I had more photos out, it would destroy me so I hid them.

I know, it's no excuse and I'm sorry. I was weak and heartbroken. I hope one day you will understand. When you get home, you'll find a box of photos in the attic.

Hamish, please don't think I ever resented you. I never once did. But seeing you was a reminder of what I loved and what I lost, but that wasn't your fault.

After today, there's only one more day to go before you find out the truth. I hope when you read my final letter that you'll understand why I did this.

All I can tell you is I was protecting you.

Until tomorrow, Ma.

"Protectin' us?" Hamish muttered under his breath.

"Screw that," Douglas said, snatching the letter from Hamish and shoving it aside. "I want you to tell us what you know. Now."

Chapter 22

♥

The relief of telling his brothers the truth was short-lived. Tension filled the air inside, making the already small space feel even smaller. The storm had them all on edge, but Hamish's confession added to the unease. Morsels of food lay discarded on the table from their lunch. Angus sat in a seat, shoulders slumped, not looking at Hamish. Hamish sat on one end of the sofa with Douglas on the other end. He sat right on the edge, his right leg bouncing up and down as he glanced around the small suite.

Unlike their bungalow, which was big enough that they weren't on top of each other, this suite had a bedroom and bathroom, and everything else was in the cramped living area. A sofa, TV, some storage space and mini-fridge, a small table and three chairs, and two small cots collapsed against a wall for them to pull out when they slept.

The cyclone intensified outside with even stronger winds and heavy rain pelting against the shutters. The waves of the usually calm ocean crashed on the shore. It could be worse, he supposed. No one knew how bad this cyclone could get, and they were safer here.

As the silence extended between them, the guilt of keeping the secret only grew. He thought he'd done the right thing honouring their mother's wishes, but his brothers' extended silence implied they didn't see it that way.

"I said I'm sorry," Hamish said when the silence entered a new hour. "Are you goin' to stay mad at me forever?"

"Sounds good to me," Douglas snapped, throwing him a glare as he got to his feet and paced the small space like a caged lion.

"I understand *why* you did it," Angus said slowly and diplomatically, always the logical one. "But it doesn't make it right."

"I was just followin' Ma's—"

"—wishes," Angus finished with a nod. "Yes, we know but, Hamish, she's dead." He said this softly and lowered his gaze. It was still a sore topic. "People state wishes, I get that, but do you know what happens when you dinnae follow them?"

"Bloody nothin'," Douglas growled. "Wishes be damned, you should've told us, Hamish."

"I know and I've already apologised. What else do you want me to do? I cannae fix what's been done. Stayin' mad at me won't fix anythin'."

Douglas groaned and sat, but then stood again almost immediately, clutching his hair.

Hamish realised being cooped up wasn't helping the situation. It made Douglas more irritable than he would've been in any other situation. Out of all three of them, Douglas hated staying indoors the most.

"Yeah, well, you should've thought of that before you kept it from us," Douglas let his arms fall to his side and he turned to Hamish. His eyes were dark but not angry. He looked sad. "We've always told each other everythin'." His tone betrayed the sadness. Clearing his throat, he said more gruffly, "So, yes, I will hold this against you." He started pacing again.

Another moment of silence passed before Douglas added, "I just can't believe you were goin' to sit on it until the 'big reveal' and let us find out like that. Hell, what was *Ma* even thinkin' by doin' that?"

Angus nodded. "I agree. How hard was it to tell us years ago that he'd died? I know Ma was heartbroken, but wouldn't it have helped *her* to share it with her sons?"

Hamish shrugged. He couldn't argue that point.

"And I wouldn't have assumed he was just a deadbeat who didnae want to be a father," Douglas said, that sadness back in his tone again.

The tension in the room lifted a little and Hamish breathed easier.

"That's what this is really about, isn't it?" he asked. "You feel guilty for makin' the wrong assumption, and you're miffed that Ma didnae tell us earlier?"

Douglas sighed and finally plopped into a chair. "I suppose so. It *is* sucky, right?"

"Yes," Hamish said. "If it's any consolation, I considered tellin' you because I thought it was a terrible way to reveal it. Then I thought you'd want to find out that way because it was what Ma wanted for us."

Angus rolled his eyes, and he smiled. "I'm pretty sure I can speak for Dougie when I say this, but we're not *that* sentimental. We're only here because Ma had already booked everythin'. We would've been happy to read about it in a letter."

Hamish nodded along with Douglas and finally the tension in the room dissipated all together as they all got onto the same page. They never could stay annoyed at each other for too long. Hamish vowed to never keep a secret from them again. It was a stupid mistake made with good intentions, but he should've known they'd hate learning on the day.

"I guess she wanted us to see his grave," Hamish said. "And meet the people who had such a big impact on their relationship."

"But she could've done that and let us do this holiday on *our* terms," Angus said.

"Perhaps," Hamish said, "but I've quite enjoyed followin' their journey."

"Me too," Douglas said with a shrug.

Angus snorted a laugh. "Yeah, but you two have had bonny lassies you've been able to enjoy some activities with. It sucks not havin' Skye here."

Silence fell again, this one more comfortable. At least they'd made a breakthrough.

Another two hours passed, and Douglas started pacing again. This time even Hamish was getting angsty, and so was Angus, who was the only real homebody here. They'd already searched the suite for board games or anything to do, but apart from a deck of cards, they came up empty-handed. They'd played a game of poker already but quickly got bored.

The storm continued to intensify, the waves of the usually calm ocean crashed on the shore and debris hit the walls of the building. Hamish switched the TV onto the weather channel. The large cyclone cloud slowly passed over them. While the eye would still miss them, the edges covered the entire island. The twenty-four-hour forecast showed it should pass by morning. He hoped he could leave the room tomorrow.

As the hours dragged and it reached dinner time, they removed some pre-cooked meals from the fridge and ate them in silence as the wind continued to howl and the rain hammered the shutters. The lights flickered but the power hadn't gone off yet, so they kept the weather channel on. The cloud moved over the island in a north-west direction, avoiding Fiji all together.

"Bloody hell I'm *bored*," Douglas complained for the umpteenth time after they'd finished eating and cleaned up.

On cue, the bedroom phone rang. The three of them sat up straight, eying it suspiciously.

"I'll get it!" They said in unison, leaping to their feet and making a grab for it. Douglas picked it up first.

"Let it go," Angus cried, reaching for the receiver.

"No, I got it first," Douglas huffed, holding it out of reach.

While they bickered, Hamish walked around and snatched the phone from Douglas' hand. "Hello?" he said into the receiver as Douglas punched his arm. "Ow, Dougie, stop it!"

"What was that all about?" a familiar voice said on the other end.

"Tenika!" He grinned and lowered the receiver. "It was for me after all."

Tenika's laughter sent pleasurable sparks across his skin. "Sounds like you boys are as bored as we are. Care to come to our suite?"

"I thought we were 'encouraged to stay in our rooms'?"

"Emphasis on 'encouraged', not enforced. So, are you boys coming or not?"

He grinned and Hamish called out to his brothers, "Hey, who's up for goin' upstairs to see the girls?"

"Hell yes!" Douglas said, fist pumping the air and making a beeline for the door.

Angus nodded eagerly and followed.

"I take that as a yes," Tenika said on the other end with a chuckle.

"Aye, it is. See you soon."

Hamish sat on the sofa with Tenika next to him, Angus on the end, and Brenda and Douglas on the floor. While the power miraculously stayed on, they spent the rest of the evening watching movies and eating Tenika and Brenda's food. When they ran out, Angus retrieved the stash from their room.

After the amount they'd received, they didn't think they'd eat it all. Now he wondered if they'd have enough. Hopefully, the restaurant would open again tomorrow.

Despite watching movies, there was a general sense of unease hovering over them. The roaring cyclone was relentless. Every time something hit the shuttered windows, they jumped. The movies were a distraction, but they never drowned out the raging storm.

When it neared midnight, the lights gave a final flicker, and the power went out. The girls cried out at the interruption as they couldn't see the ending. A moment later, light from Angus' phone torch lit up the room as he got to his feet.

"Well, I'm gonna go back to our suite and claim the bed before either of you muckers can," he said, making his way to the door.

A chorus of goodnights followed Angus as the door clicked shut and darkness shrouded them again. Tenika snuggled into Hamish's side with a contented sigh and he tightened his arm around her, in no rush to move.

"Bed sounds like a really good idea," Douglas said, turning his own phone torch on and sending Brenda a knowing wink.

She grinned and jumped to her feet. "Sounds like a plan." She took Douglas' hand and pulled him to his feet, all but dragging him to her room.

"Please keep it down," Tenika called.

"Put some music on," Brenda called back with a giggle.

"We have no power."

"Improvise."

Hamish chuckled and removed his own phone. "I've got us covered." He unlocked it and opened the Spotify app.

"Thank God," Tenika said with a soft laugh. "It's nice being technology free. I didn't want to have to succumb to it because of a technicality."

Hamish found a playlist and tapped play, turning the volume up a few notches. When he heard Brenda giggling, he adjusted it a little more. He put his phone aside, the glow from the screen bathing them in a faint light. He stared down at Tenika, memorising the way her curls settled on her forehead and her eyelashes rested against her cheeks. Being alone with her was the best and worst thing that could happen.

He swallowed and willed his racing heart to slow down. He wanted nothing more than to suggest they go to her bedroom, but how would she take it? *Especially* after her newest memory. Instead, he played it safe and put the ball in her court.

"If you want to go to bed, I can leave." She shifted a little and looked up at him through her lashes. Captured by her gaze, he held his breath expectantly. He didn't want to leave, but he would if she told him to.

Her eyes betrayed the truth before she even spoke. "I'm getting tired but," she lowered her gaze, "I don't want you to leave."

He blew out a slow, shaky breath. His heart skipped and stuttered inside his chest as he reached out to tilt her chin so he could look into her beautiful eyes again. Eyes that would forever live in his dreams. He didn't know what she saw in his, but she appeared to grow braver before him. She moved from her position next to him and straddled his lap. The light from his phone made her look almost ethereal.

His breathing quickened as he reached out to run his hands down her arms.

She leant in and nibbled his earlobe, sending a shiver across his skin and down his spine. "I want to be with you," she whispered in his ear, moving her kisses down his neck.

He moved his hands to her hips, his fingers finding solace under her flimsy t-shirt and touching soft skin. Goosebumps rose under his fingers by his touch, and this was nearly his undoing.

He groaned when something occurred to him. "I didnae come prepared," he said, pulling away. He hadn't intended for this to happen.

"It's okay," she sat back to unbutton his shirt, "I've got an IUD." Her gaze met his, suddenly uncertain, and she stopped with the buttons. "The IUD helped my painful and heavy periods. I haven't been with many people. I-I'm clean."

A strange groan sounded from the back of his throat as he reached up to place his hand on the back of her head and pulled her down to kiss him. "So am I," he said against her lips.

She pulled back and started on his buttons again. She got one undone, but her trembling hands made her fumble. Losing patience, she ripped it open, and a couple of buttons pinged across the room. She grinned at him, and he chuckled, making short work of removing it. He watched her swallow as she reached out and trailed her fingers down his chest, over the light definition.

His breath caught the closer she got to his belt buckle. She stopped and fiddled with the metal as she looked at him through her lashes, her chocolate pools dark and full of desire.

"We can stay here, or we can go into the bedroom," she said.

He didn't even have to think. In the bedroom he'd be able worship every single inch of her stunning body. He left the music playing but positioned his phone torch to light the way, then he grabbed her thighs and stood with ease, lifting her with him making a beeline for her bedroom with her giggling in his arms.

Chapter 23

♥

When dawn broke the next day, Tenika woke after very little sleep with dull light shining into her bedroom through the partially drawn curtains.

After such a loud and stormy night, the first thing she noticed was the silence. No wind. No rain. No birds chirping. Just eerie silence.

The second thing she noticed was the heavy weight around her middle. It took her a few seconds to realise it was an arm. Another few seconds after that, she realised what, or rather *who*, it was.

She gently rolled over, her heart skipping at Hamish's sleeping form, his breathing steady and even. His eyelashes, a little lighter than his red hair, flared out against his cheeks. She could spend the rest of her life waking up next to this man and watching him sleep.

Last night had been unplanned but she had no regrets. She and Brenda got bored quickly, and the knowledge the boys were so close made the decision easy. Once Angus had left, and Brenda and Douglas had gone off, Tenika knew without a doubt she didn't want to wait any longer.

She was falling for this man.

Falling, hey?

No, she had already fallen. He had her heart and if anything went wrong, she'd never be the same again. No man would ever compare to Hamish McNeill.

She closed her eyes and memorised the events from last night. He was so attentive and gentle yet didn't hold back on the passion. He'd made her feel so special, so loved, so *worth* something.

She reached out to run a hand across his stubbly cheek and jaw.

He stirred and his eyes fluttered open, a large, beaming smile spreading across his face.

"Good mornin'."

When he leant in to kiss her, she gasped and recoiled, covering her mouth. "Morning breath!"

Hamish laughed and grabbed her around the waist, pulling her flush against him. "I dinnae care about that. Come here you stunnin' woman." He made short work of kissing her again and even shorter work of repeating what they'd done last night.

There was no hope for her now.

Tenika woke a couple of hours later, blissfully sated, and ready for whatever life was ready to throw at her.

Or so she thought.

As her eyes adjusted to the brighter light in the room, and her brain flickered to life, one thought came crashing to the forefront of her mind and she sat up with a gasp.

Hamish sat upright, looking at her in sleepy bewilderment. "What's wrong? Are you alright?"

"The reunion," she said, turning to him with wide eyes.

"What about it?"

"It's tonight."

Nausea washed over her, and her stomach rolled. Bile rose in her throat and didn't stop. Covering her mouth with her hand, she shot out of bed with the sheet wrapped around her and sprinted to the bathroom, vomiting into the pristine toilet bowl.

She'd been fooling herself, thinking she was ready for this. Yesterday she was carefree and ready to take on the world.

Today the memories of her school years flooded her mind. Never being enough. Always being the laughingstock. She could still vividly remember the pain in her ribs after they kicked her. The pain in her lungs when she was running out of air. The fear when she lost the strength to push Zachary off her. Not to mention the emotional pain.

What the hell had she been thinking? Why had Brenda been so insistent that Tenika attend? Was she in on some elaborate plan too?

Now you're being paranoid.

She flushed the toilet and sat back, breathing heavily as tears coated her cheeks.

A gentle knock sounded on the door followed by Hamish's voice, "Are you alright?"

She sniffled and wiped the tears away. She didn't want him to see her like this.

"I-I'm fine," she stammered, drawing in a shuddering breath.

She heard more voices on the other side, one male, one female. Presumably, Brenda and Douglas.

"Nika," Brenda said a moment later, her voice laced with concern, "can I come in?"

"No, I'm okay. I'll be out in a few minutes." She bunched up some of the sheet and buried her face in it to silence the sobs.

She wasn't okay, but she had to be.

And this was why she knew Brenda would never be one of them. She was the one person who'd always been there with a shoulder to cry on at the worst times.

When her tears wouldn't abate, she untangled herself from the sheet and stepped into the shower.

She'd just ruined such a great evening and morning. What would Hamish think now?

She gasped and a little shriek escaped her lips when the bathroom door opened. Hamish poked his head around it, and she instinctively covered herself, suddenly feeling so exposed even though she had no reason to.

"I don't want you to see me like this," she said, tears streaming down her cheeks.

"Why not?" He stepped inside, shutting and locking the door behind him.

Fully clothed, he stood in front of the shower door, staring at her with compassion. All her awkwardness disappeared as she shrugged and burst into tears again.

The reunion terrified the hell out of her, but why? Davina had changed so much and the other two hadn't shown up. Maybe it was the memories. They were still so real, and she feared it would happen again.

"Can I come in there?" Hamish asked.

This time she nodded. He undressed, then stepped into the shower and held her against his chest under the stream of warm water. It wasn't sexual, but there was something so comforting and loving about it.

She lost track of time as he let her cry. When she'd calmed down, he washed himself and her while not saying a word. He didn't need to. His actions spoke volumes.

"I'm sorry," she said a few minutes later when they were drying off.

Hamish stopped drying himself and captured her gaze. "You have nothin' to be sorry for." He reached out with his towel to wipe away a drip that had dropped from her hair onto her shoulder. "You realise you dinnae have to go tonight?"

She nodded and hung her towel up, spotting a pile of clothes on the cabinet next to the basin. She turned to Hamish with a smile. "Thanks for the clothes."

"You're welcome."

"I know I don't have to go," she said. "But I think I need to. Even though Zachary and Belinda aren't here, the closure will do me good. It just snuck up on me that's all." She bit her bottom lip. "I'm sorry if I ruined anything. We'd had such a good night and morning—"

He held a finger against her lips, silencing her. "You didnae ruin anythin'."

When they were dressed, he said, "I'm goin' to dash back to my room to get a fresh change of clothes."

"Okay. Do you want to come back for breakfast? We have some food left and should be able to feed all five of us if Angus wants to join."

"I'd like that. How about I check if anythin' has reopened? If the restaurant has opened, I might be able to pick up some basic supplies."

"Sounds good." She turned to open the door then turned back and said, "Hamish, thank you for everything."

He came up to give her one last lingering kiss, then they left the bathroom together. Tenika stopped in her tracks when she saw Angus, Douglas, and Brenda at the table with plenty of food before them. It looked like bread and some leftover pre-made meals, but it was more than Brenda and Tenika had. Angus talked to someone on his phone, which was propped up in front of him.

Brenda glanced between Tenika and Hamish, a knowing but happy smile on her face.

"It's about time you got up." She winked at them. "And look, Angus brought more food."

"Saves me a job," Hamish said.

Angus, looked up with a grin. "The restaurant reopened so I grabbed what I could. Good mornin' by the way. Hey Tenika, come and meet my girlfriend, Skye."

"I'm goin' to change," Hamish said. "I'll be back in a few."

He disappeared and Tenika stood behind Angus. On the screen was a beautiful Scottish woman with rosy cheeks, brunette hair, and a smile that lit up her stunning grey eyes.

"Hey Skye," Tenika said, waving awkwardly at the camera. "It's nice to meet you."

"Aye, you too! I've heard a lot about you. I think you'll do for our Hamish."

Tenika laughed, her cheeks growing warm. "Thanks. I heard the happy news. Congratulations."

If it was at all possible, Skye's smile grew wider, and she held a hand against her still flat stomach. "Thank you, Tenika. Angus and I are fair chuffed, though it was a surprise."

"You can say that again," Angus said. "Hey, speakin' of, I had some ideas for names…"

While Angus and Skye got talking about baby names, Tenika grabbed herself a coffee. With her back to the table, she focused on breathing. She needed to be around these wonderful people today, but she also needed a moment to pull herself together.

"Hey," Brenda said coming up behind her, "are you okay?"

Tenika smiled at her friend. "I am now."

Brenda squeezed her arm, then joined Douglas at the table.

Yes, Tenika *was* okay, and she'd be even better once the reunion was over and she could finally enjoy her holiday. And her new relationship.

Chapter 24

♥

The power was restored by mid-morning, and they received the all-clear to leave the resort. Tenika, usually more than happy to stay indoors, was a bundle of nervous energy and thankful when they heard this announcement. With Hamish and his brothers helping to tidy up and repair the bungalows that had borne the brunt of the storm, Tenika dragged Brenda along with her.

Stepping outside the main entrance of the resort, Tenika stopped and breathed in the cool, pungent tropical air. As she glanced up at the sky through the trees, Tenika was surprised to see a lot of blue as the clouds parted. There was still a breeze, but nowhere near as strong as during the storm last night. She and Hamish barely slept from the noise and…other things.

Something poked her in the ribs, and she yelped, turning to Brenda with a scowl. "What was that for?"

"That silly grin on your face. Stop it, it's sickening." She was smiling though.

"This was you only a few days ago. If I had to tolerate it, so do you."

Brenda chuckled. "Fair enough. I'm happy for you, Nika. Are you sure you're okay? After this morning, I mean."

Her cheeks flushed at the memory of how easily she'd fallen apart. She thought she had it together. Interestingly, after her breakdown she felt calmer. Maybe she'd needed to release the pent-up emotion. Now she was ready for the reunion and eager for it to be over.

It was time to move on and make something of her life.

With Hamish.

She breathed out a sigh and smiled. "Yeah, I'm good. C'mon, let's go check out the damage and see if we can help."

There were people everywhere, locals and visitors alike, working to tidy up the debris. Already the area around the resort was mostly cleared so she and Brenda made their way to the beach on the southern side. Before they even stepped through the trees, they saw lots of debris on the sand. Palm fronds, bark, and snapped palm trees. All the structures appeared to be intact.

Spotting Taito talking to a group of locals, Tenika headed his way with Brenda following. He glanced over and waved at them with a large smile. She hoped that was a good sign. The group walked off and proceeded down the beach.

"Good morning," Tenika greeted Taito. "How is everything looking?"

Taito stopped and placed his hands on his hips. "Pretty good according to reports. We were fortunate it was a weak one and got off lightly. There was a little damage to the bungalows but nothing too drastic. Though I fear our crops might not have fared so well, but I haven't heard for certain yet." He muttered something under his breath and glanced heavenward as though praying.

"Have you ever had a really bad cyclone?" Brenda asked.

Something passed over Taito's face as he appeared to disappear into a memory. When he spoke, he sounded distant. "Many years ago, the island experienced a category four. These were the days when we were still a small community, and no tourists visited. We evacuated to Fiji and when we returned, we barely recognised the island. I pray we never experience that again."

He swallowed, glancing up and down the beach. The mood changed and Tenika sent Brenda a look of reprimand. Brenda only shrugged and mouthed, "How was I supposed to know?"

Tenika cleared her throat. "Can we help at all?"

Taito looked at her for a long moment, then he blinked and his cheery smile was back in place. "I think we've got all the tidy up covered. Although, if it's no hassle, could you meet the seaplane? It will be here any minute. There's one more guest arriving for tonight's event, and there are a couple of people coming from Fiji to offer their help. If you could send them to the resort, I'll be ever so grateful."

Tenika's spine stiffened. "Tonight's definitely going ahead then?"

"We moved it indoors since we didn't know what the weather was doing, but yes it's going ahead. Perhaps we'll light a bonfire afterwards."

Tenika nodded slowly, her stomach knotting up. *Don't be silly, you knew this was happening.*

Taito looked at her expectantly and she realised she hadn't answered his request. "Um, of course it's no hassle, I'll happily meet the plane."

"Thank you, Tenika." He went to walk away then turned back. "One last thing. If you see the organiser of the reunion—Davina, is it? —Please tell her Litia needs to talk to her about the plans for this evening." With a wave, Taito turned and walked away.

"You okay?" Brenda asked.

"I'm fine. Come on, let's go meet the plane."

She and Brenda walked in silence, so Tenika took the moment to pull herself together. What if the reunion wasn't so bad after all? Best case scenario it'll be a pleasant night and they'll all move on as new people. Worst case, Zachary and Belinda gate crashed, and all hell broke loose.

Not helping.

"Sooo…" Brenda said, breaking the silence after a few more minutes passed.

Tenika glanced over at her. "So what?"

Brenda rolled her eyes. "Last night. How was it?"

"Oh." There was no stopping the silly grin spreading across her face. "It was good."

"Only good?" Brenda stopped and grabbed Tenika's arm.

Her cheeks grew hot as she freed her arm and folded them across her chest. "It was great, mind blowing even."

That was how sexually active Tenika *wasn't*. She'd never had these conversations with Brenda. She didn't share her first and last encounter with her because it wasn't memorable. Besides, Tenika had always been a traditional woman, never wanting to put herself out unless it was someone special.

She never understood what she saw in her ex. If she was honest, it was likely she wanted to get her first time over with. How pathetic. She wondered now if Zachary's assault had a bigger impact on her actions, but she didn't realise it.

Brenda did an excited jig on the spot. "I knew it! Now tell me everything, and I mean *every*thing."

Tenika looked at her friend in horror. "You can't be serious!"

Brenda's face was deadpan. "Every. Single. Detail."

Tenika gulped and considered how to get around this when a familiar buzzing sound interrupted her thoughts.

She glanced up at the sky. "Saved by the plane."

Brenda shook her head but smiled. "Come on then, let's go."

They broke into a jog and made it to the pier as the seaplane landed and skied along the water to the dock. They stayed at the end of the pier, watching and waiting. After a few minutes, the doors opened. A couple of Fijians disembarked and Tenika was about to walk up and greet them when another figure exited. She gasped.

"Is that—?" Tenika squinted to see better.

"What?" Brenda asked. "Who?"

When she saw the face clearer, her heart stuttered to a stop. "Oh my God."

"Who is it? Am I going blind? I can't make them out."

"Oh my God!" Tenika repeated. Ignoring Brenda, she dashed down the pier waving her arms in the air.

The figure turned holding bags but then stopped when he spotted Tenika. He dropped the bags again, waving and grinning then ran towards her.

"It *is* you!" Tenika cried, jumping into Travis' arms and embracing him tightly. Even though they spoke often, she hadn't seen him for nearly two years.

He laughed and wrapped his arms around her, spinning her as though she weighed nothing.

"What are you doing here?" she asked when she was back on her feet, stumbling and grabbing his arm for support. "I hadn't heard from you so I thought you weren't coming. How's Kylie? Has she had the baby? What did you have? A boy or a girl? I can't believe you're here!" And she flung herself at him again.

"Whoa, calm down," Travis said with a chuckle, pulling back. "Breathe."

Tenika glanced behind her and beckoned Brenda who was already halfway down the pier. "Brenda, look, Travis is here!"

Brenda ran over and embraced him too.

When the excitement died down, Tenika said, "So? What's the deal?"

Travis laughed. "So many questions." He answered her by counting off on his fingers. "I didn't think I'd make it because of the baby, that's why I'm late. I would've arrived yesterday, but the storm hindered that. I wasn't even sure I'd make it today, but it didn't end up being so bad. Kylie is good, and yes, she's had the baby, a boy we named Marcus. I almost didn't come, but she's got family staying with us while I'm away. I'm only here for one night because I have news. I thought you should know before the reunion since you're going technology free and all that."

Tenika hugged him again, bouncing up and down. "Oh my God, I'm so happy! Congrats Daddy!" She pulled away and his cheeks were bright red. "Make sure you tell Kylie congrats from me. I can't wait to meet Marcus." She stopped when she remembered his last sentence. "Uh, what's the news?"

His eyes sparkled and a slow smile spread across his face. "So, get this—"

"Tenika? Is that you?"

She spun around and her jaw dropped. "What are *you* doing here?"

It was a Fijian from the seaplane who she had to direct to the resort.

"Nika, who's that?" Brenda asked.

"My name is Adi," the woman said clasping her hands in front of herself.

"She's my aunt," Tenika said between clenched teeth. "The one who wanted nothing to do with me."

Brenda's arm slipped through Tenika's and Tenika gave it a squeeze in thanks.

Adi had the decency to look sheepish. "I apologise for the way I behaved when we last spoke. I am here as part of a small support group from Fiji. We heard about the storm, so we brought some supplies, and we wanted to see if the island needed any help."

Tenika had to stop and process this. This didn't match the same woman she'd met. The same one who'd shown such anger and all but threw her out and told her to never come back. This woman was completely different.

Not ready to deal with her, Tenika focused on what she'd promised Taito she'd do.

Pointing towards the trees and the path that led to the resort, she said, "Just follow the signs to the resort. There may be a free cart around if you don't feel like walking. When you arrive, ask to speak to Litia or Taito."

Adi nodded and, with her gaze on the pier, turned to leave. Tenika didn't have time to breathe a sigh of relief when Adi turned back again.

"Tenika, I had no way of contacting you, but I regret how things unfolded in Fiji. This is a fortunate turn of events, running into you like this, and I would like to talk to you again. There are things you must know."

Tenika held her head high and shrugged. "Sorry, I'm busy." Then, with Brenda's arm still through hers, turned and left with Travis following.

Chapter 25

♥

With their itinerary cancelled for that day too, after breakfast, Hamish spent the rest of morning with his brothers and some locals, helping to clean up and repair the bungalows. Tenika and Brenda helped with the clean-up on the other side of the island, and they planned to meet up at the reunion.

The debris spread far and wide, the structure damage minimal. The thatched roofs only required a few minor repairs.

By mid-afternoon they finished. After being told they could move back into the bungalow, the three of them walked to the resort to grab their things.

When they entered, Litia handed over their letter of the day. "The suite is free for the rest of your stay if any of you need space." Then she smiled and rushed off.

Back in the suite, but before they gathered their things together, Hamish sat on the sofa. "Let's read the letter first."

Angus sat beside him with a nod. Douglas snatched the letter from Hamish's hand but remained standing, leaning against a wall. He started reading.

My dear boys,

I write this letter with a heavy heart and a lot of hindsight. As I was reflecting on the second to last day of our journey, something came to me. A memory I must've locked away, too afraid to admit it meant something.

This day when we woke up, something felt...off. It's hard to explain but your father and I didn't want to go anywhere or do anything. There was a heaviness inside both of us...an uncertainty of sorts. Like something was going to go wrong.

Douglas stopped reading, his eyes wide as he looked at Hamish and Angus. No one said anything but Douglas drew in a breath and continued.

I've noted down our planned itinerary and I hope you have fun, but I can't tell you our experience as we didn't go. We spent the day together. Lazed in bed, ordered room service, went for a swim, and just enjoyed each other's company.

But as I write this, I realise what that feeling was. Dread. Maybe an omen of some kind? We didn't know what was going to happen. How could we? But deep down we knew something wasn't right. I only wish we had foresight.

I'm saying too much.

"He didnae...kill himself, did he?" Angus said in a shaky voice.

Hamish shuddered and looked at his two brothers, but they all shrugged. It was a possibility, but why? If, according to Ma, their life was so great, he'd have no reason to.

"I dinnae want to speculate," Douglas said, then continued reading.

I'm sorry to drag this out, but I promise it'll be worth it. Tomorrow you'll find out the truth, and as I relive it, my heart is breaking all over again. I've never stopped loving or missing your father, but I have many regrets. The biggest one is not including his memory in your lives, but I can't do anything about that now.

I only hope you can move forward knowing the sort of man he was, and what he could have been.

Have fun today, my boys. Enjoy every second of your life because you never know what tomorrow is going to bring.

Ma

"Well, that's—" Douglas shook his head, and put the letter on the table. He looked pale and slightly haunted.

"Ominous?" Angus offered.

Douglas shrugged but nodded. He shook his shoulders, pushed himself off the wall, then searched for his bag and packed his things. Even though they hadn't spent the night in the room, he'd still managed to leave items in various places.

No one spoke about the letter. There was nothing to say until the truth came to light tomorrow. Perhaps then there'd be more to talk about. Right now, Hamish felt heavy and unsettled about what to expect. If the tension in the room was anything to go by, Hamish suspected his brothers felt the same way.

"I think I might take Litia up on her offer and stay here for the rest of the trip," Angus said, breaking the tense silence between them. "If you two dinnae mind?"

"You sick of us already?" Douglas asked irritably, zipping his backpack and placing it next to the door.

"Of course not." Angus said. "I've really enjoyed spendin' time with my bros again, but you're both goin' to want some privacy with your new women, right?"

Angus looked pointedly from Hamish to Douglas.

Douglas lost his irritableness, and he smiled. "Thanks, bro. I—"

"I've got dibs on the bungalow," Hamish interrupted, laughing at Douglas' crestfallen expression. "Sorry, Dougie, you were too slow, just like the day you were born."

"Hey!" Douglas took two long strides towards Hamish and tried to punch his arm, but he moved out of the way with a bellowed laugh.

This broke the tension and resulted in an all-out war between the brothers play fighting like they used to when they were younger. It never got violent, but it always resulted in sore heads, bruised arms, and bruised egos as they tried to outdo each other on insults.

"Alright, alright," Douglas said, breaking out of the group with a laugh and rubbing his head where Angus had been rubbing it hard with his knuckles. "But tomorrow night I want the bungalow for our last night here. It's only fair."

"Okay." Hamish rubbed one bicep than the other where he'd been hit hard.

Then the reality came crashing down as Douglas' words sunk in.

Our last night.

He'd tried, and succeeded too well, in not thinking about the end of their journey. From the moment he met Tenika, all he'd wanted was to enjoy every second and not think about what awaited them. But it was ending too quickly, with no confirmed plans in place.

He swallowed and looked at Douglas who appeared as shell-shocked as Hamish. It took a few seconds for Angus to realise what the sudden silence meant, but then his eyes widened, and he nodded.

"That went fast," Angus said.

"Too fast," Douglas muttered. "I'm goin' to drop my things off, then find Brenda." He looked between Hamish and Angus as though wanting to say something but shook his head instead. He walked to the door and picked up his backpack.

"Everythin' okay?" Hamish asked.

"Fine," Douglas said too quickly.

Hamish let it go.

"Thanks, bro," Hamish said to Angus. "It's nice you're doin' this."

Angus shrugged. "It's not that difficult. Hamish, have you spoken to Tenika yet?" His pointed look made Hamish writhe.

"Haven't had a chance, but I hope to tonight."

"What about you Dougie?" Angus asked.

Douglas grunted, muttered something, then stormed out of the room.

Angus turned to Hamish. "What was that all about?"

"I cannae be sure, but I have a feelin' he's freakin' out a bit. I'm not sure whether he or Brenda have even spoken about what happens after this."

"Sounds familiar," Angus said.

"Tenika and I have talked about possibilities," Hamish defended. "Just nothin' concrete." He grabbed his own bag, checked everything was inside, then zipped it up. "Sorry you won't be attendin' the reunion tonight."

"Dinnae worry, it sounds borin' anyway." He grinned. "I'll chat to Skye then watch some TV." He shuffled on the spot. "What do you think we're goin' to find out tomorrow?"

Hamish shrugged, slinging the strap of his backpack over one shoulder. "I dinnae ken. Most likely *how* he died, but I hope Ma explains why it was kept secret for so long. Nothin' makes sense right now."

"Does Taito know we know?"

"He knows *I* know, but that's it. He looked so defeated that I'd found out and asked me not to say anythin'. I dinnae want to completely ruin it for him. I think he feels like he's doin' Ma one last favour."

"I guess that's why you didnae tell us."

Hamish nodded. "Pretty much, but I'm glad I did in the end. I hate keepin' secrets."

"And you suck at it. You gotta work on your poker face, bro."

Hamish chuckled and walked to the door. "See you in the mornin'."

· ❤ · ❤ · ❤ · ❤ · ❤ ·

An hour before he had to meet Tenika, Hamish sat on a chair on the deck outside the bungalow overlooking the ocean. Douglas had returned from seeing Brenda and had gone for a swim before he had to get ready.

Hamish found it surprising how quickly the weather had returned to normal. If he hadn't helped with cleanup and repairs, he would've questioned if there was any cyclone at all. It was humid, sunny, and idyllic, like nothing had happened.

As he gazed out over the ocean, his thoughts drifted to Tenika and their night together, a smile spreading across his face. In the space of twenty-four hours everything had changed. Again. There'd been so many missed opportunities to talk to her about their future and he couldn't wait to sit down with her and discuss it later tonight. His heart pounded just thinking about it. Last night had been...wonderful. She was everything he'd ever looked for in a woman and more.

The way she fit in with the island, the people, and looked so happy, he couldn't take her away from it. And the longer he stayed here, the more he liked it too. He'd never love the humidity, but he'd deal with it.

Scotland would always be his home, but this was his future.

Half an hour later, Hamish went inside to shower and freshen up. He had brought no formalwear to the island, but Tenika had assured him it was a relaxed event. It was too hot to wear trousers, so he settled on shorts and a button-up shirt. He only brought two with him, the other now had buttons missing. He smiled at the memory and prayed the evening would go fast so he could do it all over again.

Hamish combed his hair back, then left the bathroom. "You ready yet?" Hamish joked to Douglas who tapped his foot impatiently as he dripped saltwater on the floorboards.

Douglas scowled. "How can I be ready if you're hoggin' the bathroom? Move your arse and let me shower. I'll be ready in ten minutes." He pushed past and slammed the door.

True to his word, in ten minutes he was ready and they walked the short distance to the resort. School alumni filled up the entry area. Apart from the beach party a few nights ago, there hadn't ever been too many people in one place. There were more than Hamish expected.

Hamish spotted Tenika with Brenda and another man near the entrance to the restaurant where the reunion was now taking place. Since the resort didn't have a ballroom or function room, they had to improvise. Davina, the organiser, appeared relaxed as she flittered about talking to and greeting people.

Tenika looked stunning in another bula dress that was a different colour, her hair pinned back elegantly. Hamish couldn't wait to remove each pin and run his fingers through her curls.

When she spotted him, she grinned, then got the attention of the man next to her and pointed. Who was he? She waved Hamish over, so he elbowed Douglas in the ribs and jutted his chin in their direction. Douglas followed as they made their way over.

"You made it!" Tenika said with a wide smile when he stopped in front of her, her eyes bright. Something appeared different about her tonight. She looked lighter somehow. Carefree. What was different?

"You look stunnin'," Hamish said, leaning in to leave a lingering kiss on her cheek and catching an intoxicating scent of tropical flowers.

Tenika grabbed his hand and squeezed it. "There's someone I want you to meet." She gestured to the man who stood ramrod straight, arms crossed over his chest, eying Hamish cautiously. "This is Travis. I told you about him, remember? He arrived this morning."

Hamish nodded, breathing a sigh of relief. The man who saved Tenika's life. The caution made sense now. He'd seen the absolute worst and was protective of her. If anything, Hamish respected the man even more and wanted to prove he was nothing like those who hurt Tenika.

"Travis, this is Hamish and one of his brothers, Douglas."

Douglas greeted him, then joined Brenda. Hamish held out his hand and Travis eyed him warily, mouth down-turned, gaze judging, but unfolded his arms and took it. He was tall with dark blonde hair and weathered skin, but his hazel eyes were kind, even if they were cautious. Hamish appreciated he looked out for Tenika.

"It's great to meet you," Hamish said.

Travis' lips lifted in a small smile as his grip tightened on Hamish's hand and pumped it up and down. "It's nice to meet you too." He let it go. "It's good to put a face to the name. Tenika's barely talked of anything else today."

Hamish grinned and looked across at a blushing Tenika, who only shrugged.

"I've heard a lot about you." Hamish flexed his fingers. Travis had a firm grip.

"Good." Travis met his gaze and smiled easier this time even though his eyes displayed an unspoken warning.

Hamish liked him already. Anyone who cared for Tenika the way Travis did had a tick in his books.

When the crowd started moving, they moved along with it into the restaurant. Fifteen round tables, each seating ten people, surrounded a makeshift dancefloor. The doors leading onto the terrace were open, letting the balmy breeze inside.

White tablecloths covered each table with beautiful centrepieces of tropical flowers, fruit, and candles. Bamboo placemats with a menu in the middle, cutlery, and napkins folded into fancy designs marked the place settings.

Tenika had a skip in her step as she held his hand tight and led him to a table at the back, Brenda, Douglas, and Travis following.

They settled at a table with five other people Hamish had never seen before in his life. He had Tenika on his left and Travis next to her. On his right was Douglas and Brenda. Tenika, Brenda, and Travis chatted to the other five alumni, any nerves from earlier appeared to be long gone. Someone whistled and silence settled over the room. Davina wandered to the front, no longer looking calm like she did earlier. Now she appeared nervous and on edge.

"Good evening, everyone!" Davina called. "I don't have a microphone so please bear with me. Can you all take your seats please?"

While everyone found somewhere to sit, Hamish picked up a menu. His stomach rumbled. It all looked delicious.

"Hey, bro?" Douglas asked.

"Hmm?"

Douglas plucked the menu out of his fingers. He stared into his brother's serious eyes.

"What's up?" Hamish asked, sensing this was important.

Douglas looked over his shoulder where Brenda talked to another alumni. He leant closer to Hamish, then said in a low voice, "I was thinkin' of askin' Brenda to come back to Scotland with me. Is that a stupid idea?"

Hamish stared at his brother. Was this what he wanted to say earlier?

"You do you, Dougie. But for the record, I think it's a great idea. Do you think she'll agree?"

Douglas swallowed and shrugged. "No idea, but I want to ask her tonight."

Hamish grinned. "She'll certainly keep you on your toes."

Douglas nodded but the smile never left his face. Hamish looked at a glowing Tenika. She glanced over at him, her permanent smile only growing wider. His breath caught and three special words popped into his mind. Words he couldn't say here, but desperately wanted to.

Later, perhaps.

Chapter 26

♥

Tenika shuffled in her seat. Even though Travis had told her everything, it sounded too good to be true.

"Are you okay?" Hamish asked from beside her.

She smiled apologetically and forced herself to sit still, folding her hands in her lap. "I'm fine." She wanted to tell him, but didn't dare. What if Travis heard wrong?

She trusted him as much as she did Brenda, and he insisted he heard the news from a reliable source, but Tenika couldn't settle. She wanted to hear it from Davina, certain it would come out tonight. After all, Davina had always been an attention seeker. If there was any part of the old Davina there, she'd want the sympathy points.

"Are you nervous about tonight?" Hamish coaxed.

She shrugged one shoulder. "Not anymore, I just want it over with."

I want to spend the night with you, she thought, meeting his gaze. She could've sworn he'd read her mind by the smouldering in his eyes.

She'd spent the afternoon with Travis, catching up on things they'd missed and reminiscing on old times. The good old times at least when they weren't at school. Swimming at the local pool, hiking, seeing the occasional movie at the cinema in the next town over. There wasn't a lot to do in the small town she lived in, so they made their own fun. Walks and hikes were the main thing they loved doing together. Enjoying nature and the freedom to be themselves.

Davina called everyone's attention a second time, and Tenika turned to the front. Staff flitted in and out, the sounds and smells from the kitchen making her stomach rumble.

"Thank you all for coming tonight," Davina said when everyone had found their seats and quietened down. "Ten years is a long time and we've all changed so much. I hope everyone is doing great."

A light, half-hearted applause sounded. Davina continued talking but Tenika zoned out. She glanced around at the blank expressions of these people. It was hard to believe they all went to school together. Many she didn't even recognise. Others she did but they were strangers now. Brenda and Travis were the only two she kept in touch with.

Why am I even here?

A week ago, she dreaded the reunion. Afraid of what to expect, of facing her past. The fear of it happening again had been forefront in her mind. Even earlier in the day she still had those fears. But at this moment...nothing. No fear. No dread. She had the closure she needed thanks to Travis.

Now she wanted to leave. Be anywhere but here.

Of course, this did nothing for Tenika's agitation. She shuffled in her seat again and ran her hands over her dress. Now all she wanted was for Davina to reveal all, then Tenika could leave. She had better places to be.

With Hamish.

"—the main reason I wanted to do this," Davina was saying, "was because of how much I've changed. I know I wasn't liked, and I did some bad things, but I'm a different person now. I wanted to prove to you all—"

"It's all about you, isn't it, Davina?" someone spoke up.

Tenika swivelled her head around and found a woman with brunette hair standing with her hands on her hips. She looked familiar but Tenika couldn't remember her name.

"It's always about you," the woman continued. "Do you even hear yourself? I, I, I, that's all we're hearing coming out of your mouth, so many 'I's'. *You* were a bad person and *you've* transformed. *You* organised the reunion so *you* could prove *you've* changed."

"Candice," Davina chuckled nervously, "I'd really appreciate it if you didn't interrupt. I'm trying to make a point."

"Then make it," Candice shot back. "I'm not here to remember what you did to me and so many others. I'm here to prove that you and your gang didn't destroy me."

Davina's face turned red, her hands folded in front of her as she kept her gaze lowered.

Tenika glanced between the two women. *Candice Hunter.* Yes, she remembered her now. Although she realised with shame that she had no idea she'd been bullied too. It was so easy in school to get caught up in her own problems. Who else was bullied?

Heaviness settled in her gut when a new realisation hit her square in the chest. Were all these people victims too? Or supporters of victims?

Tenika glanced at Travis, then at Brenda, both wearing wide-eyed expressions. This had taken a turn neither of them expected.

"How does this reunion affect any of us?" Candice continued. "You do realise we only came because it was a crazy cheap holiday, and you were footing most of the bill thanks to your rich family."

Davina's mouth opened and closed. "I-I-I'm—"

The crowd started booing, catching on to Davina's overuse of the word 'I'. Tenika winced and caught Brenda's gaze. This wasn't supposed to happen.

"Do something," Brenda mouthed.

"What?" Tenika mouthed back.

Brenda shrugged and Tenika flicked her gaze to Hamish and Douglas, who sat stock still, stunned at the goings on around them.

When Travis started booing too, her spine stiffened. "Travis," she hissed.

"C'mon, she deserves it," he said.

"No, she doesn't." Gritting her teeth, Tenika pushed her chair out and stood. "Everyone be quiet, will you!"

The booing and taunting continued. Davina stood at the front, eyes shining with moisture, her chin wobbling. The dark side of Tenika almost got pleasure out of it. Wanted Davina to suffer, but the compassionate side couldn't bear it. They were supposed to be better than that.

"Quiet, please!" Tenika tried again to no avail.

A loud, ear-piercing whistle cut through the sound, shutting everyone up. It came from Douglas, who'd broken out of his surprise and she sent him a smile of thanks.

All eyes were on Tenika.

"I never expected *you* to take her side," Candice called out.

She had to make this good before they turned on her too. She might've been a victim in school, but she could easily become an enemy now if she wasn't careful.

"I'm not taking her side," Tenika said. "But will you all listen to yourselves? How are any of you better than Davina and her gang were in school? You're adults now. You should know better." She pointedly looked at Travis, who slunk down in his seat.

"Davina organised this reunion for a reason, and I think the least we can do is listen to *why*. In case you didn't notice, there are two people missing. That's got to say something, doesn't it?"

Silence fell over everyone as they nodded in agreement. Tenika took her seat again and breathed a sigh of relief.

Hamish squeezed her hand and leant in to whisper, "Look at you go."

She grinned at him and squeezed his hand back.

"Hey, I'm sorry about before," Travis said. "I got too caught up in the moment. You've always been the more forgiving one."

Catching his apologetic gaze, she smiled. "It's okay, I understand. I guess I feel bad for her after what you told me."

"Who *are* you?"

"The new Tenika Ballentine." She pulled her shoulders back, meaning every word.

She was a new woman who took crap from nobody and no longer lived in the past.

"Thank you, Tenika," Davina said, her voice trembling. "I'm sorry if it sounded like I was making this about me. That wasn't the intention. What I meant to say was that during my years of self-discovery, I realised who I'd hurt in school. So, while a part of me *did* organise this for selfish reasons, my focus was to apologise so I could help others get closure too."

When no one reacted harshly, Davina's shoulders slackened.

"Today I found out something that really put everything into perspective," Davina continued.

Tenika sat up straight. This was it!

Davina cleared her throat. "It confirmed that cutting my sister and Zachary off, and starting a new life, did me multiple favours. Not only did I realise just *how* horrible I'd been as a person, but I also dodged a very large metaphorical bullet."

More murmurs but Davina didn't elaborate, much to Tenika's surprise. A sense of pride made her chest expand. She and Davina would never be friends, but seeing her in a different light, as a new person...wow! How could she *not* be proud? Davina really had changed.

"What I really wanted tonight to be about was a fresh start for all of us. I can't make up for past wrongs, but I hope a heartfelt apology and a promise to continue being the best version of myself will be enough to move forward. Let go of the past. Forgive and forget. That's all I want." She took a moment to take a breath, then added, "Enjoy your evening, and your meal." Her voice broke on the last words, and she managed a wobbly smile before disappearing out to the terrace.

"Well, that was a letdown," Travis muttered. "I'd hoped she would announce it for everyone to hear."

But Tenika barely heard him. "Excuse me," she said, then stood and weaved her way through the tables, past chairs, and onto the terrace.

She found Davina on the end facing west. Though the tropical foliage blocked most of the view, the last rays of daylight dappled through the trees. The sky was mostly blue with a few lingering clouds lined in pink.

Davina's floral maxi dress fluttered in the breeze as she stood at the balcony, her hands resting on top as she stared out over the tropical garden.

"So, it's true then?" Tenika stopped about a metre away.

Davina spun around, wiping her cheeks and sniffling. "I don't know what you're talking about. What are you even doing here? You have no reason to speak to me ever again."

"You're right, but I feel a strange sense of concern. It wouldn't be easy finding out your sister and ex are in custody for crimes that could give them both life in prison."

Davina's face turned red as her chest heaved and she spun around, a sob catching on the breeze. Her shoulders lifted as she drew in a breath but then they shook with silent sobs.

It was weird standing here with her after all that had happened, but Tenika meant it. She *was* concerned. She didn't specifically mention the crimes, not sure how Davina would react. But according to Travis, Zachary was being pinned for multiple counts of rape with Belinda as an accomplice. She apparently lured the women to their home where it happened. There were possible murder charges too, but investigations were ongoing.

It was all quite shocking.

To think, they were gone from her life for good! The freedom she experienced was euphoric.

"Go on then," Davina said through sobs. "Tell everyone. Let them mock me and make fun of me. You saw what they were like earlier. They'll have a field day with this."

"I wouldn't do that, Davina. If they find out, it won't be from me." Of course it was tempting. *So* tempting. But she didn't want to stoop to that level.

Sighing, Tenika stepped closer until she stood beside Davina at the balcony.

"I only found out today," Davina said, her voice barely audible. "I received a phone call. The police want to talk to me when I return to Australia. Since I'm related and everything, I guess they want to see if I know anything. Having not seen them for ten years means nothing."

Tenika nodded. "I suppose it's what they have to do. Make sure they've got all the information they can."

"I may have to talk about what happened in school," Davina said, regret flittering across her features.

Tenika's spine stiffened. "Why would it have anything to do with what's happening now? It was so long ago. We were kids."

"It connects to who they are as people. Maybe it'll explain why they are like they are now. Who knows, it may lead to other victims." Her face grew pale when she added, "Not everyone RSVP'd to the reunion, Tenika. It may mean nothing, but it may mean something."

Tenika shuddered at the implication. That Zachary might've gone after some girls in school. It was complete speculation, but it made her think.

"Obviously I don't know for sure," Davina added. "But it is a possibility."

"I understand," Tenika said softly. "Say what you have to say and if they need to talk to me…" She trailed off and swallowed, shrugging a shoulder. "Well, you know how to contact me now."

Davina drew in a deep breath and wiped her tears away. "Why did you never report us? To the school or the police?"

There was that question again. Tenika's face burned hot. Her adoptive parents never pushed her about it, but Travis and Brenda did. She meant what she'd told Hamish. She was scared. The thought of it was all too overwhelming so she didn't. She was so young too, and didn't know any better. Though it seemed no one else did either.

If she needed to talk about it now to help two criminals get what they deserved, she wouldn't hold back.

"I was scared," she said simply, "of what might happen if I drew attention to it and you got away with it. If I kept silent, it meant I didn't aggravate the situation."

Tenika met Davina's gaze and her face crumpled. Tenika didn't want to be mean or too direct, but they were words that had to be spoken.

"I really am sorry, Tenika," Davina said.

"I forgive you." The words were out before Tenika could stop them, but she meant it.

The bombshell had altered something inside her. No more grudges. Be more forgiving. Davina was trying, and Tenika needed to acknowledge that. They wouldn't be instant besties if Tenika forgave her. It just meant she'd be free of the pain of the past.

A bright smile broke out on Davina's face. "Thank you." Then she lunged forward and embraced Tenika.

It was over just as quickly, and Davina dashed back into the restaurant, but a strange sensation washed over Tenika and tears stung her eyes. This was *true* closure.

She stayed out on the terrace for a little while longer until the sun had set and darkness set in. She wasn't sure how much time passed, but eventually Hamish came looking for her. He strode over, his brow furrowed.

"I was worried about you. Are you alright?" he asked. "Travis is a little frantic too after Davina returned and you didnae."

Tenika laughed despite herself and grabbed Hamish's arm, holding onto it tight.

"Everything is great. Let's go inside and I'll let Travis know I'm not locked away somewhere."

Hamish tutted and squeezed her arm. "Dinnae even joke about that."

She looked up at him and his mouth was downturned.

"Sorry." She leant up to kiss his cheek. "I didn't mean to make you, or anyone for that matter, worry. I've got something to tell you, but I promise things couldn't be better."

His expression lightened and he nodded. "Alright."

"Hey, how about we go somewhere after we've eaten? I'm ready to ditch this party."

"I've already organised to have the bungalow to myself for the night if you're interested."

She nodded eagerly. "I'm very interested. We have a lot of talking to do."

His eyes flashed. "And a lot of other things too."

When they stepped back inside and went back to the table, a very flustered Travis and Brenda gave her a stern talking to. While they ate, she told them everything and realised she had exactly who she needed in her life right here, right now.

Chapter 27

T enika dropped Hamish's hand and ran along the beach, arms outstretched, the evening breeze cool on her skin as it whipped past her. The full moon shone on the water and bathed the sand in a beautiful silvery glow. She stopped and faced the ocean, the breeze tangling her dress around her legs.

Tenika spun on the spot and giggled. She could see an entire future ahead of her. So much to do, so much to see, so much to achieve. Life looked exciting. It had meaning.

At last.

This night couldn't have been more perfect if she'd tried.

Except...

She turned and watched Hamish's approach. He stared at her with such intensity, a half-smile on his face, that if she hadn't already realised she was in love with him, she would've fallen right there and then. His red hair caught in the moonlight, shimmering like molten copper, the strands glowing. Red hair really was becoming in the moonlight. As he drew closer, his piercing green eyes sparkled.

Her Scottish hero.

Only one thing would make this night completely perfect.

When he stopped in front of her, close enough to smell his delicious woodsy scent mixed with the salt of the ocean, only one word came to mind.

"Stay," she said.

Hamish took one step forward and wrapped an arm around her waist, pulling her flush against him, his warm breath fanning her face.

"Yes," he whispered gruffly, then claimed her lips.

Her heart leapt and raced and fluttered all at once as he staked his claim. One simple word would forever live in her memories and dreams. He chose to stay on this island with her even before she talked about her plan.

He was certainly a keeper.

"Do you really mean it?" she whispered when they pulled away.

"Wherever you are, I want to be."

"But I have an idea—"

He kissed her again. "Whatever it is, it'll always be yes. So long as you're there."

Tenika groaned as they fell to the sand, barely losing contact. She ended up on top of him, their kisses growing intense. She remembered Brenda's words a few days ago and she couldn't stop the giggle from escaping.

"What's wrong?" Hamish asked, brow creased.

"It's not you," she said with a chuckle. "I just remembered Brenda saying she didn't recommend sex on the sand."

Hamish grinned, then swiftly rolled them over, so he was on top. Breathless, she stared up at him, taking in his handsome features, ethereal hair, stunning eyes, and knee-weakening smile. She truly loved this man.

He kissed her again, then pulled back. "Aye," his voice was rough, "I can see it would be unpleasant. Sand everywhere."

He got to his feet and helped her up.

"Did you say you had the bungalow to yourself?" she asked. When he nodded, she impatiently added, "Well, what are we waiting for?"

"Wait," he said with a soft smile, pulling her to him so they stood side by side facing the ocean. "Let's remember this moment. Commit it to memory as the beginnin' of our future."

Tears of happiness pricked her eyes as she did just so.

With her arm around his waist and his around her shoulders, she stared out over the ocean and the reflection of the silvery moon. The waves lapped at the shore, the balmy breeze caressing her skin, the sky a blanket of diamonds.

Struck with an idea, she turned to him. "Let's go swimming!"

A slow smile spread across his face as he nodded and lifted one leg to remove a shoe, followed by the other, his gaze fixed on her.

She grinned and grabbed the bottom of her dress, pulling it over her head, leaving her in nothing but her shoes, underpants, and bra. After kicking off her shoes, she waded into the water, still tinged with warmth even though it was late and it'd been a cooler day.

"You coming?" she asked, turning back when the water was waist high.

Hamish was staring after her, holding a shoe but quickly snapped to action. He dropped the second shoe, then removed his shorts and shirt, before coming after her in his boxers.

She swam out a little deeper where she could still touch the sand, but the water was just below her shoulders. Turning, she found Hamish only a few metres away, grinning as he came up to kiss her so thoroughly it made her head spin.

"You can do that anytime," she murmured when he slowed the kiss and pulled away.

He chuckled, then lifted his hand to her hair, removing the pins holding it in place. "I've wanted to do this all night."

"Don't drop them."

He tutted, then winked and pinned them to the waistline of his boxers.

"Clever," she said with a laugh, turning with her back to him so he could continue removing the pins.

When he'd removed all of them, she ducked under the water. "That's better," she ran her hand over her hair and massaged her scalp.

"Beautiful," Hamish said.

Her cheeks glowed as he leant in to kiss her again. Was this really happening? Was this their future now? Here? On this island?

Even if it was, she still wanted to share her plan. "I was thinking a year here, then a year in Scotland."

His eyebrows furrowed as he cocked his head to the side.

"Us. Together. Maritimo Island."

A slow smile spread across his face. "I already said I'd say yes to anythin', but that is a great plan. I hadn't thought that far ahead. All I know is that you weren't ready to leave here, and I wanted to be with you. It was a no brainer."

"What about tomorrow?"

"What about it?"

"What if everything changes?"

He shook his head so vehemently she believed him. "That won't happen. The only thing that will happen for sure is I'll need to return to sort a few things out, but I'll be back here in no time."

"I'll have to do the same."

"Well then," he reached for her hand, "it's a plan."

Excitement skirted along her skin.

He leant in to kiss her, slow and sensual, making it clear where this was heading.

"Shall we go back to the bungalow?"

She swallowed and drew in a breath. "Yes."

They waded back to shore and Tenika gasped.

"What's wrong?" Hamish asked.

She pointed at the partygoers spilling out onto the beach where a bonfire was being built up. She grabbed her things and held the dress against herself to offer what little decency she could manage.

"Um, there's no way I'm going to get this dress on while I'm soaked."

Hamish, not at all fazed, shrugged and picked up his own things. "We'll make a run for it. Race you!"

He dashed off, not giving her a chance to argue. "Not fair!" she called, but ran after him, not caring if anyone spotted her.

Hamish woke early and turned his alarm off before it disturbed Tenika. It was only five-thirty a.m. but he had to meet Scott and his brothers at the resort at six. No jog today.

An unexpected heaviness weighed in his stomach. What *would* today bring? When Tenika had asked him if anything would change, he was so sure nothing could ruin their plans. But after he and Tenika had made love last night and she'd drifted into a deep sleep, he had lain there for ages thinking about this question. Had he been too quick to dismiss it?

There were no certainties, and Ma had built up this last day to reveal something big. What if it changed everything? In an ideal world, they'd get the last letter, learn how their father died, then bid both parents goodbye.

He leant over and placed a kiss on Tenika's shoulder, her skin soft and warm under his lips.

"I love you," he whispered, enjoying the way the words rolled off his tongue so easily.

He'd tell her soon, when the time was right.

Picking up his phone, he tapped the screen but there was nothing there. Had Douglas asked Brenda to return to Scotland with him? He'd half expected a message with the outcome. Hopefully, no news meant good news.

Tiptoeing to the bathroom, he showered and changed in record time. He located the box that held Ma's ashes they'd brought with them, then left a good morning note for Tenika suggesting they meet up for dinner.

He arrived at the resort five minutes before six a.m. and Scott was already there. Angus arrive next, followed by a grinning Douglas. The same grin Hamish was certain he wore. It was a loud and excitable five minutes as he and Douglas shared their news, Angus watching on in amusement. When Scott beckoned them to start the hike up the mountain, they were high on life.

Surely nothing could ruin this day.

Chapter 28

Even Angus wasn't complaining as they hiked. They talked and bantered until it got steeper, and they needed to reserve their energy. It was just after seven-fifteen a.m. when they reached the top. In just a couple of days, the team restored the whole lookout area, leaving some foliage, but nothing remained hidden anymore.

Hamish's heart stuttered when his eyes drifted to the gravestone. It appeared someone had replaced it. It was still marble, but it looked new and had a new epitaph.

In loving memory of Duncan Angus McNeill.
Beloved husband to Isla.
Father to Hamish, Douglas, and Angas, who he never got to meet.
Dearly loved, never forgotten.

Tears stung Hamish's eyes. He swallowed and tore his eyes away to take in the area. Scott stood to the side, looking sombre. Krishneel and Ratu stood beside him, along with some other locals. Taito and Litia stood next to the gravesite.

Hamish glanced at the timber barrier that ran along the cliff edge, then turned to Douglas and Angus. Their eyes said it all. They were all thinking the same thing. Hamish didn't give it a thought the day he'd stumbled across the grave, but now it all made sense. Why Ma had been so devastated.

It was all so tragic.

"Welcome McNeill boys," Taito said, and Hamish turned to him.

Taito looked at all three, recognition passing across his features. Seemed it wasn't just Hamish who didn't have a poker face. His brothers didn't either.

"I told them about the grave durin' the cyclone," Hamish explained. "I'm not good at keepin' secrets and I couldn't lie to them."

"We still dinnae ken what really happened," Douglas added. "I mean, I've got an idea but I could be wrong."

Taito nodded, his lips lifting in a small smile. "I shouldn't have asked you to keep that secret, Hamish. I apologise. The last letter I got from your ma asked me to oversee this journey with Litia and I took it seriously. Wanted to do everything as she'd stepped out, but I know now it's not always that simple."

"If it's any consolation, we pretty much threatened death if he didnae tell us," Douglas admitted.

Taito chuckled. "There are no hard feelings. I suspected by the time you got here you would all know, so it made preparing for today much easier."

Litia stepped forward holding a familiar envelope, this one thicker than the others.

"This isn't the last letter," she explained when Hamish took it. "There'll be one more tomorrow. I think she knew the three of you would need some time to think things over."

"Do we open it now?" Hamish asked.

"Not yet," Taito said. "First, I think it's important to know what happened, then you can read about why they were here."

"It wasn't *just* a honeymoon, was it?" Angus asked.

"You'll find out soon enough," Litia said kindly, moving to stand beside her husband, who looked weepy, and looped her arm through his. "Everyone loved your father, especially those here today."

All the others had their heads bowed and hands folded in front of them.

Taito took over. "He was easy to love. The life of the party. Easy-going, carefree, always ready to have a laugh. Your ma was such a shy thing when she arrived, but she came alive around him. She became just as loved as your Da." Taito paused and wiped his eyes. "They were so happy. It wasn't just the honeymoon love either. There was so much more there after all they'd been through in such a short time—" He shook his head and pressed his lips together. "You'll read about it in the letter. But their love was *real*, the forever kind."

A lump formed in Hamish's throat as he stared at the gravestone. Was that what he and Tenika had? What about Douglas and Brenda? Angus and Skye?

"On their last day here," Taito continued, his voice hoarse, "they came up here for one last hike. Your ma was setting up a picnic in the spot you were at recently and heard a scream."

Hamish bristled and held his breath in anticipation, even though he'd already guessed.

"When she came back," Taito wiped away a couple of tears, "he was nowhere to be seen. All she saw was a ragged edge where it had been smooth. When she inched closer and peered down—" He shook his head and covered his eyes with his large hand.

"He'd fallen?" Hamish finished. That was what he'd guessed, but what if he was wrong? What if—?

Taito nodded and Litia took over. "The edge of the cliff gave way. They were our third lot of guests after we opened the island to tourists.

The first two hadn't come up this far, more interested in the island and water sports. The locals came here often, but they never got close enough to notice any weakness."

"We'd had a couple of days of heavy rain," Taito said when he'd composed himself. "It's possible it had been weak, but of course we didn't know." He puffed out a sigh and shook his head. "Your da, bless him, was a thrill seeker and loved heights. He wouldn't have thought twice about getting close for the best view, having no idea of its weakness."

Hamish swallowed, a shudder traipsing down his spine. What a terrible way to go. So much life ahead for him and Ma. A future together, and to go…like that. So suddenly.

"Da," Angus cried out, then sat in front of the headstone, resting his hand on top of the marble as he silently cried.

Hamish caught Douglas' gaze. His eyes were watery, but he held himself together.

"Your ma was devastated," Litia said. "There was nothing we could do. By the time the rescue team got to him, it was too late. We think he died on impact."

Hamish sat beside Angus, and Douglas followed.

"Please read the letter," Litia said softly. "And stay here as long as you need to. If you get hungry, there's food and drink in a basket on the table where you ate last time."

"Thanks, Litia," Hamish said.

She disappeared with the others, but Taito lingered.

He came over and rested a hand on Hamish's shoulder. "I'm very sorry, lad. I carried a lot of guilt for many years after the accident."

"It was hardly your fault," Douglas said.

"I know that now, but those 'what ifs' haunt you forever." He squeezed Hamish's shoulder and took his leave.

Hamish sat with his brothers in silence for a few minutes. The birds had returned after the storm, their birdsong catching on the soft breeze rustling the nearby leaves and plants. Faint voices sounded as the group hiked down the hill, but they soon disappeared.

"Shall we spread the ashes now?" Hamish asked. "I thought over the cliff edge, so they'll scatter over the water."

His brothers agreed and they got to their feet, stopping at the wooden fence. Hamish removed the ashes and they took turns scattering them over the edge. They drifted away on the breeze and onto the water.

They stood in silence for a few minutes before returning to the gravesite and standing in front of the headstone. There was a sense of finality hovering over them, but Hamish was happy Ma was at peace.

"What a way for Da to die," Douglas said.

"He had so much goin' for him," Angus added.

"Do you want to know the rest?" Hamish asked, waving the envelope. "I'm not sure what else Ma has to say after that, but I'd like to know."

"Go ahead," Angus said.

Hamish breathed in deeply then ripped open the envelope, removing the wad of paper.

My dear boys,

So now you know the truth and why I was so devastated. I'm sure you've thought it, because I did too, but it wasn't suicide. Your father was happy, I have no doubt of that. He wouldn't have done that, even though things were bad back in Scotland.

And this takes me to what I must tell you next.

Our trip to Maritimo Island wasn't just a honeymoon. It was an escape. We needed to go somewhere far away where a particular person wouldn't think to track us. We were only going to stay for a week, then we'd planned to travel before returning to Scotland undercover.

I can already imagine your impatience, so let me fill you in.

"Why can it never be simple?" Douglas grumbled, proving Ma's point. "This better bloody be worth it. I'm over the secrets."

Hamish continued reading.

I mentioned in a previous letter that your father wanted to run a distillery. Let's just say it's in your blood in more ways than this. You see, the McNeill family ran a distillery for many years called McNeill Family Distillery. It was passed down from generation to generation dating back to 1715...

"Bloody hell," all three said at once.

Hamish looked at his brothers, who wore the same shocked expression. How had they never known this? They knew their whisky, it was in their blood but had never come across a McNeill Family Distillery. They would've questioned it if they had.

McNeill was a common surname, but that wasn't the point. They still would've been curious.

"Keep readin'," Angus prompted impatiently.

Hamish cleared his throat.

In the early days, the oldest son would inherit the distillery. The McNeill family line has a lot of men, but one generation did not. Your great-great-grandparents only had daughters, so they changed it so that the oldest child would inherit it, and it's stayed that way. If the oldest passed away, it would then go to the second oldest, and so on.

Your father was the second oldest of four children. Two younger sisters and an older brother.

The two sisters were conjoined twins, but they unfortunately passed away not long after they were born, leaving only his brother, Alasdair...your uncle. Naturally, as the oldest he'd inherit the distillery, but in high school he decided he didn't want to take over the family business and wanted to study law instead. Your grandfather respected his wishes and changed his will so that your father was the benefactor instead.

A couple of years passed, and McNeill Family Distillery boomed. The whisky that had been ageing for many years became one of the best. It was forty years old. The McNeill's had always been well-off enough to be comfortable but never rich. Until then.

Alasdair, in his first year of university, caught wind of this and lost interest in studying law. He wanted money, and lots of it. Your father and him had never been close. They were very different. Alasdair was money hungry, but your father wasn't. He just wanted a comfortable life. He was passionate about whisky though, which Alasdair wasn't.

When Alasdair approached your grandfather stating he'd changed his mind, he was told no. The will change was clear and documented with Alasdair's signature. Your father was the official benefactor, and Alasdair had missed his opportunity. Alasdair would be next to inherit after your father if he didn't have any children, which at the time he didn't.

"Oh no," Douglas said. "I think I know where this is heading."
Hamish shivered and continued reading.

Alasdair didn't react well. He went off on a tirade and threatened he'd take over the distillery no matter what it took. He'd always been short-tempered but had never been violent or angry before. Everyone assumed he was speaking out of anger so didn't take it seriously.

He cut himself off from the family and it went quiet. A couple of years later, your father turned eighteen, which was the legal age to inherit and run the distillery if anything happened to his father. This is when he and I started dating. We were going out for about six months when your grandfather was involved in a terrible car accident one night when his brakes failed. Because of how serious it was, the police attended the scene, and the car had to be inspected.

Your grandfather survived with serious injuries, but nothing long lasting. A few months after that, your father was involved in a minor bicycle accident when the chain broke. No one thought much about these at first.

It was only when police reported back a couple of months later stating the brakes to your grandfather's car had been tampered with, that suspicions arose. Unfortunately, there was no proof it was Alasdair, and he denied having anything to do with it.

Over the next year or so, your grandfather and father were both involved in a lot of 'accidents'. The police were always involved, but since they couldn't find any evidence against Alasdair, and he always denied any involvement, they never took action.

In the end, fearing for their lives and ours, your grandparents closed the distillery permanently and moved away to London, where they still are....

"Wait," Douglas said. "They're alive? I was expectin' the evil uncle to murder them." He turned wide eyes to Hamish. "We have more grandparents."

"This is soundin' like a soap opera," Hamish muttered.

"Keep readin'," Douglas probed. "I want to know what happened."

...though I have no idea where they are living. All I have is a phone number. We agreed to cut contact and lay low until Alasdair revealed himself or...died. Only then could the phone number be used.

It's why your father and I married so young. Our honeymoon was our safe location, and we planned to travel before finally returning undercover to Edinburgh. When he died, I still returned undercover because I had no idea if Alasdair knew of my existence. I wasn't taking any chances.

My boys, this is why I never told you about your father, or your family history. I was never sure when or if it would be safe. I didn't want any of you digging around and uncovering the past, which could have hurt many people, including yourselves.

The only reason I am telling you now is I recently received news that Alasdair had passed away from cancer at a hospital in Portree. He left behind a wife but no children. Your grandparents were the ones who reached out to me, telling me it was safe. When I told them they had triplet grandsons, they were so happy and eager to meet you all.

After this journey, I want the three of you to visit your grandparents. Your grandfather would love to see the distillery thriving again, but he's getting on now and can't do it himself. He'd be happy to talk business.

Your dreams of running a distillery are literally at your fingertips.

This is a lot to take in so I'm going to sign off here and you'll receive one last letter tomorrow. I only hope this gives you the answers you've been looking for.

With love, Ma

Silence stretched over them as Hamish and his brothers stared at the gravestone of their father. A man who was forced into hiding because of an evil brother. Hamish would never have thought that a possibility!

But it was and he realised with overwhelming dread that he should've taken Tenika's concerns more seriously.

Everything had changed.

Chapter 29

♥

Still in a daze, Hamish put the letter aside and flipped through the remaining pages. Photos, news articles, adverts, information, all about the McNeill Family Distillery. Some photos had their da in them and Hamish was still struck by how similar they were in looks.

"Guys," Hamish said after he'd skimmed through the information, "look at this."

He handed the papers to Douglas first, who handed Angus a page one at a time after he'd looked at it.

"And to think, this could be ours," Angus said incredulously.

Douglas' eyes went wide. "The letter said they only closed it, right?"

Hamish nodded.

"So then, what's the bet there's still some whisky agein' in barrels?"

Hamish went numb. Not about the ageing whisky, that was any whiskey lover's dream. No, it finally hit him hard that he had to tell Tenika. What was he going to say? *Hey, so it looks like we might inherit a whole distillery and I have grandparents I never knew existed, and I don't think I can stay here now. Sorry. Nice knowing you.*

Bloody hell.

His chest tightened and he scrambled to his feet. He ran his hand through his hair as he moved away from his brothers and the grave, needing some space to breathe. To think. To figure out where to go from here.

The timing couldn't have been worse.

"Hey, you okay bro?" Douglas called.

"Yeah, fine," Hamish waved him off.

He turned his back on them and stared out at the stunning view of the ocean and the small islands dotted around, wanting to drink it all in and commit it to memory. This could've been his home. Was it too much to hope that it was still a possibility? Before he considered worst-case scenario, he needed to speak to Tenika.

There *had* to be a way around this.

His return to Scotland had a longer timeframe on it now, but he didn't know *how* long. No idea what would happen once he met his grandparents. Maybe nothing. Ma only hinted at 'talking business'. What if it was simply waiting until their grandfather died? Deep down he suspected that wouldn't be the case. His grandfather had been waiting for over thirty years for this moment. Why would he want to wait any longer?

One letter from his mother and his family had grown. Another set of grandparents. Their family was a close-knit one and he and his brothers frequently caught up with the grandparents on their ma's side. To meet anyone from Da's side...Hamish never thought it would be a possibility.

Could he convince Tenika to swap the years they visited Scotland and go there together first? It only solidified in his mind they needed to talk. This loosened the knot in his stomach, and he breathed a little easier. There was no point in overthinking it right now.

"Hey, you okay?"

Hamish spun around to find Angus standing behind him, his brow creased in worry.

"It's Tenika, isn't it?" Angus added.

"We finally talked last night, had it all sorted. I was goin' to stay here for a year but now...this."

His eyes widened. "It doesn't have to change anythin', does it?"

"It changes everythin', Angus."

Angus eyed him warily but nodded. "Well then, you better go talk to her. I'm sure you'll figure it out. Do we have anythin' else on today?"

"Not accordin' to the itinerary."

Visible relief washed over Angus. "Good, I'm goin' to veg out and do nothin' for a while. Skye might be awake, so I'll talk to her. She'll want to know what's goin' on. You want to eat first? Dunno 'bout you, but I'm starved."

"Me too." Hamish's stomach let out a loud grumble and he chuckled. "Let's go check out what Litia left for us. Hey Dougie," Hamish turned to Douglas, who sat cross-legged in front of the grave. "We're goin' to have somethin' to eat. You want to join us?"

Douglas shook his head but said nothing, so Hamish left him to it. He had to deal with it his own way. They'd leave him some food.

As he and Angus sat, the knot returned in Hamish's stomach. Why did this feel so final? Last night he saw his future laid out before him. Now it was all so unclear.

Tenika sat at the table on the balcony with Brenda, eating the continental breakfast delivered via room service. Tenika was sure her smile was just as big as Brenda's. After telling each other about their respective nights, an undercurrent of excitement hummed around them.

"I can't believe Douglas asked you to go back to Scotland with him," Tenika said, wiping her fingers on a serviette.

Brenda's eyes widened. "And Hamish is staying *here*? Holy crap, Nika! Who would've thought we'd be here a week ago?"

They sat in companionable silence for a few moments, the scent of coffee wafting up to Tenika's nostrils every time the breeze picked up across the balcony. She drifted into a dreamland, reminiscing on her night with Hamish. She'd barely slept for two nights now but didn't care. Life was great and she was so excited at what lay ahead.

Brenda suddenly breathed in sharply and Tenika's head whipped up. Her friend's face was pale, and she looked panic-stricken.

"Brenda?" Tenika sat up straight. "Are you okay?"

"It's *only* been a week," Brenda whispered, her eyes growing wider with each word. "Oh my God, Nika, am I *insane*? How can I be following this...this stranger back to Scotland? And he is a stranger, really." She started breathing heavily. "My family is going to *freak*! What am I doing, Nika?"

Tenika shuffled her chair around, so she sat next to Brenda and took her hand, squeezing it. "Brenda, look at me." When Brenda met her gaze, chest heaving with each breath, Tenika spoke calmly. "You're a grown woman who's fallen in love. Yeah, it's quick but it's *real*." Brenda nodded, eyes brimming with tears, but still breathing too fast. "Hey, what you've got with Douglas is amazing and genuine. Your family will love him."

"But it still doesn't change the fact that it's happened so fast. I've had no luck with men for so long, but to meet someone *here* of all places—" she shook her head in disbelief, "—it's unbelievable. Almost too good to—"

"Stop, don't say it." Tenika squeezed Brenda's hand again. "You need to get out of your head. Where's the woman who's always encouraging *me* to take a leap of faith? I think it's safe to say the McNeill brothers are a good bunch."

Brenda breathed out a slow breath and her shoulders slumped. "Yeah, they are, aren't they?" She ran her hands down her face, her smile wobbly and her eyes wide, but she was breathing slower. "Holy crap, that emotional freak out was intense. I know you're right, and I know what Doug and I have is real—"

"Ah, you're already shortening his name. It'll be Dougie soon enough." Tenika chuckled and let go of Brenda's hand. She reached for her coffee and sipped it.

"Nah." Brenda smiled affectionately. "He's just Doug to me."

"Aww." Tenika held a hand over her heart. "You're too sweet."

Brenda's cheeks turned pink, but a sappy smile crossed her face. "I know we agreed no technology while we're here, but I think I'm going to have to call Mum and Dad today." She got to her feet and went to find her phone.

Nerves knotted in Tenika's stomach as she thought about the big reveal. How was it going for them?

"Hey." Brenda returned holding her phone. "Thank you for talking me down."

"Any time." She sighed when a thought crossed her mind. "The only downside of all this? We're going to be so far apart."

They'd been friends for so long, never going a day without seeing each other either in person or online. Life was supposed to change after high school but it didn't for them. Not much at least. They got jobs and moved out of home, but nothing *big* happened until now. Tenika felt so unprepared.

"Hey." Brenda sat back down and placed her phone on the table. "You won't get rid of me that easily. We'll still chat or text daily. And just think, if things with Doug work out and if things with you and

Hamish work out, we might be *sisters*." Her eyes lit up, a large grin spreading across her face.

Tenika laughed and wiped away a stray tear. "That would be amazing, but until then, we could go a whole year without seeing each other."

"In the flesh perhaps, but you're not getting out of seeing me on a video call *at least* once a week. I'm not letting you forget this mug."

Tenika smiled. "I love you, Brenda. You're my best friend and you've never let me down."

"Oh, stop it," Brenda's chin wobbled. "You're going to set me off. I love you too, you silly goose. Now come here and hug me before I start blubbering."

They both stood and met in an embrace, blubbering anyway. They still had a week together, but after everything that happened overnight, it felt like the right time to have this conversation. It gave them time to prepare for what was ahead.

When they pulled away, they laughed and wiped away their tears.

"Are you seeing Hamish today?" Brenda asked once they were seated again.

"We're going to have dinner tonight. Until then, I'm meeting Travis on the pier before he leaves. Then I want to talk to Litia about staying on the island and if she has a job on offer. I've got loads of ideas for the resort."

Brenda grinned and looked at her with pride. "I'm proud of you, Nika. Say 'see ya' to Travis for me. I'm going to call Mum and Dad."

They finished eating then went their separate ways. When it neared ten-fifteen a.m., she had to rush to the pier as Travis' flight was leaving at ten-thirty. He was already there when she arrived, standing on the dock in front of the plane with his bags by his feet. Davina was also there along with three other alumni. Ratu picked up bags and stowed them away.

"Travis!" Tenika called as she ran down the pier.

He spun around and even from a distance she saw relief on his face. He said something to Ratu then turned and ran to meet her.

"I didn't think you'd make it," he said as they met for a tight embrace.

"I'm sorry. Brenda and I got talking."

They pulled away and Travis shook his head good-naturedly. "You two still natter on, don't you?"

She swatted his arm. "Don't be a stranger, okay?"

"I won't, but same applies to you. Make sure you pop by the farm before you move here for good." He gave her a pointed stare.

She lowered her face to hide her flaming cheeks.

"I'm not silly," Travis said with a soft smile. "I've never seen you more at home."

"I was going to tell you." She looked back up at him.

"What about your new man?"

She paused. "We're figuring it out." She wasn't sure why she hesitated. "Hey." She reached for his hand. "You don't have to worry about me so much, you know? I'm a new woman."

"I know, but you're like my little sister and I'm always going to worry about you."

Ratu called out to say they were boarding, and Travis sighed.

"That's your cue," Tenika said.

He nodded and leant in to kiss her forehead affectionately. "Take care, Tenika."

"Thanks again for coming." She blinked away tears.

He gave her hand a quick squeeze then rushed off.

"Send my love to Kylie," Tenika called after him. "And give Marcus a big hug!"

When he reached the plane, he turned and gave one last wave before disappearing inside the cabin. Davina was the last to board and she looked back too, catching Tenika's eye. She held up her hand, smiled brightly, then disappeared.

Chapter 30

♥

Tenika approached the reception desk where Eroni sat, head down, tapping at the keyboard. "Hey, is Litia around?"

He stopped and looked up. "She's in the office."

Tenika thanked him, then slipped in behind the desk. Knocking on the door once, she turned the handle and stepped into the small office. She stopped short when she saw her aunt there, sitting opposite Litia. She hadn't seen her since her arrival the day before and intended to keep it that way. As far as Tenika was concerned, there was nothing left to say.

Both Litia and Adi looked up and Tenika froze in the doorway. "Oh, sorry, I'll come back later."

She rushed out from behind the desk, ignoring Eroni when he asked if she was okay. Annoyed that she couldn't talk to Litia yet, she made a beeline for the pool area instead. If she was fast enough, she could escape through the trees without Adi catching up with her.

"Tenika, wait!"

Or not.

Tenika stopped in front of the pool chairs and lifted her eyes heavenward. *Damn it.* She turned as Adi approached wearing an apprehensive smile.

"I'm glad I ran into you again. I'm flying home later today and I really hoped to—"

Not in the mood, Tenika interrupted, "Look, I appreciate your apology from the other day, but I don't have time for this."

She turned to leave again but Adi's next words stopped her in her tracks, "Your grandparents wish to meet you."

Tenika stumbled to a stop, her heart leaping into her throat. She had grandparents? It made sense, of course, but she hadn't let herself think too much about what family she might have. It hurt too much knowing she'd never get to meet them.

"They're my parents," Adi elaborated. "They only learnt about you...recently."

Tenika spun around. "How did they not know I existed? Did you not tell them?"

Adi gestured to a couple of deckchairs next to each other. With people leaving in small groups during the coming days, guests still packed the pool area getting in one last swim.

Adi sat and indicated Tenika should sit too. "I'd like to explain. I do not wish to keep you from your family any longer. It was wrong of me to think I could do so."

"Then why did you? How is it possible they never knew of my existence?" Tenika took the seat facing Adi.

"One thing you must know about Fijian culture is that we value tradition and family above all else. Especially our family who lives in a smaller village, as you saw recently. Each generation follows the same traditions, and it has worked for many years. But Hana, your mother, had a desire to see the world. To escape tradition and culture. She found it...suffocating."

Adi stretched her legs out. "I lived and breathed the culture and tradition, so I did not understand my sister." She shook her head, staring ahead through the palms leading to the beach. "When she announced she was moving to Australia with her boyfriend, it tore the family apart. He wasn't from a village. He was from the urban area and not like us."

"They didn't share the same traditions or cultures?" Tenika asked.

"No, they did not. They had modern amenities, technology, encouraged to have an education and a career. He put ideas into Hana's head of an exciting life full of travel and fun and there was no changing her mind."

"I don't see how that's such a bad thing," Tenika said gently. "I understand the importance of your culture and the traditions, but everyone should be allowed to choose the life they want to live."

Adi pursed her lips into a thin line. "Yes, I suppose you are right. I see that now, but I did not see it back then. No one in our family had done anything like this before. Hana was the first to break tradition, and it nearly destroyed my parents."

She stared at her hands.

"While Hana was away, I had to rebuild the family. My parents were shells of themselves, but over the next two years they adapted and we slipped back into our traditional ways without Hana. Her absence was noticed but we coped. Then she contacted me after you were born claiming she and her boyfriend needed financial help. I couldn't let her waltz back into our lives without a second thought of how it would affect our parents."

Tenika saw where Adi was going, but she couldn't agree with how it was handled.

"Unmarried? A child out of wedlock?" Adi shook her head and held a hand over her heart. "My parents had only just recovered from her leaving. If I'd let your parents come back with a child, they wouldn't have coped. Tradition was so important to them and this went against everything they believed."

"It was you," Tenika said, turning cold at the thought. "You told her she had to give me up for adoption?"

Adi's face was full of regret. "It was not an easy decision, Tenika, but my parents were still so emotionally weak. They would have been able to accept Hana's return with her unwed boyfriend, but a child out of wedlock would have put them back to where they were."

"Yet they died upon arrival and your parents would've been devastated anyway. It seems counterintuitive to me. All of that for nothing."

Adi fell silent.

"Well?" Tenika coaxed.

The silence continued.

Tenika stared at her aunt for a moment. Was that guilt? She gasped when the dots connected. "No! You never told them she died?"

Adi's chin trembled but she held it together. Her strength impressed Tenika.

"I wanted to surprise them," Adi explained. "But when I heard about the accident, I knew it would've killed them. They'd already lost her but in their minds she was alive in another country. I didn't have the heart to confess the truth."

"But they clearly know now because you said they want to see me."

Adi rubbed her temples and got to her feet, pacing the ground in front of the chairs.

"When you visited recently, some of the local villagers recognised you."

"How is that possible?"

Adi stopped and looked at Tenika with a wistful expression. "You're very much your mother's daughter, Tenika."

Tenika had only ever seen one grainy photo of her parents so she couldn't say for sure if she agreed or not.

"I wouldn't say you're a spitting image," Adi continued, "but you have her hair and her eyes, her most notable features. It only took one person to notice. Then it eventually came back to me via my parents, and it all came out."

"How did they react?"

Adi sat again and shook her head. "How you'd expect, I suppose. They were devastated to learn of Hana's death, excited to learn of your existence, and disappointed in me for hiding this secret for so long."

"But they didn't fall apart like you'd feared?"

Adi shook her head.

"Oh Adi—"

"I am fully aware of my wrongs." Adi's face was stony, but pain was evident in her eyes. "I am riddled with regrets, but there is nothing I can do to change the past. That is why I am happy I saw you again. If I can do anything to make this right, I want to."

Tenika couldn't believe the mess her aunt had made. She understood to a point, but it didn't make it right. Adi *was* right about one thing. Nothing would ever change the past, which gave Tenika a new determination to live her best possible future. She couldn't wait to start it with Hamish. They had so much to achieve.

"Do you know my grandparents on my father's side?" Tenika asked.

When she started searching for her father's family, she'd come up blank. They must've moved, but before she could dig deeper, she found a lead on her mother's side and never returned to the search.

"I'm afraid not," Adi said. "Like I said, he was from the urban area and we did not know anyone there. In fact, we never even met your father."

Did his family even know he'd died? The thought of them never knowing what happened to him made her so incredibly sad. She'd have to make it a goal to find them and tell them what she knew. She understood all too well how important closure was.

All this family talk made her miss her adoptive parents so much. They couldn't conceive, which was why they adopted her, and they'd given her a happy and idyllic life.

"Tenika," Adi said, "I want to apologise again for how things ended in Fiji. For blaming you for your parents' death. It was wrong of me."

There was still a pang of anger deep down, but Tenika pushed it aside. Instead, the little box she kept closed inside her heart, just for her family, opened a little. It wasn't too late after all, and she wanted to embrace this.

"Apology accepted," Tenika said. "But no more secrets, okay?"

Adi nodded, a smile stretching across her face. "Of course. And I hope you will come back to Fiji soon to meet your family. We are small though, it's just me and my husband and your grandparents. I never had children." Pain passed across her features, but Tenika didn't push the topic. "You will be warmly welcome."

"I will. I'm thinking of settling here on Maritimo Island for a while, so I'll pop over soon and visit. Perhaps we can exchange contact details? I assume you've modernised a little since I was born?"

Adi chuckled. "We don't have much, but I have a phone and an email address."

After exchanging details, Adi said her goodbyes with the promise of keeping in contact. Tenika, still in shock at the revelations, stayed put for the moment. She had a lot to think about and come to terms with.

Chapter 31

♥

L ong after Angus left, Hamish stayed at the table picking at the food. He wasn't sure why, he'd eaten enough to be full, but he was on autopilot.

Hamish got lost in his thoughts as he enjoyed the view. He contemplated what awaited him back home. First stop, London. He made a mental note to check the itinerary to see if he needed to contact the airline to make amendments.

Foliage rustled nearby and he looked up as Douglas stepped through. His face was blotchy, his eyes red and puffy. Hamish said nothing but gestured to the remaining feast splayed out in front of him.

"I hope you're hungry," Hamish said. "Angus and I have had our fill but there's still too much."

Douglas smiled weakly and sat, taking a chicken skewer. "Thanks, I'm famished now." He ate in silence for a few moments, then asked, "What are you still doin' here anyway?"

"Just thinkin'."

Douglas finished chewing. "What do you think about everythin'?

Hamish reached for a piece of watermelon, then changed his mind and sat back. "I think it's a damn shame what happened to Da, but

I guess I'm excited about what's to come. We could have a whole distillery left to us, Dougie."

Douglas picked up the slice of watermelon Hamish didn't take and ate it. "Yeah, I know, and I was excited about it, but I've been doin' some thinkin'. If it's closed, is it still viable for business?"

"I dinnae ken, man."

"It all just seems too good to be true, that's all." Douglas put the rind on the table.

"You dinnae believe Ma?"

"I dinnae believe she knew everythin'. It just seems weird to close a distillery and leave it for thirty years. Our grandad could've sold it for a ton if the whisky was takin' off."

Hamish shrugged. "Maybe he always hoped to reopen but it took longer than expected. There are a few lost distilleries around Scotland."

Douglas nodded. "Yeah, maybe. I mean, it all sounds great but I dinnae want to get my hopes up."

They continued small talk as Douglas ate. By the time he finished eating and left, there was barely any food left. Hamish tidied everything up by putting it back in the basket to be picked up later, then got to his feet. As he admired the stunning view, he considered what to say to Tenika. How would she react? Would she agree to go back to Scotland with him? He really didn't want their...whatever this was...to end here. Now. Ever.

He had images of a long future together. Between Scotland and Maritimo Island. Maybe one would become a holiday destination they visited yearly. Married one day, with a kid or two. Red hair and brown skin, or dark hair and pale skin. A boy and a girl? Two little mini-me's.

A smile remained on his face as these thoughts consumed him. So caught up, he lost track of time and when he checked next, it was early afternoon. Douglas would've already made it back to the resort. Hamish would have to make tracks soon to meet Tenika for dinner.

He turned to leave when he heard footsteps draw closer. He spun around as the foliage parted and Tenika appeared. His heart leapt at the sight of her, and he smiled. Rushing forward to kiss her, he breathed her in, and cupped her face, wanting to commit everything to memory.

Could he dare to hope that she'd put her plans on hold for a year? For him?

"What are you doin' here?" he asked when he pulled away, keeping her within the circle of his arms.

"I ran into Douglas as he returned, and he said you were still here. Thought I'd take a chance at running into you on the way down, but clearly you haven't left yet."

"I got caught up, just takin' everythin' in. It's hard to believe I'm leavin' tomorrow."

The words lingered in the air between them. Tenika's questioning gaze met his. Heaviness settled in the pit of his stomach.

"It's bad news, isn't it?" Tenika asked, worrying her bottom lip. "The letter, that is. You can talk to me." She stepped forward and took his hand.

Telling her now was probably the best idea. It would mean it was out in the open and they could enjoy their final evening together.

"Actually, it was the opposite. My da's parents are alive and live in London. Long story short, they owned a distillery, which they had to close but never sold. Ma implied in her letter that my grandfather would likely want to reopen it but he'd want our help. He might even sign it over to us."

Tenika's eyes lit up and she embraced him. "Oh my God, that's amazing! It's what you've always wanted, right? And you don't have to start from scratch."

Hamish smiled wryly and rubbed the back of his neck. "Aye, but—"

Tenika's smile slipped and she took a large step back. He missed her absence and reached for her, but she only took another step away.

She stared at him wide-eyed but said nothing.

"I cannae stay," he said in a rush, needing to get the words out. "There are things I need to do, and I dinna ken how long they'll take."

"Surely it's—" She drew in a breath. "—it's only temporary, right?"

He stepped forward again but this time she didn't step away. He reached for her hands and held onto them tightly. "Tenika, we need to talk. I need to explain."

He heard her breath catch. "It's *not* temporary?" Her beautiful eyes were pools of molten chocolate as large tears dripped down her cheeks. His heart broke in two. There had to be a way to salvage this.

"I dinnae ken for sure, but it could be a while." He squeezed her hands and stared into her eyes as he implored, "Come to Scotland with me first. Your plan still works, we just need to swap it around. This...*us*...doesn't have to end here."

His heart raced as he said the words aloud, positive this could work.

Until Tenika shook her head. "Yes, it does." She removed her hands from his and wrapped her arms around herself, pacing the ground in front of him.

"What do you mean?" He turned cold. Not even the intense humidity or the dapples of sunlight through the trees could warm him.

"Oh Hamish, I'm so happy for you, but—" She sniffled and wiped her tears away. "—I can't go because I found some of my family too. My aunt I told you about in Fiji, the one who blamed me for my parents' death?"

Frozen to the spot, he managed a nod.

"She turned up yesterday. I didn't get a chance to tell you. We spoke today and she apologised and said my grandparents want to meet me."

Now she was smiling, and Hamish tried to smile too, but struggled. Could the timing be any worse?

"Hamish, this is a dream come true. And I spoke to Litia before and she's got a job for me here, and a place to stay, and—" She stopped and stared at him, her mouth opening and closing. "We can't save this, can we?" She deflated before his eyes.

At first he didn't think they could. He nearly agreed with her. Until it came to him.

"Yes, we can! We can do long distance."

It wasn't ideal, but if it meant saving their relationship and still being with her, he'd do it. Would she?

"We could chat every day, video call as often as we can, visit when—"

Her answer came when she shook her head and his heart shattered into a million pieces.

"I can't do that," Tenika whispered. "I'm sorry, Hamish, but long distance fills me with dread."

"Brenda's agreed to go to Scotland with Dougie. Are you endin' the friendship with her?" He sounded more irritable than he intended.

Tenika averted her gaze and took a step back. "It's not the same."

"How? You're still keepin' in touch with someone who's in a different country. I dinnae see any difference at all."

"It's completely different!"

"How?"

Her chin trembled. "Because I don't love her the way I love you!"

The words hit him like daggers but then soaked into his skin and made his heart swell with love for this woman. She loved him!

"Brenda's my best friend, and I love her platonically, that's why it's much easier with her. But you?" She shook her head. "Not being able to touch you. To see you every day. Wake up with you. Share the same bed, the same shower, have breakfast together...it'll destroy me, Hamish."

A strange sound emanated from the back of his throat. He gathered her in his arms and kissed her senseless, pouring every ounce of heartbreak and love into it. Hoping he could convince her it was worth it. He believed they had the strength to survive a long-distance relationship.

He pulled away, panting slightly and rested his forehead on hers. "Dinnae do this. We can make this work, Tenika."

She moved back, still holding onto his hands, her pain-filled gaze connecting with his.

"It's the wrong time, Hamish. I love you, I meant that—"

"—but not enough to do this long distance."

It was a statement, not a question.

She winced and stepped back, letting his hands go. "Let's face it, I'm probably going to lose contact with Brenda." Her laugh sounded strangled and held no humour. "I need to at least be in the same country as the people I love. Brenda, Travis, my adoptive parents, there's a reason they're the only people I'm close to."

"You can change it. In this day and age, it's not difficult to have friends all over the world."

She said nothing and the stubborn expression on her face was the answer he needed. She *wouldn't* change. He shoved his hands into his pockets, gritting his teeth. Was it possible for his heart to shatter even more? Because his just did. He scuffed his shoe along the dirt, shoulders slumping.

"I'm so sorry," Tenika said.

The last thing he felt was her hand squeezing his arm. The last thing he heard were her footsteps walking away.

Out of his life.

Chapter 32

♥

Tenika swiped away tears as she ran down the mountain, her feet slipping and sliding on the ground. She'd brought this on herself. What the hell had come over her? Truthfully, long-distance *did* fill her with dread, but Hamish was worth it. Yet her bloody mouth had a mind of its own.

She was an absolute idiot!

And to imply she didn't love him enough to do long-distance? *Ugh*! What had she done?

Her feet slid out from under her, and her heart leapt into her throat. Grappling for something, anything, she grabbed a hanging vine and came to a stop. The vine creaked and groaned from the branch above. Heart pounding, sweat dripping down her face, limbs shaking, she steadied herself and leant against a tree.

Wiping her brow, she closed her eyes and focused on slowing down her racing heart. Deep breath in. Hold. Release slowly. She did this a few times until she composed herself, but the tears were relentless. She'd messed up the best thing that had ever happened to her.

Should she go back and talk to him? Apologise?

Why bother? A little voice inside her head taunted. *It's not like he told you he loved you back.*

She drew in a sharp breath. That was telling in itself...wasn't it? Sniffling, she removed a tissue out of her trouser pocket and wiped her cheeks and nose dry. She couldn't go back. If she did, what was the likelihood he'd listen anyway? She'd come across completely unhinged! She had to live with her mistake, no matter how much it hurt.

With a firm nod, she reconvened her hike down, slower this time, and pushed aside all thoughts that tried to make her see sense.

When Tenika arrived back at her suite, Brenda was nowhere to be seen so she enjoyed the silence by wallowing for a while. She flopped onto the sofa, staring out the open balcony doors. From this vantage point, she only saw the shimmering, turquoise ocean.

What *had* she done? The question ran around her head.

Nothing made sense anymore.

What if Hamish hadn't told her he loved her because the timing was wrong? After all, she'd just told him their relationship was over. Not really the right mood for confessing love.

She grabbed a pillow and held it close to her chest.

Before she'd gone searching for Hamish, everything was so clear. She'd found Litia and spoken to her about her plans. Everything had fallen into place. Litia offered her a job, and a place to stay, like it was meant to be. Tenika was so excited to tell Hamish, she couldn't wait until dinner, which was why she'd gone looking for him.

Then Hamish had shared his news, and everything crumbled. Their plans were useless now. Yes, he'd asked her to go to Scotland with him, but how could she? It would mean putting her own plans on hold. Selfish? Yes, but the biggest factor was not being able to do the long-distance relationship.

As she rested her chin on top of the cushion, it occurred to her what the problem was.

One moment their journeys had become one, the next they'd forked off onto different roads. It didn't look like there was any chance of them joining again.

Were they doomed from the beginning but couldn't see it? In hindsight, it *had* all been so surreal. Too good to be true—they were the words Brenda nearly used earlier. Maybe she was right after all. Tenika had left her reservations behind and taken a leap of faith, but look where it left her?

Perhaps she could've handled it better, but it had all happened so fast. She hadn't expected to turn up and for things to end...like this. It was meant to be a confirmation. To cement their new future. So much for the big reveal not changing anything.

Fresh tears coated her cheeks and plopped onto the cushion. This situation only proved one thing: she wasn't ready for a big life change. She thought she was. Hamish helped her believe she was, but now she knew different. After all, it wasn't normal to limit who she had as friends just because they didn't live in the same *country*.

There were deeper issues there. Ones she needed resolved before committing to such a big change.

She lost track of how much time passed but the light coming through the balcony doors turned a golden tinge, indicating it was getting late. It must've been close to dinner time, but she had no appetite. When would Brenda be back? Tenika had the awkward task of telling her friend what happened. If she hadn't already heard.

On cue, the front door opened, then shut again seconds later with a loud *bang*. Tenika jumped and turned on the sofa to see Brenda storming into the room, her eyes ablaze. No words were needed. She knew.

Brenda hadn't even spoken yet, but Tenika shrunk back as Brenda stomped over and hovered over her, her frizzy hair even more so in the humidity. Her eyes were wide and angry. Rarely one to lose her cool, she was a terrifying figure.

"So let me get this straight," Brenda said with surprising calmness. "You meet a hot, *Scottish* guy who is seriously head over heels for you and you throw it in his face when it all gets too difficult?"

Tenika opened her mouth to respond but Brenda held up a hand, silencing her.

"I'm not done." The edge to her tone made Tenika shiver. "I've always tried to be understanding, Tenika. You've had it tough. I get that it's difficult to trust and let people in, but things were different this time. What I don't get, is—" Her eyes fluttered closed and she pinched the bridge of her nose as she drew in a slow breath. "What I don't get is how you can confess you love him, then say you don't love him enough to do a long-distance relationship?"

"It—"

Brenda held up a hand again. "Still not done." She paced the floor in front of the sofa. "Then you spout some rubbish about only wanting to be in the same country as people you like?"

"Love," Tenika corrected and instantly regretted it when Brenda glared at her.

"That's even worse! So, what, were you just going to let me fly away to Scotland and then forget all about me? Was that your plan all along?"

Tenika bit her tongue, not wanting to make the same mistake three times. But Brenda rolled her eyes and waved a hand. "You can answer."

Tenika threw the pillow aside and stood, walking over to the balcony doors but not stepping outside. "No, that wasn't my plan," she said, her back to Brenda. "But I might've told Hamish that it was likely we'd lose contact." She winced at her thoughtless words.

There was a scoff but nothing else. When Tenika turned, Brenda had disappeared. She heard a noise from Brenda's bedroom. Tenika went over to find Brenda had placed her case on the bed and was throwing items into it.

"Oh, come on, Brenda," Tenika said. "Now you're being silly. We still have another week here."

"No, *you* have another week here. I'm leaving. I'll spend the night with Doug and I'll go home tomorrow." She opened a drawer and took an armful of clothes out of it, transferring them to her case.

"But your flight is booked for next week."

"It's not that hard to reschedule flights, you know?" Brenda snapped, then she glanced up at Tenika. "Look, I'm willing to give you the benefit of the doubt. I received third hand information from Doug who heard it from Angus who heard it from Hamish. But I know you, and it all sounds pretty accurate. If I do have anything wrong, please enlighten me."

Tenika shuffled from foot to foot, her stomach sinking. She had no words. Everything was unravelling, all because of some stupid words she said without thinking.

Brenda shook her head and turned to grab some items from on top of the dresser. When she turned back to the case and dumped them in, she said, "I'm so sick of this friendship being so damn one sided, Tenika. Through school it was either me or Travis saving you from the bullies, but what did you ever do for us? We were targets too, as were so many others. You were at the reunion, you saw it. But no, you were so damn hard done by, you couldn't help anyone else. You had to go into hiding like the sissy you were."

Tenika gasped. "That's not fair!"

Brenda stopped, breathing heavily. "No, what's not fair is that you're unwilling to make the effort for a friend, for a *man*, because it's just too damn hard." She straightened her spine and held her head high, holding eye contact with Tenika.

Emotion bubbled up and Tenika suddenly felt boxed in. She needed air. "Fine," she said through gritted teeth. "If you're going to be like that, I don't need you in my life." She spun on her heel and stormed to the door.

"Yeah, run away," Brenda called after her, "like you always do."

Tenika opened the door and slammed it after her. For a moment she leant against it as she breathed heavily, tears filling her eyes. Her heart crumbled inside her chest. Not only had she lost such a wonderful man, but she'd lost her best friend too.

She pushed away from the door, walked past the elevator and took the stairs to the ground floor instead. Brenda's words ran around her head. She didn't want to believe them, but as she was transported back to her school days, she couldn't deny the truth. She *did* go into hiding at school rather than helping others. As an adult, she *did* run away when things got too hard.

She only attended the reunion because Brenda talked her into it. She would've avoided it otherwise. Put it in the 'too hard' basket. She'd never been taught how to deal with this sort of conflict.

She'd had all the support she ever needed, and was thankful for it, but it had stunted her emotional growth. When she was bullied, rather than being taught how to stand up or fight back, her adoptive parents cocooned her in a safety net of soothing words and promises to protect her. While Travis and Brenda nagged her about going to the police, her parents didn't push her. Told her it was okay if she didn't want to.

Being in that cocoon had been a wonderful feeling, but she'd never considered how it would affect her as an adult. It explained why she wasn't a very good friend. She was excellent at comforting words but sucked at resolving conflict.

Brenda moving away terrified her. It scared her even more to try a long-distance relationship with Hamish. It was unchartered territory, so it was easier not to try.

On the ground floor, she stopped at the exit door and caught her breath. Where to from here? Might as well do what she did best.

She pushed on the door and made a beeline for the exit leading to the pool area. As she stepped outside, she came face to face with three brothers who she'd come to love on different levels. One in a way she never thought possible.

But she'd screwed it all up.

There was no stopping the tears as she looked at each one, her heart breaking at the disappointment they wore on their faces. Disappointment at *her*. She broke free and muttered a half-hearted apology as she pushed past them and ran away from the resort.

Chapter 33

Hamish watched Tenika disappear. Her heartbroken expression would forever remain etched in his mind. How could he leave her to deal with this alone?

His feet moved on their own accord to go after her, but was stopped by two hands, one on each shoulder. Douglas on his right and Angus on his left.

"Leave it," Douglas squeezed his shoulder. "She's done enough damage."

"No." Hamish writhed free of their grip and turned to them. They wore the same concerned expressions. "I just need to see if she's okay."

Angus pursed his lips. "She didnae see if *you* were okay."

Hamish took a step back. "Dinnae use that tactic on me. You dinnae ken her like I do. She's dealin' with a lot of stuff right now."

"And that makes it okay to hurt you?" Douglas snapped.

Hamish rubbed the back of his neck. "No, of course not, but I—" Emotion clogged his throat as he turned to glance out over the pool and through the trees. Tenika was nowhere in sight now. "I cannae leave things like this." Tears burned his eyes when he turned back to his brothers, his shoulders slumping in defeat.

"Come on, bro," Angus said, placing a hand on his shoulder again and navigating them away from the doors. "Leave it for now."

With no fight left in him, Hamish let his brothers lead him to the tidal restaurant. Taito and Litia had set it up as a last goodbye. This did nothing to improve Hamish's mood. It only brought back memories of their first night when everything was so new and exciting.

When they arrived, there were a handful of remaining reunion guests dining there too. Brenda turned up at some point, but Hamish wasn't paying attention to the time. She seemed to be in a dour mood too. She sat next to Douglas, her face set in a permanent scowl, and she barely spoke to anyone. Had she and Tenika had a fight?

Hamish glanced out over the ocean where the sun had sunk below the horizon. Even the sunset was lacklustre this evening. The colours were dull. Lifeless. Just the way he felt.

They were a silent group on the way back to the bungalow after dinner. Brenda joined them, which confirmed Hamish's suspicions she and Tenika had a falling out.

"Do you mind if I stay the night? I'll share with Doug." Brenda looked at Douglas who nodded. "I promise we won't get up to any funny business."

"Says who?" Douglas quipped with a wink.

Brenda laughed but it was forced. Even his brothers weren't themselves. Was it the general gloom that came with the end of a holiday? Or was Tenika's absence missed by them too? Hamish realised she probably had no clue how much she'd come to mean to all three of them. She'd fitted into their family so well, as had Brenda. Ma would've loved them both.

Back at the bungalow, Hamish kicked off his shoes, put in his earbuds, then set his playlist to shuffle. Retrieving the itinerary, he checked the stopover details. If anything had to change, now would be the best time to do so because of the time difference.

He needn't have worried. Ma had factored everything in, just like she'd done for the entire journey. She'd booked their flight to Edinburgh to leave London a week after their arrival, which gave them time to recover from jetlag, visit their grandparents, and anything else that may need to be done.

With that off his mind, he tucked the itinerary away and moved out onto the deck at the back of the bungalow, overlooking the ocean. He sat on the deck, his legs hanging over the edge. The tide was out so his feet didn't touch the water.

The night was dark and balmy, the sky littered with stars and the moon entering its final quarter. In the distance, he saw the spot where he and Tenika had swum in their underwear last night. When everything was so certain and full of hope.

So much had happened since. His heart clenched at the memory that she wasn't in his life anymore. It all happened so fast.

But he wouldn't wallow. He had so much ahead of him in Scotland. Grandparents to meet. A dream to fulfill. He would use this experience to spur him on. To remind him that while this heartbreak hurt like hell, it didn't have to stop him from living life. Besides, Ma's journey wasn't over yet and he owed it to her to complete it. It was just so bloody unfortunate that Tenika's own journey went a different way.

Why couldn't she put her plans on hold?

This question had been running around his head since she left him standing at the top of the mountain. Had he asked too much? He understood she'd found family and had sorted a life here with Litia, but something else was missing.

He shook his head and removed his earbuds, placing them inside their case. It would drive him insane if he kept thinking about it.

He got to his feet and went back inside. Douglas and Angus argued over something, and Brenda was laughing. It was nice to hear laughter again and it helped him feel a little lighter too. He went to investigate only to find the three of them tangled around each other in a game of *Twister*.

"What *are* you doing?" Hamish asked.

Brenda shrieked and lost her balance, falling to the ground. She knocked Douglas' arm, which sent him toppling beside her. Angus remained in his noodled position, though he wobbled precariously when Douglas' leg hit his ankle.

"I won!" Angus shouted, fist pumping the air with one hand, then promptly fell flat on his face.

Everyone burst out laughing and even Hamish managed a chuckle.

"That was your fault, Hamish," Brenda accused, pointing at him, but she was smiling.

He held a hand against his chest, feigning surprise.

"Don't deny it, you scared the crap out of me. Alright." She jumped to her feet and picked up the dial. "This calls for round two. This time you're joining us, Hamish."

He held up his hands. "No thanks, I'll pass. I'm tired anyway. We have a long trip ahead of us, so I need some sleep before I dinnae get any at all." He never slept well when he travelled.

"Wuss," she joked after him.

He smiled at her over his shoulder, then disappeared to get ready for bed. When he was done, he climbed under the covers and put his earbuds back in, knowing he wouldn't sleep with the racket going on behind the wall.

Truthfully, he wasn't really that tired, and it was still early, but he missed Tenika more than ever. The temptation to find her and talk it out was strong, but he didn't. He couldn't handle another rejection.

Only sleep would give him some peace.

Of course, when he went to bed, he hadn't considered the fact he would dream about Tenika. When his alarm blared at six a.m., he was bleary-eyed and unrested after a night of too many dreams that now seemed impossible.

He dragged himself out of bed, hollering to his brothers and Brenda, who answered in groans and curses.

After showering, he opened the back doors of the bungalow to let the cool, morning air inside. As he packed his things, the morning light seeped in, and his brothers started grumbling. Soon enough they both stomped around like the morning people they weren't, and Douglas had a hard time getting Brenda out of bed.

"If you're always this difficult to wake up, I'm seriously questionin' our relationship," Douglas muttered.

Hamish chuckled under his breath as Brenda retaliated, "I'm already questioning it after you stole the covers last night."

With everyone awake now, and Brenda and Douglas bickering light-heartedly, Hamish's heart grew heavy. He was happy for his brother, but he couldn't deny there was also a bit of envy there too. He thought he and Tenika had that.

Yet despite the heaviness in his heart, he also felt lighter somehow. He'd gone from never knowing who his father was, to finally having answers. That constant unknown had lifted. A thrum of excitement coursed through his veins. There'd always be a space in his heart for the woman he loved and lost, but he wouldn't let it defeat him.

If he'd learnt anything on this journey, it was that life was too short to have regrets or hold grudges. It was time to bring Da's dreams to fruition.

Half an hour later, the four of them trudged out of the bungalow, down the jetty and across the sand. Litia and Taito waited for them on the path with two carts. A lump formed in Hamish's throat. The time had come to say goodbye. Would he ever see them again? Hamish would keep in contact, but he wasn't sure if he'd ever come back.

When they stopped, Litia came up, hugging Hamish and his brothers. Taito followed but gave them a handshake and a slap on the back.

"It's been so wonderful seeing you three again," Litia said, her eyes shimmering with unshed tears. "Don't be strangers. You're always welcome." She handed out an envelope. "Here's the last letter."

Angus took it and slipped it inside his satchel. "Thank you. We'll read it on the plane." He then kissed her cheek and strode over to a cart, loading his luggage into the back.

Douglas and Brenda said their goodbyes and loaded their things into the vacant cart, setting off seconds later.

Litia threw Hamish a questioning glance.

"It's a long story." He smiled sadly, but didn't elaborate. He gestured to the bungalow behind him. "We left the key on the table inside. Let me know if we owe anythin'."

"Your ma had it all covered. You don't owe a thing." She came in for one last hug, holding on tight. "If it's not too much hassle, we'd love to hear how everything goes."

"I'll keep you updated. Thank you, Litia, for everythin'." He turned to Taito who stood to the side. "And you too, Taito."

Hamish gave them a wave before putting his luggage in the other cart where Angus waited, then joined him in the front. Angus set off but didn't say a word. This suited Hamish just fine as he wasn't in a talking mood. He had a lot to think about.

Despite the excitement in his veins, there was still hollowness deep down. He missed Tenika. He always would. But she'd made her choice, and he respected that.

A few minutes later, Angus stopped behind Douglas on the path opposite the pier and dock where they first arrived. Hamish glanced around once in the off-chance Tenika might've come out to say goodbye.

Of course she wasn't there, and why would she be?

He muttered under his breath and got out of the cart, removing his luggage from the back. When he was on the dock next to the plane with his brothers and Brenda, he glanced back once more. Strange, he felt close to her somehow. Like she was close by. Was it because she was part of the island now?

When Ratu announced they could board, his brothers went first followed by Brenda. He went next, one leg on the step, the other still on the dock, but he had to look one last time.

She *was* there! Standing in front of the trees, arms wrapped around herself, her knee-length yellow dress wrapping around her figure.

His breath caught.

His heart stopped.

An overwhelming urge came over him and he turned to Ratu with what he was certain were wild eyes. If he didn't do this, he'd regret it.

"Can you give me five minutes?"

Ratu breathed in through his teeth and checked his watch.

"*Please*?" Hamish begged. "I promise I won't be longer than that."

Ratu took off his cap, scratched his head then nodded. "If you're not back in five, I'm leaving without you."

Hamish sped off. He sprinted across the pier, onto the sand, making a beeline for Tenika. As he drew closer, he noticed tears coating her cheeks and his heart broke. He hoped so much that she could find happiness. That's all he wanted, was for her to be happy.

Her eyes widened as he stopped in front of her, breathing heavily.

"I couldn't leave..." He drew in a breath to slow his breathing. "Without...without..."

He took her face in his hands and kissed her for all he was worth, filling it with every single emotion. Love. Passion. Frustration. She didn't draw back. She reciprocated with the same urgency. For a moment, the world disappeared. It was just the two of them in paradise, the balmy breeze caressing them, the salt from the ocean mingling with their kiss. It made him want to fall to his knees and beg, just one last time, that she come to Scotland with him.

She was the first to pull away, looking dazed, tears still coating her cheeks.

"I love you," he blurted because if he didn't say it, he'd regret it forever. "I need you to know that. I desperately want you to come back with me, but I understand you cannae."

The plane propeller spluttered to life, and he glanced back to see Ratu in the cockpit. He had time, but not much.

"I wish you every happiness, Tenika." Then with a final, tender kiss on her forehead, he turned and sprinted back to the plane.

She never said a word.

He boarded with time to spare and clipped his seatbelt around his hips. He looked back to see Brenda glancing longingly out the window. He still didn't know what went down between them.

Douglas and Angus stared at him with raised eyebrows in silent question.

Hamish shrugged. "No regrets."

And he didn't have one. He'd fought and failed. The ball was in Tenika's court and if she didn't play it, then so be it.

Chapter 34

♥

After many hours of flying and stopovers, the plane started its descent into London's Heathrow Airport. From Maritimo Island they'd flown to Fiji, then to Melbourne. They spent the day there before flying out that evening to London via Kuala Lumpa.

Angus jabbed Hamish in the ribs with his elbow from the middle seat. Hamish paused his music and removed his earbuds, turning from his position of staring out the window. Angus held the envelope Litia had given him. He noticed the Maritimo Island Resort logo on the top left corner for the first time. It probably stood out now because they were no longer there.

His heart grew heavy.

"I forgot I'd put this in my satchel," Angus said. "We should read it before we land."

Hamish nodded and Angus woke a sleeping Douglas who grumbled before sitting upright, wiping away some drool from the corner of his mouth.

"What is it?" Douglas asked, using his thumb and index finger to rub his eyes.

Angus waved the envelope at him. "Thought you'd want to be awake for this."

Douglas removed a bottle of water from the pocket of the seat in front of him. The shape had distorted from the pressure inside the cabin. When he unscrewed the lid, the bottle popped back into shape. "Go on then." He sipped his water and put the bottle back.

Angus ripped open the envelope and pulled out a single sheet of paper.

My boys,
You're nearly at the end of your journey and this will be the last letter you receive from me.

Angus dropped his hands and swallowed. Hamish nudged him and raised his eyebrows in silent question, asking if he was okay. Angus' eyes filled with moisture, but he nodded.

He started again.

I know you three had a lot to come to terms with and I hope you can understand why I kept your father's identity a secret. It killed me to do so, but you must know by now I was only keeping you all safe. Alasdair was capable of anything, and I didn't want to take any risks.

If you've got a hotel booked in London, cancel it. Your grandparents are expecting you. In fact, they're so eager to meet you, they'll be at the airport to greet you. From there they'll take you back to their house and they'll fill you in on everything you need to know.

The plane jumped as it hit an air pocket in its descent. Angus stopped reading and looked at Douglas then Hamish.

"Have either of you booked anythin'?"

Douglas shook his head, and Hamish said, "Me either. I was goin' to figure it out after we landed."

Angus nodded and continued reading.

I'm sure you all have a lot of questions and from here, your grandparents will answer them. All I want to say now is embrace this new venture. You're not only fulfilling a dream the three of you have shared for years, but you're also fulfilling your father's dream too.

Whatever you do from now on, make it count. Life is too short to live with regrets. Angus, you already have someone special, but Douglas and Hamish, if either of you find that special someone, savour every single moment with them. If you have a little tiff, which is inevitable in all relationships, be ready to forgive, forget, and move on.

"It's a bit bloody late for that," Hamish muttered.

Douglas peered at him, brow furrowed in question, apparently not hearing him, but Angus grimaced in sympathy. Frustration bubbled low in his belly. Frustration at himself for not going after Tenika when he had the opportunity and frustration at his brothers for stopping him. Most of all, frustration for not handling the whole situation better.

It'd been so damn long since he'd been in a relationship, he thought giving her space was the right thing to do. Now he wasn't sure.

Angus continued reading.

Most of all, live life to the fullest and be happy. Don't let anything or anyone hold you back.

I love you all so very much, never, ever forget that.

Ma xx

Silence settled over them as Angus put the envelope away. Hamish turned to stare out the window again, now seeing the English houses coming into view as they descended closer to the runway. His mind tumbled over his thoughts. Ma said to have no regrets, but he had a big stinking one. So much for that.

Finally, the plane landed, taxied, and stopped. Before too long, Hamish followed his brothers to the exit of the plane. As they stepped through the door into the tunnel that would lead them into the mayhem of Heathrow Airport, a violent shiver ran down Hamish's spine. London was having a cold snap with snow forecast any day. As much as he loved the cold, the change from humid Maritimo Island was intense.

Once inside the airport, hordes of passengers from various flights walked alongside, or overtook them as they navigated the long hallways, following the signs to the luggage carousel.

It was so strange being back in the land of the living. Life on Maritimo Island was so different. Quieter, for starters. But more relaxed too. There weren't the normal pressures that came with living in a big city.

If things had turned out differently, he had been so ready to live on the island. If Tenika had said yes to joining him, they would've gone back once everything was sorted. Of that he had no doubt.

But it wasn't to be.

She was so quick to end it when one hurdle got in the way. What was with that?

He gritted his teeth and shook his head, willing himself to stop thinking about Maritimo Island and a certain woman who he'd left behind.

Angus and Douglas chatted animatedly, but Hamish hung back and followed. After picking up their luggage, they followed the signs to customs and passport control. Hamish had nothing left and he flagged. It wasn't just jetlag either. The further Tenika was from him, the heavier he felt.

In line at passport control, Douglas was texting Brenda and Hamish scowled at him. Who would've thought Douglas, the most uncommitted of the three, would settle before Hamish? Brenda had promised to get started on her visa immediately and be in Scotland within a matter of weeks. *She* didn't have any concerns about it.

Why is she able to do it so easily, yet Tenika can't?

This was going to drive him insane. It had been going around his head for the entire flight. He shoved it aside, along with his bitterness, but it never strayed too far. He hoped after some much-needed sleep and a few days of relaxing, the pain would lessen.

The line moved and they were standing at the front to be called next. Within a matter of minutes, their passports were stamped, and they made their way through to arrivals. Hamish cast an eagle eye around the crowd of eager people waiting for friends or loved ones to arrive.

Would he know his grandparents when he saw them? He'd never seen a picture, but would it be one of those instinctual things?

As they approached the end of the cordoned off area, Hamish glanced around at the sea of faces, but no one jumped out. Angus stopped suddenly and grabbed Hamish's arm.

"What?" He glanced over and saw Angus had grabbed Douglas' arm too and they stared straight ahead, jaws hanging open.

Hamish whipped his head around to the left where he hadn't looked, and his eyes widened. Their grandparents stood only a few feet away. There was no mistaking them. In fact, even though Angus and Douglas had resemblances to Ma and Da, they also shared similarities with their grandfather.

They both appeared to be in their seventies, but they looked strong. Healthy. Full of life. He had a feeling they hadn't always been like this, and he was relieved they could finally enjoy their life after what they'd suffered through.

Grandad was tall and broad, his red hair and bushy beard streaked with grey. His green eyes sparkled and creased at the sides. Grandma was more petite. A slight woman, she came below his shoulders and had hazel eyes and short hair which was now fully grey. Her skin was pale, but her cheeks were rosy.

Her face lit up as she held onto her husband's arm and patted her hand against it in excitement.

Hamish's worries flew from his mind as he broke into a grin and legged it the final distance. Grandma held her arms out to him. He flew into them, welcoming the grandmotherly warmth that overwhelmed him, much like Ma's. He missed Ma so much, especially her hugs. This was second best. Seconds later, there was commotion next to him as his brothers noisily greeted Grandad.

It was a boisterous and happy reunion. Everyone talked over each other, unanswered questions flew around, but no one seemed to care.

When the excitement died down, the five of them stood in a circle to the side, grinning like fools with tear-streaked cheeks.

"Look at you three," Grandma said, her hand sitting over her heart. "The McNeill blood is strong in all three of you. And you." She came up and took Hamish's face in her hands, her eyes shimmering with tears. "You are a spittin' image of your da."

Hamish smiled and warmth washed over him.

"Thank goodness none of them took after Alasdair," Grandad muttered.

"Shush you," Grandma said, swiping his arm. "We dinnae talk about him."

"Yes, yes, well, come on then. We have our car and we'll take you back to our place. I'm sure you'll want to rest."

Angus yawned on cue.

"Yes, that would be great," Hamish said. "It's been a long trip."

Grandma looped her arm through Hamish's. "Of course it has."

They stopped talking as they exited the airport and followed their grandparents to the car. Once on the road, Grandad started talking excitedly about all things whisky.

When there was a gap in conversation, Grandma turned in her seat from the front.

"Forgive him. Callum's been talkin' about the distillery nonstop lately. He's eager to get it runnin' again."

"*I* dinnae want to run the bloody thing, Elspeth," Grandad grumbled. "I'm too old, but these boys will do a grand job. Did you know McNeill blood is actually whisky?"

Grandma smiled and rolled her eyes good-naturedly, settling back into her seat. Hamish and his brothers laughed.

"It's true!" Grandad insisted, looking at them in the rear-view mirror. "I cut myself once and it was the colour of deep copper!"

They chuckled again and Grandad continued to prattle on about his beloved distillery, the history of it, and his excitement at seeing it open for business in the future.

In a daze, Hamish sat back and listened to Grandad talk. Slowly but surely, a new excitement grew deep inside Hamish. Excitement at making a dream a reality. Not many people had this opportunity, and he wanted to embrace it with open arms.

Chapter 35

♥

He loves me.

Tears trickled out of the corners of her eyes as Tenika stared at the ceiling, listening to the waves lapping at the shore through her open window. She'd been locked up in the room for two days now. Or was it three?

She couldn't remember. Everything was a blur.

Ever since Hamish had kissed her, told her he loved her, then disappeared back to Scotland, she hadn't been the same.

He loves me.

Those words played in her mind every day and echoed in her dreams at night.

She grabbed the spare pillow and covered her face, screaming into it. That's all she'd been able to think about. And what did she do? Stand there like a goddamn fool and didn't say a thing. Just let him disappear.

Of course, she'd always known it. His actions, his words, his looks, all said it. But hearing the words was so different. Finally, she understood what Brenda meant. That Tenika never did anything for anyone else. She only knew how to protect herself. While that was important, she'd yet to find the balance of protecting herself for the right reasons while opening her heart to others.

Doing so meant putting them before her. It meant being self*less*. God alone knew she wanted to be, but she'd be at risk of getting hurt again.

She forced herself into a sitting position and threw the pillow aside, waiting for her cotton wool head to stop spinning. Today she had to get some fresh air. Staying in her room and living on room service wasn't healthy. She'd finally read that Agatha Christie book, but she didn't remember a thing about it. Perhaps reading while depressed was a bad idea.

There'd been knocks at her door a few times, but she never answered. After the first knock, she put up the 'do not disturb' sign.

Wallowing isn't fixing anything.

As though reading her mind, a knock sounded at her door. This time a familiar, concerned voice called through. "Tenika, it's Litia. Are you okay?"

Her heart tugged, and she berated herself for letting herself get so low. How could she ever do better if she didn't do anything about it?

She padded over to the door and opened it.

Litia took one look at her before sighing. "Look at you, girl." She shook her head. "I was wondering where you were. Have you been cooped up here?" She peered into the room, her nose wrinkling.

"Just relaxing," she lied.

Litia gave her a look that said she didn't believe her. "Now that all the guests have left, it's quiet around the resort. Would you like to join me for breakfast and a walk?"

Tenika nearly declined, but the look in Litia's eyes told her she wouldn't take no for an answer. It might've been fifteen years, but

Tenika always found her easy to talk to. Perhaps talking to someone else, an outsider, would help.

"Sure," Tenika said. "I just need to shower and change first."

"I'll meet you downstairs."

Half an hour later, she met Litia at reception, and they went to the restaurant for breakfast first. There was no buffet laid out now the guests had left, but the chef prepared breakfast for them. They sat on the terrace overlooking the rainforest with the ocean in the distance, drank coffee, and ate pancakes with local fruit.

After one cup of coffee and a couple of pancakes, Tenika felt a little more alert. The warm sun on her skin was heaven and she closed her eyes to bask in it.

"Would you like to talk about it?" Litia asked softly.

Tenika didn't move at first, just enjoyed the warmth on her skin, but words and emotions bubbled inside her, needing release. She opened her eyes, poured another cup of coffee and took a sip.

"I made a really dumb mistake," she said, then didn't hold back.

She told Litia everything. Not just from the last three days, but her entire life. Litia knew bits and pieces of Tenika's past, but not how bad it got in the later years.

Litia was just as attentive as she'd always been. She listened, nodded, and said all the right things. For the first time in a long time, Tenika felt lighter. Even during the happiest times with Hamish, there was still *something* weighing her down. She only noticed it now because it was missing.

When she stopped, she drew in a long breath and released it slowly. Litia said nothing at first, so Tenika sat in silence, letting the woman digest everything. Tenika's coffee had gone cold, but she sipped it anyway.

A few wispy white clouds floated across the otherwise blue sky. The balmy breeze caressed her skin, and she rubbed her arms.

"We all make mistakes, Tenika," Litia finally said. "But I firmly believe every mistake, or every decision, is made for a reason. Even down to poor Duncan's death."

Tenika paused. "What actually happened?"

"You didn't hear?" Then she shook her head. "Oh, of course you wouldn't have."

Tenika grimaced. *I never had the chance to ask.*

Litia revealed all and Tenika's heart broke for Hamish and his family. What a devastating way to lose someone!

Yet here I am letting him go because...because I'm a bloody idiot!

"The worst part," Litia said on a sigh, "is that Isla and Duncan had argued that morning. I don't remember what it was about, Isla told me later, but it was so long ago now. I remember it was meaningless and stupid, but they'd gone on the hike to walk it off. They never got around to properly sorting it out and Isla lived with that guilt." Litia paused. "I never told the boys this. I didn't think they needed to know. Isla and Duncan loved each other so much, a petty argument like that wouldn't have broken them. If the accident hadn't happened, I'm certain they would've come down the mountain the best of friends again."

Tenika swallowed. "Why are you telling me this?"

"Because petty arguments happen. Misunderstandings are a normal part of life, but you need to learn how to deal with them quickly. Don't let them become big problems."

Tenika ran her hands down her face. "But how?"

Litia looked at her in amusement, her lips twitching. "Do I need to spell it out for you?"

"Obviously! I told you, I run away from conflict not *into* it."

Litia reached over and patted her hand. "No one can avoid conflict forever. Brenda is your best friend and she loves you. Don't lose that friendship over a silly argument. Distance can't destroy a friendship like that. I've got friends in Australia who I rarely see but we speak often. And you and Hamish?" She shook her head, her eyes shimmering brightly. "I saw how close you two were. You reminded me of Isla and Duncan. Two perfect halves that make the same whole." This time she curled her fingers around Tenika's hand and squeezed tightly. "If you love him, don't let him go."

Tenika's heart leapt into her throat. "I can't just run after him...can I? I've got a life organised here. I have to see Travis and my parents—"

Litia squeezed Tenika's hand again. "Yes, go back to Australia before doing anything drastic. And this island is not going anywhere. You'll have a job and a place to stay whenever you're ready. Do what you must and take your time."

Tenika swallowed and nodded slowly.

"Eroni has some ideas he wants to implement, which will bring in some regular visitors but it may take some time. He's excited to have a righthand woman—that's you—so just make sure you *do* come back."

Tenika nodded again. Now that she could think clearer, she knew what had to be done.

"Okay," Tenika said, releasing Litia's hand and getting to her feet. "Will I be able to catch the plane to Fiji today?"

"That should be fine but let me reach out to Ratu. You go get yourself organised and meet me at the dock in half an hour."

Tenika kissed Litia's cheek, determination coursing through her. "Before I go, I have one idea for the resort." When Litia nodded for her to continue, Tenika added, "You should enquire how to make this a regular stop for cruise liners."

Litia's eyes widened. "Cruises? Oh my! They can hold thousands of people. Would we even be able to cater for them?"

"I don't know what's involved, but you may be able to suggest smaller cruises. I would think you'd have some control over who can visit. They normally take bookings onboard, so you can limit how many people take part in activities. As for anyone else visiting the island, it'll be a great income boost for the community."

Litia sat back, contemplating. "I see what you're saying. I will think about it. Now, you go and get yourself sorted. Keep me posted on how things go."

"I will. Thank you, Litia."

"Thanks, Dad." Tenika smiled up at her father when he placed a cup of tea in front of her.

He squeezed her shoulder as he passed, but his smile didn't reach his eyes. She glanced across at her mother as she dunked her teabag. Even across the table, Tenika didn't miss her watery eyes.

They sat at a six-seater setting under a pergola area that overlooked the garden. Mum's pride and joy. As a professional garden designer, she'd designed theirs. There were fruit trees that produced apples, lemons, oranges, peaches, and apricots. Not to mention an array of vegetables—potatoes, carrots, corn, cauliflower, pumpkin, and spinach. The garden itself had an Australiana vibe. When the weather was good, they often ate out here.

When Tenika arrived in Melbourne that afternoon, the dry heat consumed her. After a week and a bit, she'd acclimatised to the humidity of Maritimo Island and now realised she didn't like dry heat.

Now that evening was setting in and the sun dropped in the sky, a tinge of cool spread across the garden.

She'd gone straight to her parents' home once she'd landed. Her arrival was a surprise and she appreciated their warm welcome. It'd been nearly a month since she last saw them, and nearly two weeks since she'd spoken to them because of her no technology pact. She still hadn't turned her phone on, but she would soon.

She'd told them everything that had happened on the island, even down to her revelation thanks to Brenda's honesty. They listened, didn't judge, and consoled. Just like they always had. Yet she saw the guilt on their faces. She hated to be the cause of it, but they needed to know the truth.

"We just wanted to protect you," Mum said, using a teaspoon to remove the teabag and wrapped the string around it to squeeze it. "We never thought it would have this outcome. You were our only child. We had so much to learn."

She placed the used teabag on a plate in the middle of the table, then used her fingers to wipe underneath her eyes.

"I know, Mum." Tenika held her cup between her hands and left the teabag in the water. The stronger the better. "And I can't tell you how much I appreciated that. No one could've known this would happen, but I can learn from it, right?"

Despite her lack of emotional growth, they'd never let her down. How could she blame them when they did what they thought was best?

If she had a child, she imagined she'd want to protect them at all costs, too. Wrap them up in cotton wool and tell them everything would be fine, so long as she smothered them with love and support. There was nothing wrong with that, but she'd learnt that guiding them on how to stand up to the bad guys was also important.

Images of mini-Hamish's appeared in her mind again and hope filled her. Strapping young boys with red hair and green eyes. Could she save this? She had to try. She so desperately wanted to get on with life. With Hamish, hopefully, and his family. But also with Brenda and her parents. One big, happy family.

Mum's nod was barely visible, but it was there. Dad stood a few feet away inspecting the lemon tree. He turned back holding his own mug and came to stand behind Mum, placing one hand on her shoulder.

"What's your plan then?" Dad asked, sipping his coffee.

"I need to see Brenda next," Tenika said. "Then I need to figure out what visa I need to live in Scotland and work. All within a matter of days, hopefully."

It seemed like an impossible feat, but she was up for the challenge. She had a small amount in savings, but if she stayed a while and picked up some work, she could build it back up again. As much as she wanted to get out of hospitality, it was a great skill to have when working abroad.

Dad tutted but winked. "Trust you to fall for someone on the other side of the world."

"You'll love Hamish. He may be inheriting a whisky distillery so who knows, maybe he'll bring some whisky back with him."

Dad's eyes brightened. "Now, that I can get behind."

If he'll come back with me.

Tenika shuddered at the thought because last time they had this discussion, it hadn't ended so well. Yes, it was her fault, but she'd had a huge reality check. Long distance wasn't for her, but if she had to stay in Scotland with him for a while, she would. She realised now that changing their plans to reverse them didn't have to be a problem. It had only freaked her out initially because it wasn't what *she* wanted.

She cringed. She'd been so selfish. But not anymore! She was going to be more selfless and wiser.

"Why don't you invite Brenda for pizza?" Dad suggested. "We haven't seen her for a while either. And if she's moving to the other end of the universe soon, it might be our last chance to see her."

"Good idea," Tenika said. "I'm going to go over and see her now and I can pick the pizzas up on the way back, if you like? Tell them I'll be there in about an hour."

"I'll order now," Mum said. "What would you both like?"

Tenika and Dad gave their preferences, then Mum disappeared.

Tenika finished her tea, then said, "Hey Dad, can I borrow your car?"

Dad nodded and threw her the keys, which she caught with one hand.

On the way to Brenda's, Tenika went over and over in her mind what she'd say. Nothing she came up with sounded good enough. Maybe she should settle for a simple 'I'm sorry, I'm a selfish cow, but I promise to do better?' Better than nothing.

When she stopped outside of the modern apartment complex where Brenda lived, Tenika sat in the car for a moment, gathering her thoughts. They were disrupted a few moments later when she saw movement a few feet away. As the figure drew closer, Tenika realised it was Brenda. No time to think, she jumped out of the car and acted on instinct.

"Brenda!"

Brenda yelped, her feet even lifting off the ground. She glared at Tenika, hand over her heart, panting. "What the actual hell, Tenika? You scared the living crap out of me!"

"I didn't realise crap was actually 'living'."

Brenda stared at her deadpan. *Not a good time to crack jokes.*

"What are you doing here, Tenika? Shouldn't you still be on the island?"

Okay, so she hasn't forgiven me yet. Think fast!

She blurted the first words that came to mind, "I'm a sorry cow and I will selfishly do better," then blinked and shook her head. What the hell?

Brenda pursed her lips as though trying not to smile. "You're not entirely wrong." She placed her hands on her hips.

Tenika winced. "That came out wrong, but I suppose there's some truth to it." She huffed out a sigh and tried again. "Brenda, I'm sorry. I'm a selfish cow, but I promise I'm really trying to do better. That's why I'm here, to prove to you that our friendship means more to me than anything. I'm sorry for all the times I wasn't there for you. I hope we can move past this."

Brenda didn't budge. She stared at Tenika through narrowed eyes, lips pursed.

"What about Hamish?" she finally asked.

"I'm going to stow away in the luggage compartment and go to Scotland to grovel."

Brenda's eyes widened comically. "Nika! That's illegal—"

Tenika grinned. Not just because she succeeded at a joke, but because Brenda called her 'Nika' again. She only used her full name when annoyed.

"You bitch," Brenda said with a laugh, then came forward and pulled Tenika in for a hug.

They stood like that for a couple of minutes and Tenika vowed to always do better. *One down, one to go.*

"I forgive you," Brenda said when she pulled away. "But that means when I go to Scotland, you can't just ditch me. I'm freaking out about this move, Nika, but I'm doing it because I love Doug. I still need my best friend."

"I know you do, and I promise I won't ditch you. Now, were you going somewhere? It's just Mum and Dad are ordering pizza, and you're invited."

"I was only going for a walk because I was bored, but pizza sounds so much better. Then you can tell me how you're going to get Hamish back."

Chapter 36

♥

"Dougie, hurry up!" Hamish called, banging on Douglas' door.

"I'm comin', I'm comin'!" he called back, opening the door with the phone glued to his ear.

Hamish rolled his eyes with a grin. "Is that Brenda, *again*?"

Douglas flipped him the middle finger and kept talking as he went out to the car. Angus returned to Edinburgh yesterday after he received a call from Skye. Something about an appointment she wanted him there for. With everything done in London, his leaving wasn't an issue.

It had been a week since their arrival, and today Hamish and Douglas were returning home too. Grandad was flying back with them, but Grandma was staying in London for a while longer. They would move back to Edinburgh permanently, but Grandma had things to finish in London first.

Grandad came down the stairs, zipping up a satchel over his shoulder. "Ready Hamish? The taxi will be here any minute."

"Nearly. Were's Grandma?"

Grandad pointed towards the kitchen.

"I'll be there in five," Hamish said, then went to find her.

It had been a fantastic week with their grandparents. They'd flicked through albums with a lot of photos of Da in his younger years. Even some of Alasdair slipped through, but every time he popped up Grandma did her best to move on quickly. She'd move the conversation along, but Hamish was curious and wanted to know more about his uncle before he'd turned bad.

Grandad enjoyed talking about the good days, what Alasdair used to be like, and so he'd share stories later at night when Grandma was asleep. If his brothers weren't there, Hamish relayed them later. He found it so sad that jealousy had changed him so drastically and changed the course of their lives.

Still, nothing could change the past and despite the wasted years, Hamish wanted to enjoy as many years with his grandparents as he could.

"Grandma?" Hamish called when he entered the kitchen and couldn't see her.

"I'm out the back."

He pushed through the door leading to the backyard. It was a small yard with a patch of grass, some rose bushes, shrubs, and a medium-sized vegetable patch. Being winter, it was bare right now but it would come alive in spring. He hoped whoever bought the property would love it as much as Grandma did.

Hamish found her weeding the pumpkin patch, kneeling on a cushion in front of it. He worried about her overdoing it, but every time he offered to help over the last few days, she always shooed him off.

"Shouldn't you be gone already?" she asked, smiling up at him. "Callum and Dougie already said goodbye. You dinnae want to miss your flight."

"I told them I'd be five minutes. I just wanted to say goodbye, and make sure you'd be okay on your own?"

"I'll be fine, laddie." She got to her feet and turned to stand in front of him, craning her neck up to look at him. "You do worry, dinnae you?"

He shrugged. "I care about you, that's all."

She took his hand and patted it. "You are a sweet boy, so much like your father." She went misty-eyed and he choked up too.

"I'll be fine, I promise," she added, a catch in her voice. "The neighbours will help if I need anythin'. Once I'm organised here, I'll be over. You're needed there, trust me." There was a secretive twinkle in her eyes, which he didn't understand.

"Alright," he leant down to kiss her cheek. "We'll make sure we have everythin' organised back in Edinburgh for your arrival." He glanced around the yard. "You'll miss your garden, I'm sure."

"Aye, but it became a much bigger job than I expected. I'm quite lookin' forward to startin' again and keepin' it smaller." The taxi horn beeped from the front. "Off with you, laddie. Dinnae keep them waitin'. I'll see you in a week or so."

He gave her one last kiss on the cheek, then rushed out to the waiting taxi.

After they landed in Edinburgh, they stopped off at Hamish's house first to drop off some things. He'd inherited Ma's house, much to his brothers' disappointment. He'd never got the chance to purchase his own, whereas Douglas and Angus had.

Ma had talked to all three of them about it before she passed and while they all agreed, his brothers were still a little salty over it. Hamish never gloated about his good fortune, wanting to keep things normal between them. If he could pay it forward one day, he would.

Which was why he'd offered for Grandma and Grandad to live with him. They'd agreed on the proviso that it would only be temporary as they wanted their own space. Hamish dropped Grandad's things in the spare room. He'd have to make up the bed and give the room a quick clean later.

Grandad looked around the room, then peered out the door and down the hallway where Douglas leant against a wall. "Not bad," he mused, stroking his beard. "Needs some work though."

"I know," Hamish said. "I haven't had time to think about it. If you fancy a project, I dinnae mind if you want to get your hands dirty. Just tell me what you need."

Grandpa rubbed his hands together. "Well, maybe I will. I quite enjoy buildin' and restorin' things."

Douglas pocketed his phone and pushed off the wall. "Are you two ready? Angus just sent a text sayin' he'll be at the distillery soon so we should head on over when we can." He gave Grandad a pointed look.

Hamish checked his watch. One p.m. "I'm happy to go now. Shall we grab some lunch on the way?"

Everyone agreed and headed out to Hamish's car in the garage. An hour later Grandad directed Hamish to take a right turn. After another ten minutes of driving along narrow winding roads, a dilapidated distillery came into view behind a security fence. The building was old and traditional, constructed with stone and a dark slate roof. It looked the same as the photos he'd seen, just more rundown. Hamish's heart pounded in his chest. His breath caught.

This is it. Our future.

He drove a little further, crossed a small bridge over a babbling brook then turned into the driveway of the distillery, through an automatic gate. They were waved on through by a security guard.

"What's with all the security?" Douglas asked from the backseat.

"Protecting our assets," Grandad said simply. "It's costed me a bloody fortune over the years. Yet another reason to get this place up and running again."

They entered a large open space that was once a car park. Hamish stopped a few feet from the main doors, next to Angus' car, but stayed put as he stared out the windscreen. There were security cameras on the front of the building, adding another layer of security.

"There she is," Grandad said wistfully. "McNeill Family Distillery." His sigh was long and deep. A thirty-year-old sigh that had been waiting to be released.

"It's beautiful," Douglas said from the backseat sounding choked up. Then he got out of the car but left the door open. He ran up to the old building and inspected the outside, touching the walls, the door, the windowsills, anything he could reach.

"Are you comin'?" Grandad asked, opening his door.

"In a minute," Hamish said, his voice sounding hoarse.

Grandad patted Hamish's arm, grabbed his satchel, and stepped out, closing his door after him. Hamish's gaze never left the grand, old building. All he heard was his own breathing and the trickle of the brook behind the car.

They were only about half an hour out of Edinburgh. The surrounding landscape was lush and green, and the distillery stood perfectly positioned in the countryside at the base of snowcapped mountains. For decoration, two sets of three wooden whisky barrels stacked on top of each other in a triangle shape sat on either side of the door. The windows had been boarded up and all signage removed, though there were spaces where signage once was.

Hamish unclenched his hands from the steering wheel, swallowing over the lump in his throat as he opened his door. He stepped out of the car, his boots crunching on the light snow from the previous night and the crisp air stung his warm face.

He shut his door and Douglas', then glanced behind him where the brook twinkled in the afternoon sunlight as it flowed past rocks. Beyond it were gentle rolling hills with peaks and valleys covered in snow, with winter grass and heather swaying in the breeze. The sun melted the snow in places and new sprigs of vegetation peeked through.

He breathed in fresh air and smiled. *It's so good to be home.* He missed Tenika so much his heart ached. He even missed Maritimo Island, but nothing could beat this. Wherever he ended up, Scotland would forever be in his blood.

He wasn't sure if the heaviness in his heart would ever go away, but he was so ready for this new venture. This was where he needed to be right now. Distilling whisky with his brothers and fulfilling theirs, and their father's, dream.

He turned when he heard his name called. Angus had stepped out from inside the distillery and joined Douglas and their grandfather. He waved Hamish over. He'd expected Angus to meet them but didn't realise he'd seen the inside already. Weren't they meant to do the tour together?

A niggle of annoyance irritated him, but he bit his tongue. It wasn't the right time, and why did it matter anyway? He was here now.

"You made it," Angus said with a wide grin as Hamish approached. "Wait until you see inside. It's amazin'. We have a lot of work ahead of us though."

"Why did you go in first?" Douglas asked, echoing Hamish's thoughts.

Hamish bit back a smile. Although what was with the weird face Angus was pulling? He glared at Douglas, widening his eyes a little too wide and mouthed something Hamish couldn't make out.

Douglas cleared his throat and backpedalled. "Right, shall we go in?"

What was that all about?

Grandad went ahead and Douglas followed, then Angus, and finally Hamish. They stepped into an entryway with a musty smell. The stone floor was dusty, which lifted with their movements and tickled his nose.

Grandad stepped up to a door but didn't go in. He gestured inside. "First stop, visitor centre and tastin' room."

When no one moved, Hamish looked at them. Angus and Douglas wouldn't make eye contact, and why was Grandad trying not to smile? Hamish shrugged and went ahead. Everything was in musty darkness apart from streams of light coming in through gaps of the boarded-up windows. Specks of dust danced in the beams of light.

There were tables and chairs for tasting, empty shelves for stocking whisky, and a reception desk for purchasing. He could imagine the shelves stocked with the finest whisky from the McNeill Family Distillery.

"Check out the shelves behind you," Grandpa coaxed from outside, somewhat impatiently.

Hamish glanced back at Grandad over his left shoulder, brows knitted together.

"No, to your right," Grandad insisted.

"Grandad!" Angus hissed.

"What? He's takin' too bloody long."

What the hell was—?

"*Achoo*!"

Hamish spun around, his heart leaping into his throat when he saw a figure standing in shadow in front of shelves still half stocked with unopened bottles of whisky and caked in dust. It wasn't the whisky he was looking at. He took a step closer and froze. Even bundled up in winter clothes, including a hat with a pompom on it, he'd know those eyes anywhere.

"Tenika?"

Chapter 37

It took a mammoth effort for Tenika to get to Scotland as quickly as she did. A favour from her old boss landed her a job in Edinburgh along with sponsorship. Brenda and Douglas' helped with setting up this surprise. She only went through Brenda, who communicated with Douglas. Tenika wasn't ready to face the middle brother just yet.

When she arrived in Scotland yesterday, Angus and Skye picked her up from the airport. Even then, she was nervous considering she'd hurt Angus' big brother. But she needn't have worried. He was his usual friendly and forgiving self, waving off Tenika's apology with a simple, "We all make mistakes."

Skye was lovely and welcoming. Tenika hoped they'd become friends. The 'appointment' she had yesterday was a ruse to get Angus back to Edinburgh early to help with the plan. The whole family had come together to make this happen, and that's what gave her the tiniest bit of hope that Douglas didn't hate her. He would've made it clear if he wanted nothing to do with her or the plan.

Brenda had told her he was fine, a little miffed, but had more or less forgiven her. Brenda's words, not Tenika's. It was the 'more or less' that made her nervous. She wouldn't put it past Douglas to hold a grudge, so she expected it may take time for him to trust her.

Angus had retrieved the key to the distillery from his grandfather's lawyer, who kept it locked away in a safe. They arrived about an hour ago and Tenika had already had the grand tour. She'd never seen a distillery before and was blown away. There were so many big machines that did so many things she didn't understand, just to make whisky. Yet Angus was a master at explaining it all. She'd never seen him so passionate.

When he received a text from Douglas saying they were ten minutes away, he ushered her into the visitor and tasting area. He purposely instructed her to stand in front of the unopened bottles, explaining Hamish would be starry-eyed at the bottled whisky that had been aged for thirty years and sitting there for another thirty.

The rush to get her there had unsettled the dust, which was caked everywhere. It had been tickling her nose ever since, but the sneeze refused to come when she wanted it.

Until now.

"Tenika?"

She didn't know if Hamish had seen the whisky, but he fixed his unblinking gaze on her. Whereas she couldn't stop blinking, and her eyes watered from the sneeze. Her nose tingled, another one not far behind. *Oh God, I'm ruining everything!*

Although she *had* surprised him, which was all she wanted. But would he talk to her? She'd taken a risk coming all the way here without reaching out to him first. The art of surprise was what she was after, but she also wanted to prove she did it off her own back, not pressured by anyone else.

She owed him an explanation and a huge apology.

"Hi," she said with a small wave, her nose twitching as the second sneeze grew. "H...how...are...ah...ahhh...*achoo!*"

God, this dust was really getting to her.

She dug around in the pocket of her thick, winter pants for a tissue but came up with nothing. She looked at Hamish pleadingly, but he appeared to be in a daze. His gaze had moved to the bottles behind her but he hadn't moved or said anything else.

"Does anyone have a tissue?" Tenika asked, holding a finger under her nose, willing it not to drip.

Hamish blinked at her and shook his head, but he still didn't move. To her surprise, Douglas came in and handed her a tissue. He gave her an unexpectedly kind smile, then left the room again. Was that approval? She breathed a sigh of relief and blew her nose.

"What are you doin' here?" Hamish finally asked.

She wiped her nose one last time and shoved the tissue in her pocket. He wore a guarded look, not that she blamed him. Her mind raced. Had she miscalculated this? Then again, she'd left a massive scar. He'd worn his heart on his sleeve, declared his love before he left, and she did nothing. Just watched him fly away.

Think girl. You gotta salvage this.

Her nose twitched again. "I...I...ahhh...ah...*achoo*!" She fumbled for the tissue, her eyes watering like crazy. "Oh my God, I'm so sorry." Her nose and throat were clogged, making it sound like she had a cold.

This is a total disaster.

She wiped her nose and eyes, pocketing her tissue again but her bottom lip wobbled. All she wanted to do was fall into a heap and cry. On the flight over, all she saw in her mind was Hamish taking one look at her and being so happy he'd run right over, pick her up, and spin her around.

But none of that happened.

Are you being selfish again? Why should he make the first move?

She balled her hands into fists and gritted her teeth. Who knew it was so hard to break that sort of habit? Of course she had to make the first move. She needed to prove she was genuine. All in.

Impatient whispers outside the door gave her a much-needed kick. She pulled her shoulders back and stalked forwards with determination, locking her gaze with Hamish's. She stopped in front of him, and he finally appeared to break free from the trance he was in.

A small smile tugged at his lips, and he reached out for her, his hands resting on her hips. She nearly melted at that simple touch alone. She took his face in her hands and closed the distance, kissing him for all she was worth, with all the passion she could muster. And he kissed her back, returning it with the same amount of passion, then some.

She moved her arms to hang around his neck as their kiss deepened, the world disappearing for a few short blissful moments. She melded into him so naturally she wondered why she'd ever been afraid.

"I didnae think it was possible to kiss that long without passin' out," came a voice as Tenika's lungs struggled for air. She thought it was Callum, the grandfather.

She pulled back with a giggle, but Hamish chased her lips for another kiss and she caved. It had only been a week, but it was a week too long. She couldn't live without this man. Wherever they were, so long as they were together, she'd adapt.

"Come on," Douglas said. "They may be a while. Grandad, lead the way."

Hamish pulled away and rested his forehead on hers. She had to speak, but her heart raced so fast, and her head spun. She could barely form coherent sentences.

Tenika drew in a few calming breaths, and finally managed, "I'm so sorry, Hamish."

"Shh." He held a finger to her lips and leant in to kiss her again, softer this time. Slower. Full of promise. "It's okay." He dragged his lips away from hers and feathered kisses along her face and down her neck.

She groaned and clutched his hair, never wanting to let him go and wanting to remember every single detail of this moment.

"No," she breathed, forcing herself to pull away. "It's not okay." When he looked at her with bright eyes, a wide smile on his face, she found it so difficult to take this seriously. But this had to be said. She gulped and added, "Brenda had to remind me how selfish I was. I didn't want to come to Scotland with you because it interfered with *my* plans." She cringed and stepped out of his arms. "It was wrong of me, Hamish. It was a hard lesson learned, but I know now I just want to be where you are."

He came after her, taking her hands and squeezing them. "I understand why Brenda might have viewed it as selfish, but I dinnae see it like that. I see someone who was afraid, whose life was changin' so fast after bein' in a safe bubble for so long."

She swallowed and nodded. That was exactly it! He explained it in a way she'd never been able to. He truly understood. He got *her*.

"So, are we really doin' this?" Hamish asked, pulling her closer and wrapping his arms around her waist.

She nodded and his eyes lit up.

"Long distance?" He raised one eyebrow in question.

She shook her head and Hamish's eyes widened. "I'm staying here."

He grinned and whooped, lifting her up and spinning her around. She giggled gleefully. At least *that* part of her daydream came true.

"Are you sure?" he asked once she was back on her feet.

"One hundred percent sure. Litia had to remind me the island wasn't going anywhere, and I can go back anytime."

"Of course! Once we know what's happenin' here, we can go back. I still dinnae ken how long it'll take—"

She silenced him with a kiss. "That sounds perfect."

Hamish moved his arm to rest across her shoulders and guided her around to face the shelved whisky. "Now," he gestured to the shelves, "if we can find some glasses, would you like a whisky taste?"

There was a scuffle outside and seconds later Douglas and Angus came running through.

"Did we hear whisky taste?" Douglas asked.

Tenika burst out laughing and everything was good in the world again.

Callum came in unzipping his satchel, "I came prepared," and he removed five small shot glasses, setting them on a tasting table. He smiled kindly at Tenika. "It's nice to finally meet you, hen."

Hamish grabbed a bottle with a grin and the five of them stood around the table. He unscrewed the lid and poured the liquid gold whisky into their glasses.

Tenika picked it up and inhaled. It was strong and smoky, making her cough. She held the whisky away with a laugh. "Whoa!"

Callum chuckled and clinked his glass against hers. "This whisky put us on the map, hen. The batch we sold before we had to close." His sigh was heavy, but he was smiling.

"So, it's sixty years old?" Tenika asked in awe. When they all nodded, she added, "Does the flavour change much after it's bottled?"

"She's an inquisitive one," Callum said to Hamish, who smiled proudly. Callum added, "No, it doesn't change after it's bottled."

"Cheers," Angus said, picking up his glass then gulping his down in one shot. "Woo!" He fist-pumped the air.

"Cheers," the other three men chorused and followed suit.

Tenika wasn't so brave. After a half-hearted, "Cheers," she took a tiny sip and promptly started coughing, the strong alcohol catching in her throat. "Holy crap!" Her eyes watered but as the strength passed, a smoky, peaty, caramel aftertaste lingered. "Wait a minute…"

"There it is," Callum said. "Once you can get past the strength of the alcohol, the flavour makes its appearance. It takes some getting used to, but you'll get there."

"Bring it on!" Tenika said and swigged the rest. She didn't cough this time, but her eyes watered and the intensity still caught in her throat and took her breath away. "Yay!" she choked out and everyone laughed.

"She's a keeper," Callum said to Hamish.

"She certainly is." Hamish slid his arm across her shoulders and pulled her close, kissing her temple.

"Alright," Callum said, "let's start this wee tour again."

"One more glass," Douglas said, filling his glass and shooting it down. He grinned at Tenika and said, "It's good to have you back, Nika."

He promptly left, following Callum and Angus, and Tenika couldn't stop grinning. Her eyes watered and her cheeks were warm. It might've still been from the whisky, but she was pretty sure it was the fact he'd accepted her back no questions asked and adopted the same nickname Brenda had given her.

"Do you want to join us?" Hamish asked, holding out his hand.

She nodded and took it. Even though she'd already had a tour, she was eager to hear it from Callum's perspective. He gave a commentary on each room, including some historical facts. Tenika could feel Hamish's excitement coming off him in waves.

The last stop was the maturation warehouse. When they entered, silence fell over them as they glanced around the medium-sized room, stacked full of barrels.

"Oh my God," Angus whispered. "Now the extra security makes sense."

Hamish stopped and squeezed Tenika's hand but said nothing. She glanced at him, then his two brothers. They all wore shell-shocked expressions. The pieces fell into place after glancing at a grinning Callum. These barrels weren't empty! Then she breathed in, and over the musty dampness, she caught the sweet scent of ageing alcohol. Her skin crawled as goosebumps rose on her arms.

"Is that..." She swallowed as the enormity of the situation hit her. "Is all of that whisky?"

Callum's grin widened as he nodded. He pointed to the right wall. "That's the last batch Duncan made." Then he pointed to the left wall. "That's my last batch."

Douglas' hands flew to his head and he clutched his hair as he walked to one end of the warehouse and back again. Hamish let go of Tenika's hand and he and Angus followed. She left them to talk amongst themselves, their tone growing in excitement and awe as they came to terms with what they were learning.

"What does it all mean?" Tenika asked Callum.

"They can bottle and sell this," he explained. "To keep the business runnin' in the future, they're goin' to have to start distillin' immediately. Legally though, they cannae sell whisky unless it's been aged for at least three years. This stock is an excellent start for reopenin' the business and keepin' it runnin' as they start their own. If they offer tours and tastings, they'll be on the right path. Duncan and I had planned this on purpose, so we'd have somethin' to come back to. We never knew how much time would pass." His tone gained a sad lilt to it when he added, "I never expected him not to come back."

She rested a sympathetic hand on his arm. "I'm so sorry."

He patted her hand and smiled at her. "Thank you, hen. I'm so happy my grandsons can take over. To see the family distillery back in business will be a dream come true."

While Hamish and his brothers talked, Callum tapped Tenika on the shoulder and gestured for her to follow him. They stopped beside one of Duncan's barrels. Callum opened his satchel and removed what looked like a long copper pipe from a protective bag, and a glass jug. He handed the jug to Tenika, then he stepped up to the barrel and removed the cork, placing it on top of the barrel. He held a finger on the top of the tube and slid it into the bunghole.

"This is a valinch," he explained. "It acts like a siphon. Once I remove my finger from the hole on top here, I'll be able to extract some whisky. We would normally do this regularly durin' the agein' process, but this is the first tastin' in over thirty years." He winked at her and Tenika grinned. This was all so fascinating!

He did just so, then placed his finger over the hole again before removing the valinch and pouring the whisky into the jug Tenika held. Placing the tube back in its bag, he put that into his satchel, put the cork back into the barrel, and called out to his grandsons.

"Who's up for a taste of Duncan's whisky straight from the barrel?"

The three stopped talking and came over, eyes alight with excitement. Callum removed more glasses from his satchel and held them out to Tenika two at a time. She poured and the drinks were shared.

"Be warned, hen," Callum said. "This has a much higher alcohol content. I'd suggest small sips."

She nodded and inhaled. It certainly had a stronger scent, but it was sweeter too.

"Honey?" she asked.

Callum winked. "You've got a good nose on you. Spot on." He held out his glass. "To Duncan."

Everyone repeated the toast and sipped the whisky. Despite the alcohol strength, the honey flavour gave it a different touch. Took the edge off.

"Ooh I like this," she said, taking another sip. Then, feeling brave, she gave her own toast. "To the future. May McNeill Family Distillery thrive once again."

Everyone looked at her in surprise, but then grinned and chorused, "Hear, hear!" and drank again.

This sip went straight to her head, but she finished what was in her glass. She knew very little about whisky, but she had a hunch this would sell well. She glanced around at these strong men, who she was certain would eventually be her new family, and her heart burst with pride.

Without a doubt, coming here was the best decision. Her new life was only just beginning, but she was so excited to see where it would lead.

Her past was where it belonged...in the past.

Her future beckoned.

Epilogue

Twelve months later

Tenika was a ball of nerves as she rushed to get ready. Today was a big day. Not only was Hamish arriving on Maritimo Island, but they expected their first cruise! Tenika had worked with Eroni, Litia, and Taito over the last six months to bring this to fruition.

She'd spent six months in Scotland with Hamish, working at her sponsored job while helping where she could with the distillery. Hamish and his family had it under control, but occasionally she helped with marketing and social media ideas. It had been an eye opener to see the distillery go from this rundown building closed for thirty years to fully restored and gleaming ready for business.

Their first task had been to get new whisky distilling, then bottle the ageing whisky. By the time she left, it was open for business again. The leftover bottles in the visitor centre and tasting room were great for selling at a higher price because it had been so popular before the distillery closed. They found more in storage too, so this together with the new bottled whisky, distillery tours and tastings, had started earning them money.

Tenika only left Scotland early because Litia had contacted her in a flap saying a cruise company had reached out about Maritimo Island becoming a regular stop for their small cruise liner. She returned via Australia and Hamish came with her. They met up with Travis and Kylie first and finally met Marcus. Last stop was to visit her parents. Hamish easily won them over with one of the older bottles of whisky. Dad especially was chuffed. Much to Tenika's relief, they all got on well.

Tenika had a trip planned in a few weeks' time to visit her aunt and grandparents in Fiji. By then, Hamish would have settled. She'd met her grandparents a few times on video calls, but she was eager to meet them in person. She'd tried to search for her father's family again but came up blank once more. Unfortunately, she had to accept they may not be contactable.

When she left for Maritimo Island, Hamish returned to Scotland. Even though she hated the distance between them, their relationship was strong. Communication was key and they were open about everything.

Once he arrived today, he'd stay for twelve months. His brothers would run the distillery, and Hamish would manage the admin and financial side.

"Tenika, are you ready?" a voice called outside her small bungalow. "The seaplane will be landing any minute."

Tenika slipped her feet into sandals and left through the front door, embracing Litia with a tight hug. "Let's go!"

She'd moved into a small but cosy bungalow in the village. Monetary wise, the island was still growing, which meant her job didn't pay the same rate as one in Australia would. That was fine by her, and she was content living a simple life. She had everything she needed and could still save.

As she sat beside Litia in a cart, it occurred to her that soon her little home would be a home for two. Her heart fluttered and a smile remained fixed to her face.

Litia talked excitedly about the events of the day. They planned a party to welcome the cruise passengers, and there would be a huge bonfire burning all day.

Their marketing over the last few months had brought in a steady flow of new and returning guests to the island. There were families and couples travelling from all over the world for short and long stays. There was even a wedding booked in six months' time.

The island was growing with funding support from Fiji, which was where today's cruise came from. The ship only held eight hundred passengers.

Even for the smaller cruise ships, the dock had to be upgraded. The seaplane dock had been relocated from the western side of the island to the northern side, which was also closer to the resort and the holiday bungalows on the water. That meant the cruise liners would dock on the western side.

Litia continued to natter but Tenika barely heard her, too caught up in her thoughts. She peered out of the cart and looked up at the sky, hoping to spot the plane, but it wasn't visible yet. She was *so* excited to see Hamish again. Video calls were great, but just not the same.

Brenda moved to Scotland two months after she left Maritimo Island. She and Douglas had settled into their new lives and were going strong. Brenda's parents had been cautious about their quick relationship, but Douglas won them over. He'd even confided in Tenika recently, asking about Brenda's favourite gem so she suspected a proposal was on the cards. She and Brenda *had* remained best friends and moved on from that earlier blip.

Angus and Skye got engaged then married in quick succession not long after he returned from Maritimo Island. They were now proud parents to twin girls, Effie and Isla, after their grandmother. Tenika was sad she hadn't met them yet as Skye gave birth two weeks after Tenika left.

"Earth to Tenika!"

Tenika blinked. "Sorry, my mind's preoccupied."

"Of course it is. I was just saying I really hope everyone has a great time today. The activities have been booked out. The dolphin and sea turtle cruise was the first to go!"

"I can't say I'm surprised, it's a great cruise. Are all the markets ready to go?"

"Yes, and everyone's stocked up and ready for the influx."

Litia stopped and they stepped out of the cart. Tenika heard a familiar buzzing sound and when she looked up, she saw the seaplane. Her heart leapt and she turned to Litia who shooed her off with a laugh.

Tenika sprinted across the sand and down the pier, bouncing on the balls of her feet as she watched the plane land on the water and float to the dock. Ratu spotted her from the cockpit and gave her a wave and tipped his cap. When the passengers disembarked, Tenika was pleased to see some holiday goers.

Hamish was the last to disembark and Tenika ran up to him and into his arms. He caught her, laughing, and spun her around as he held her close. She pulled back to kiss him and the world disappeared.

"I missed you!" she cried.

"I missed you too." He set her back on the ground and glanced around with a smile. "It's good to be back."

"Not too hot for you?"

He grinned and her stomach flipped. "It's *always* too hot for me, but it's still good to be back. Good to be with *you*." He reached out and stroked her cheek, his eyes shining. "I've got a surprise for you later."

"Hey, me too!" A wave of nausea washed over her at the thought of what she planned. Was she brave enough?

"What is it?"

She swatted his arm. "That would be telling."

He chuckled and slid his arm across her shoulders, leading her down the pier and towards the sand where Litia stood waving.

"It's going to be a full-on day," Tenika said. "But it'll be a clear night for star gazing so I thought we could hike up to the top of the mountain."

"At night?"

She laughed at his shocked expression. "It's perfectly safe. They've even put more solar lights on the track leading up to the peak to light the way. It's become a popular spot, especially for stargazing."

He squeezed her shoulder. "It sounds perfect."

"Hamish, my boy, it's so good to see you," Litia said as they approached.

Hamish released Tenika and ran down the last part of the pier to embrace Litia. "I've missed you," he said. "How have you been? And Taito and Eroni?"

"Oh, we're fine. We're so happy you'll be with us for a while. I hear you'll be working remotely for the distillery but if you need any other work to do, we're snowed under."

Hamish stepped back and took Tenika's hand. "I'll only be doin' distillery work when my brothers are awake. I'd love a job to keep me busy at other times."

"Well then, I'll take you to see Taito later. He'll get you sorted. Tenika, the cruise will be here in an hour. Can you pass the message around?"

"What can I do?" Hamish asked.

"You can help me round everyone up." Tenika tugged on his hand and led him away, grabbing a spare cart. First stop, her little bungalow in the village to drop off Hamish's things and round people up on the way.

"Do you need to freshen up?" she asked on the drive back. When she spotted some locals, she called, "Please gather at the western dock! Tell everyone you see."

They waved, nodded, and rushed off in excited chatter as Hamish said, "No I'm fine, thanks. It was great spendin' the night in Fiji. It means I'm not so jetlagged today."

Tenika stopped the cart next to the bungalow, stepping out with Hamish following her inside. He placed his luggage in a corner and glanced around at the small space.

"This is nice," he said. "Reminds me of the bungalow I stayed in last time, just on land."

"They're all quite similar. Sorry it's so small."

He turned to her and took her in his arms. "It's not that small. I think it's perfect for us." He leant in and kissed her softly, passionately and full of promise.

Her knees wobbled and he tightened his hold on her, holding her flush against him. He gently nudged her back towards the bed and she had no power to stop him. She fell back with a gasp and he loomed over her with a sexy smile, his eyes oozing love and happiness.

"I've missed you," he said, then caught her lips once more and devoured her like he hadn't done for months.

"I've...missed...you...too," she said between kisses, barely able to catch her breath. Her heart raced, her desire growing with every kiss. She desperately needed this, *wanted* this, but now was the worst time. "But...but..." She groaned and pushed him away. "...I'm sorry, but we can't do this now."

He groaned and rested his forehead on hers. "I know, I'm sorry, I'm too impatient." He rolled off and onto his back, scrubbing his hands over his face.

She crawled over to him, smiling apologetically. "Trust me, I want you as much as you want me." He grinned and reached out to grab her again, but she moved away with a laugh. "But I really don't want to miss this momentous occasion."

She got to her feet and he sat up with a groan. "Alright, you win, but tonight..." he trailed off. His eyes flashed and her insides melted.

Her cheeks flamed and she fanned herself. "Come on," she said breathlessly. "We have people to round up."

Fifty minutes later, those who were welcoming the cruise lined up on the beach facing the dock and pier. Those giving tours stood at the front of the crowd. They held up signs advertising said tours, so passengers knew who to go to. The general welcoming committee stood behind them. Some were there to offer a more personalised island experience that didn't require a booking.

Sounding its horn, the supposedly small ship still looked so large as it slowly approached. Everyone cheered. It might've been smaller compared to the mega ships, only two decks high, but it still had all the perks.

The crew waved as they dropped anchor and lowered the gangway. As soon as the doors opened, the entire crowd of locals started waving, cheering, jumping up and down, and breaking into song. The gentle breeze carried a tinge of salt and smoke from the bonfire.

Over the next half an hour or so, the passengers disembarked. One by one, they disappeared onto their booked tours, snagged a tour guide, or strolled on foot into the island.

Tenika grinned at Hamish, grabbed his hand and dragged him away without saying a word. They wandered the paths through the island, past the resort, into the community area, past the agricultural area, checked out the beaches, the waterfall and the cave behind it, and the private beach. With people talking, laughing, bantering, and buying things, the island was truly alive.

"This is amazing," Tenika gushed turning to Hamish, who stared at her with a silly grin on his face. "What? Why are you looking at me like that?"

He kissed her then kept walking, hand in hand. "I love how alive you are here."

"You don't have any regrets, do you?"

"Not a single one. We've talked about our plans, so I'm happy."

She squeezed his hand. "Thank you, for everything."

He smiled softly. "No, thank *you*. You made the first sacrifice and now it's only fair I do the same. That's what a relationship is about, right? Givin' and takin'?"

She nodded and hummed in response. For the rest of the day, Tenika went to the resort to continue with her usual job. Hamish joined her and got talking to Taito, who put him straight to work.

The resort was also busy with tourists wanting to check it out and swim in the pool. Usually this was only for resort guests, but since they didn't have many, Litia allowed it.

By the time the day ended, and the passengers had boarded the ship, the island grew quiet again but still buzzed. While Tenika searched for Hamish, she passed locals packing up their community tables, talking excitedly.

She found Hamish and they commenced their hike up the mountain. She hadn't thought too much about the surprise she'd planned, but now that they were on their way, her stomach fluttered with butterflies. *I don't know if I can do this*. She drew in a breath and released it slowly. Yes, she *could* do this. She glanced at Hamish who stared ahead in determination. He was worth it.

Once at the top, the sun began to set, giving them a stunning spectacle. The ship had set sail and was visible in the distance. Tenika was full of excitement and hope for her life with Hamish, *and* on the island. She was so privileged to be here and a part of its growth.

"Shall we eat first?" she asked Hamish, who removed food from the basket she'd asked Scott to bring up earlier. She laughed. "That's a yes then."

He grinned. "Aye, I'm starved. Sorry."

"It's fine, I am too."

They ate and talked, never seeming to run out of things to say. When night fell and the sky became studded with stars, Tenika's nerves intensified. *It's now or never*. She and Hamish stopped talking and sat in companionable silence. She looked up at him and noticed he appeared out of sorts. Nervous even.

"You okay?" she asked.

"Of course, why?"

She shook her head. "No reason. Come with me, I've got something for you."

He stood and swallowed, his Adam's apple bobbing in his throat. "Me too."

She moved out into the clearing, which shone silver in the nearly full moonlight, a balmy breeze rustling the tropical foliage. They stopped and she turned to glance out over the ocean, breathing slowly and evenly. She could do this. Who said a woman couldn't propose? She loved this man and wanted to spend her life with him.

They'd talked about their future, and marriage was on the cards. It was a race to who proposed first, as she suspected Hamish had a plan too.

"Tenika?"

She swallowed, closed her eyes and breathed in. *Just turn, kneel, and pop the question. Simple.* So, with her eyes still closed, she did exactly that. When she opened them again, she stared into Hamish's shocked ones...who was also kneeling.

"Oh my God!" she cried and they burst out laughing. "No way. You weren't—"

"I was," and he opened the small box to reveal a stunning gold band ring with a heart-shaped diamond.

Her breath caught. "It's beautiful! But I wanted to beat you to it."

Neither of them moved.

"Now we're in a pickle," Hamish said with a chuckle.

She shook her head and grinned. "Nah, there's a simple solution."

He raised his eyebrows in question.

"We both ask." She dug into her pocket for the ring she'd bought him. A white gold signet style ring with a single diamond. "On the count of three."

He shook his head, looking slightly bewildered. "This is not how I expected this to go." He shrugged and sent her a lopsided grin. "Why not then?"

"Alright then. One...two...three..."

"Will you marry me?" they both asked.

After saying yes and exchanging rings, they got to their feet and fell into each other's arms. Hamish kept his around her waist while she rested hers around his neck and they swayed in the evening breeze. There was no music, but there didn't need to be. She inspected the ring on her finger and sighed happily.

"I love you," she whispered, pressing her cheek against his.

He tightened his arms around her. "I love you too."

In that instant, Tenika saw a real future ahead of them. All those daydreams she'd had of a life together were now a possibility. She was so much better prepared for how to handle conflicts and was so ready for this new chapter of her life.

Also in This Series

Oceans Apart, the second standalone book in the series will be released in 2025. Sign up to my newsletter to be the first to learn all about it!

Other Books by Lisa Stanbridge

Series

The **Longing for Home** series follows the story of Jane and Jacques between Paris and Australia as their relationship evolves.

Lonely in Paris – Book 1

Jane has accepted a job in Paris, but she speaks very little French. With no friends to enjoy the city of love with, she's awfully lonely. Then she meets Jacques DuPont. From a rich family, he's living the dream. Just not his own. Trapped in a life chosen by his family, he's always been alone. Until he meets Jane. The two couldn't be more opposite, yet they will fall hard. With an expiring visa, a jealous colleague, and manipulative family, their loyalties will be tested.

Troubled in Paradise – Book 2

Things are coming together for Jane and Jacques, but the news of his father's illness has Jacques troubled. When his mother and siblings beg him to return to Paris, he reluctantly agrees. Jane is loving her new life, has a new job lined up, and an old friendship has been renewed. While Jacques is in Paris, she receives some devastating news. They need each other more than ever but the pressures of distance, manipulative family and friends, and life-changing events will put their relationship to the test.

<u>Finding Our Home – Book 3</u>

They've weathered the storms of manipulative family members and the ups and downs of their evolving relationship, and their dreams of a forever home is within reach. When Jacques' brother drops a bombshell, the foundation of their dream trembles. The surprise arrival of Jane's parents is perfectly timed and Jane is elated, but her joy is short lived when she learns of a devastating lie. Jane and Jacques must overcome the unexpected twists that will force them to reconsider what home really means.

Standalone books

Abandoned Hearts is my debut novel. A heartfelt story about two broken individuals who must learn to trust again.

Finally free from her abusive ex, Claire Stone accepts a job as a live-in nurse in the small beach-side town of Busselton, Western Australia. A new life is exactly what she needs. Move away, move on, forget. If only things were that simple. Even the intriguing but abrasive son of her new patient can't shield her from relentless memories.

Michael Karalis is watching his mother die while battling his ex-wife for custody of his five year old son. He's bitter, broken, and distrustful, but Claire becomes a light in his world, despite his reservations. Two broken souls need to learn to trust again and open their hearts or they'll never find the love they both need.

Navigate to the URL below to purchase this book.

https://books2read.com/AbandonedHearts

Author's Note

Thank you for reading **Ocean's Embrace**. I hope you enjoyed it.

This is the first book in the Maritimo Island series, which I'm super excited about. Each book will feature the stunning fictional island, but each story can be read as a standalone. Some of the characters will return, but in a minor role. You won't need to have read any of the previous books to know what's going on.

This story has been through so many drafts because I could never get it *just right*. It started off as a revenge story and in a way, I'm sad it's no longer that, but I believe it's better for it. Turns out I'm not good at writing revenge. It produces too many emotions within *me*. And for me, writing is meant to be therapeutic, not rage inducing.

So when I came up with the idea of Maritimo Island and wanting to set an entire series here, I knew Tenika and Hamish had huge potential. In the original version, the reunion was a huge part of it, including Tenika's revenge. I kept the reunion, and you probably noticed I hinted at Tenika's desire of revenge, but rather than acting on it, she doesn't. I wanted to make her the bigger woman. As she said standing up in front of her peers, as adults they should know better.

And that's the moral of this story. Sometimes it's better to leave the past in the past. Let it go. Move forwards. Create a new and *better* future. Be the bigger person and make a positive impact.

Next in the series will be **Oceans Apart**, which is set for release in 2025. To be the first to find out all about it, pop over to my website and sign up to my newsletter. This story is one I wrote quite a while ago and it just needs a few tweaks to tie in the Maritimo Island location.

Now to the important thank you's!

To Pete, my ever patient husband, who's offered so much support and advice during this writing journey. I love you and I appreciate you so much.

Frances Dall'Alba, my critique partner and friend. You'll always have a spot in these thank you's because you're always the one who has the biggest impact in my writing.

My editor and friend, Danni. Thank you for the chats, the quick editing, and amazing support.

And finally, all the other countless people who have offered advice or shared knowledge, I appreciate every single one of you.

Thank you!

About the author

Lisa Stanbridge is an international award-winning author of sweet contemporary romance and romantic comedies. She guarantees an escape from reality, a few shed tears, and definitely a happily ever after.

She has been writing ever since she could string sentences together, evolving from princesses in castles, to angsty teens, and finally settling on real people going through real struggles.

She's been shortlisted in many contests, and even won some! Her biggest award is for her debut novel, Abandoned Hearts, which won 'Best First Book' in the Koru Award of Excellence, run by Romance Writers of New Zealand.

With a total of four books published, her next one is set to release in 2024 with regular yearly releases planned.

When she's not writing, Lisa works full time as a Software Tester. She reads anything she can sink her teeth into, and loves binging on TV shows, especially the British ones. Lisa loves lazy days at the beach reading or writing, but rarely swimming, and loves spending time with her husband and her friends.

Say hello to Lisa

Visit her website and subscribe to her newsletter. It will keep you up to date with:

- New releases

- Preorder links

- New cover reveals and excerpts

And lots more!

https://lisastanbridge.wixsite.com/lisastanbridgeauthor

Leave a review

Did you enjoy this book? The best favour you can do for an author is to leave a review. If you'd like to leave one, go to your place of purchase, or search for the book on Goodreads, Amazon, or BookBub and leave a review. Thank you.